# Crueltown

∽ A Drew Steele Los Angeles-Las Vegas Mystery ∽

## E.E. "Doc" Murdock

H.O.T. Press

Published by
H.O.T. Press
Los Angeles
www.hotpresspublishing.com
Established 1983

ISBN: 0-923178-20-1
ISBN - 13: 978-0-923178-20-8

# Acknowledgments

I am indebted to the members of the Ojai Writing Workshop who provided valuable feedback as I worked through the many drafts of this book. And of course, without the help of Zoe, this book would not exist.

# Crueltown

# Chapter 1

"Yes?"

"Mr. Jones, this is security at the front gate. We have a John Rudd out here. Says he's delivering a pizza, but he doesn't look like a pizza delivery guy. He's driving a beat-up looking Dodge, and he thinks your name is Smith."

"It's all right. He's making a joke. Give him a visitor parking pass and let him in."

"Okay, sir, whatever you say."

Steele clicked off the phone. He could just see Rudd out there at the gate trying to keep a straight face as he told the stern security guard he was delivering a pizza. He must be out on one of his all-night stringer runs, prowling the LA freeways searching for any kind of interesting mayhem to describe in gory detail in tomorrow's newspaper.

Steele turned back to the computer and continued scrolling through the police incident reports. Plenty of things going on tonight in LA. Not surprising for a Friday evening. But nothing that might be related to the whereabouts of the illusive Mr. Culp.

When the doorbell rang, Steele grabbed his crutches and got up to go to the door. When he looked out through the peephole, Rudd, as usual, had his eye pressed up tight against it. Always the joker.

Steele opened the door, and Rudd almost fell in. Another joke. He was grinning as he held out the pizza box. "Pizza delivery for Mr. always-working-day-and-night John Smith."

"Very thoughtful, Rudd, even if I don't eat pizza. And next time you go to the security gate, remember I'm John Jones now."

"Oh, right. I forgot. But how am I supposed to keep track of what name you're using if you keep changing it every time you move?"

"You know why."

Rudd shrugged and headed for the kitchen. "Yeah, I suppose it does make it harder for them to track you down. Sorry. Anyhow, even if you don't like pizza, I figured you could use some company while I ate it." He got a plate out of the cupboard and put a couple of big pieces of pizza on it. Then he opened the fridge. "Damn, you never have anything in here but healthy crap. Couldn't you just once have a beer or something for me?"

"There's fresh-squeezed orange juice in there. Better for you than beer." Steele tried to focus on the new reports coming up on the computer screen.

"Are you kidding? My digestion system couldn't handle anything that healthy." He came to look over Steele's shoulder while he munched his pizza. "What ya working on? A new case?"

"Uh huh. Missing-person. Guy named Kenneth Culp. A walk-away Vegas casino employee. White, middle-aged, married. They think he may have been headed for LA."

"Middle-age crisis, I bet," mumbled Rudd, his mouth full of pizza. "Younger woman involved. Has to be."

"Possibly. I did ask if any of the women he works with were missing. They said no."

"Not an office romance? Well, then I bet it was one of those hot drink girls they have over there. Last time I was in Vegas, I got to talking to this cute drink girl who kept me well stocked in beers all the time I was playing the slots. I tell ya, she was somethin' else. Really built, like out to here." Rudd cupped his hands and held them out in front of his chest to make the point. But then he frowned. "Turned out she had a watchful husband."

Steele tried to concentrate on the incident reports. Only one middle-aged. A DOA at UCLA Medical. Multiple gunshot wounds. He scrolled down to see if there was a follow-up. There was. The DOA was a black man. Couldn't be Culp.

"You're not very good company," complained Rudd. "Maybe I should take my pizza out to the pool. Seen any new women out there lately while you're swimming your morning laps?"

"None that you haven't already scared off."

"Very funny. I think I'll go out and check, just to be sure." He put a few more pieces of pizza on his plate and headed for the door. But before he got there, the cell phone on Steele's desk buzzed. Rudd stopped and turned back. "That's your mobile. Maybe it's Loren."

"No, it's the Drew Steele phone," said Steele. He glanced at the international clock at the bottom of the computer screen. "Besides, it's early in the morning in France."

He picked up the phone. "Yes?"

"Mr. Steele?"

"That's right."

"I'm here. Where are you?"

Steele didn't recognize the voice. "Who is this?"

"Why, it's Rita Culp, Ken's wife. I called as soon as I found the place. That's what you said to do, didn't you?"

Steele tried to think why the missing man's wife would be calling him. And what place was she referring to? She must be confused. "Mrs. Culp, I didn't call you. Did someone at the casino tell you to contact me?"

"I don't understand. You called me and said I should come to LA right away. You said to go to this place called Crueltown out by the harbor and then call you. I'm there now. I rented a car at the airport and came straight here. I'm right on the street you said, but it's dark and there's nothing out here except a tall fence with barbed wire along the top. Is there a gate somewhere? Are you inside?"

Crueltown again! It had been a while since Steele had heard that dreaded name. Why would someone tell her to go there, and why would they claim to be him? Something was wrong with this picture, very wrong. "Listen to me, Mrs. Culp. I didn't call you. I was hired by the casino to find your husband, but they didn't ask me to contact you. They didn't even give me your phone number."

"But why would someone say they were you? Are you telling me I came all this way for nothing?"

Rudd came back to stand by the desk. "What's going on?"

Steele held up a hand to silence him. "Mrs. Culp, listen to me carefully. Crueltown is a dangerous place. Known for crime and drug dealing. Get out of there. Drive north, toward LA. Get away from the harbor district as fast as you can."

"I'm already going north. Where should I go?"

"Just keep going until you get back to an area where there are people around. Are there any cars behind you?"

"Only one. It's kind of a dark deserted road. I don't like it here."

"Speed up."

"What?"

"I said go faster. Do it!"

"All right, I'm speeding up. But why?"

"Is the car still following you?"

"Yes, It's still back there. Mr. Steele, you're worrying me. What's going on?"

"Someone wanted to get you to the Crueltown area. Maybe they hoped you would lead them to your husband. Is that car still following you?"

"Yes, but it's dropping back. I'm going very fast now."

"Good. Keep going. Don't slow down."

He pressed the cell phone's speaker button, and handed it to Rudd. "It's the wife of my missing person. Keep her talking."

"Good evening, ma'am," said Rudd cheerfully. Uh, how are you?"

"Who's this? What happened to Mr. Steele?"

"I'm, uh, his associate. He'll be right back with you."

Steele reached under the desk to get his prosthetic foot. The footshell and shoe were already in place. He attached it to his stump and opened the lower desk drawer to get a pistol. He chose the little Beretta .32 automatic, and also a tiny pen gun. He slipped the pistol into the specially-designed holster that was attached to the prosthetic foot's carbon fiber composite ankle shaft, and slipped the tiny pen gun into its tight-fitting, pre-drilled hole. He pulled down his pants leg to hide it all, put on his other shoe, and stood up.

"Ask her where she is now."

"Uh, where are you now, ma'am?"

"I'm not sure, but I'm coming to a stop light."

"Good," said Steele, leaning close to the cell phone. "What street is it?"

"There's a sign. Wait a minute . . . Pacific Coast Highway."

"Turn left. See if the car follows you."

"All right. I'm turning. "It's . . . yes, it turned also, but it's staying back a ways. It's a silver car. New looking."

"How many are in it?"

"I can't tell. Their windows are darkened."

"Let's go," said Steele, heading for the door. "Keep her talking."

"But what about my pizza?" said Rudd.

"Leave it. Hurry!"

On the way up the stairs to the parking lot, Steele thought about that stretch of Pacific Coast Highway. There would be an endless line of no-tell motels and greasy-spoon restaurants left over from the old tourist days. "Tell her to pull into the first motel she sees."

"Damn, Steele. Wait for me. How can you move so fast with that fake foot of yours?"

"Just tell her."

"Okay, okay. Just let me catch my breath. I'm a big guy, remember?" He stopped to lean against the parking structure wall.

Steele went back and took the phone from Rudd. "Listen to me, Mrs. Culp. Pull in at the first motel you see."

"Oh, right. I will need someplace to stay tonight, won't I?"

Steele hurried to his car and was already backing out of his parking place by the time Rudd got there. Rudd barely had time to get into the passenger seat before Steele burned rubber out of the parking structure and headed for the front gate of the hillside condo complex. Rudd hung onto his seat belt with both hands as Steele shot past the two wide-eyed security guards and made a sliding turn onto the street.

Rudd managed to squeak out a high-pitched, "Jesus, what's the hurry?"

Steele handed the phone to Rudd. "Find out where she is."

Rudd caught his breath, and then said, "Mrs. Culp, are you still there? It's John Rudd again."

"What happened to Mr. Steele?"

Steele blew through a red light at speed, barely missing a rusty old pickup truck. The driver panicked and hit the brakes. In the rearview mirror, Steele saw that the truck had skidded to a sideways stop in the middle of the intersection.

Rudd took in a big gulp of air and put his hand against the dash. "He can't talk right now, Mrs. Culp. We're coming. Really fast!"

"You're coming here?"

"Where is she?" said Steele as he dodged into the oncoming lane to get around a slow-moving red Cadillac. He hit the gas again and the car's powerful engine wailed in response. This was one of those times he wished he had a stick shift, but after he got back from Iraq, he'd discovered that his prosthetic left foot made driving his stick-shift car difficult. He'd been forced to buy a car with an automatic transmission. It made this kind of fast driving through traffic somewhat less precise.

"Where are you, Mrs. Culp?" said Rudd. "Have you come to a motel yet?"

"I'm just coming to one now, but it's kind of beat-up looking. Oh, dear, the sign says, "Playboy in-room TV channel." Maybe this isn't the right place for me."

"Steele grabbed the phone out of Rudd's hand. "Pull in, and stay there. We'll be there soon. What's the name of the motel?"

"Uh, the Hideaway. I'm turning in now."

"Did the silver car follow you in."

"No. It stopped across the street. That sort of worries me, Mr. Steele. Why did it stop? What do they want from me?"

"Listen to me," said Steele, making sure he kept his voice calm. "Go into the motel office. Watch from there to see if that car does anything."

"All right. I'm pulling into a parking spot."

Steele handed the phone back to Rudd.

The last two lights before the freeway on-ramp were green, and Steele was barely able to overtake a big brown UPS truck before he had to duck back into the right lane to make it onto the freeway on-ramp. He built up speed all the way down the curving ramp, and once he was on the freeway, he began to slalom his way through the heavy evening traffic.

Rudd was again clinging to his seat belt. He held the phone against his chest and whispered, "What's the big hurry? Is she in danger?"

"She could be. Someone lured her to LA, claiming to be me. They told her to meet me at Crueltown."

Rudd let out a low whistle. "Crueltown. Not that place again. But why would anybody want her to go out there?"

"They may be trying to find her husband. Somehow they must have found out I'd been hired to find him and used me to get her to come here from Las Vegas. Ask her if she's in the motel office."

Rudd nodded. "Are you in the office yet, Mrs. Culp?"

"Yes, but the manager is on the phone talking to somebody. What should I do?"

Rudd looked at Steele.

"Ask her if she sees anyone in the parking lot. Is that silver car still across the street?"

"Look in the parking lot, Mrs. Culp? Can you see that silver car?"

"Just a second. I'll have to go to the window."

Rudd put his hand over the phone.

"She's looking."

"I'm at the window, Mr. Rudd. Are you still there?"

"I'm still here, Mrs. Culp"

"The car hasn't moved. No, wait, now they're pulling in here. They are . . . Oh no, they parked right behind my car. Oh, dear. A man in a long leather coat is getting out. He's looking inside my car. He's . . . now he's back at their car, talking to somebody inside. What should I . . . oh, now a man in the back seat rolled down his window. The man in the long coat is leaning down talking to him."

"Give me the phone," said Steele.

Rudd handed it over.

"Mrs. Culp, it's Drew Steele again. Listen to me. Don't stand in front of the window. Is there a place where you can watch that car without them seeing you?"

"Just a second. Yes, I can see them through this little window in the door, but the manager is staring at me. I think he's getting suspicious."

"Just keep watching that car. If anyone heads toward the motel office, tell the manager to call the police."

"Really? But what if they only want a room?"

"Then you can say you're sorry, that you made a mistake. Mrs. Culp, you have to realize that if someone is following you, you may be in danger."

After a moment's silence, she said, "In danger? But . . . why?"

"Those men may think you know where your husband is. Do you?"

"No. Isn't that why the casino hired you? To find him? I don't understand any of this."

"We'll talk as soon as I get there. Just keep watching that car."

"I'm not feeling so good, Mr. Steele. I think I may have to sit down. My legs feel kind of . . . shaky."

"You have to be brave, Mrs. Culp. Can you think of any reason why those men might be looking for your husband?"

"No. I didn't even think the casino should have hired you. At least not so quickly. Maybe he . . . I mean, maybe Ken just needed some time to think. Needed to get away. Lately, he's been under a lot of . . . Well, I'm . . . not sure."

Steele immediately realized Mrs. Culp didn't know about the missing money. The casino wasn't interested in finding Culp; they just wanted to get their money back. "What were you about to say, Mrs. Culp? Under a lot of what? Pressure?"

"Yes, but maybe he . . . wait . . . the man in the leather coat is walking away from their car. Now I can see him better. I think he might be Mexican, or something like that. Hispanic anyhow."

"Is he coming toward the office?"

"No, he's walking over to my car. He's trying the doors. What should I do?"

"Tell the manager to call the police."

"Really?"

"Yes, tell him somebody has been harassing you. Tell him they followed you to the motel."

Steele heard her talking to the manager, then she came back on the phone: "He's doing it. He's really scared. A little foreign man. He talks with a funny accent. I can barely understand him."

"Are you back by the door?"

"Yes."

"What is the man in the leather coat doing now?"

"He's moved away from my car. He's walking this way. No, wait, he's gone back to their car. He's talking to the man in the front seat again. Oh, God. I'm scared, Mr. Steele. What should I do?"

"Stay where you are. I'm getting off the freeway right now. I'll be there in just a few minutes." Steele dropped the cell phone into his lap and made a wide turn onto the off-ramp. He knew he was going way too fast to make the upcoming turn onto Pacific Coast Highway at the bottom of the off-ramp. His only chance was to lock up the brakes and then throw the car sideways to skid onto the street. The tires howled as he did it, but it worked: he was able to squeeze into the heavy traffic, barely avoiding clipping the rear end of a well-preserved old Chevy. He waited for his chance, then darted around the Chevy. The elderly woman in the old car stared wide-eyed as he flew past.

Rudd gulped loudly. "Wow, those are some good . . . brakes."

Steele picked up the phone. "Now listen carefully, Mrs. Culp. I'm driving a white Ford. A big car. Four doors. I'll be coming into the motel's parking lot soon, and I'll be moving fast. I'll pull up in front of the office. As soon as I stop, we'll swing open the back-seat door. You run out and get in. Do you understand?"

"I . . . I guess so. But what about my rental car?"

"We'll worry about that later."

"All right, if you say so."

Steele saw the Hideaway Motel sign ahead on the right. "There it is." He maintained his speed, waiting for the right moment to brake.

Rudd put both hands out against the dash. "No, wait, you're going too fast."

Steele braked hard, and dived into the parking lot. The front tires lost grip and he almost clipped the edge of the building, but he quickly corrected the slide and came to a sudden, tire-smoking stop in front of the motel office door. "Now!" he yelled into the phone. "Come out now. Run!"

The motel office door flew open and Mrs. Culp came running out. She was a big woman, but she was moving pretty fast.

Rudd reached back and opened the back seat door for her. She jumped in, and Rudd pulled the door closed. Steele immediately floored the accelerator to put the car into a rubber-burning drift to make it spin around in the tight parking lot. Out of the corner of his eye, he saw the man in the leather coat run for the silver car. It was a BMW 750i. If they decided to follow, it meant trouble: it was a very powerful, good-handling car.

Steele got the car straightened out just in time to slide back onto Pacific Coast Highway. He was barely able to squeeze between two of the many cars that were lined up in the right-hand, eastbound lane. The car behind him laid on his horn, but Steele ignored it and quickly moved over into the left lane. He accelerated, keeping his eyes on the rearview mirror to see if the BMW was following. If they were willing to follow even after they had been made, it would tell him a lot. It would mean they wanted Mrs. Culp badly. But why?

He saw the BMW roar out of the motel parking lot. They *were* coming.

Steele switched lanes back and forth to try to find a path through the heavy traffic, but he kept on having to slam on the brakes as he came up on slower cars. He wasn't getting much of a lead on the BMW.

Rudd turned in his seat to look back. "They're still coming. Should I call nine-one-one?"

Steele glanced in the rearview mirror. The BMW seemed to be staying back a ways. Maybe they were just going to follow to see where Mrs. Culp was going. "Let's wait and see what they do."

"But why were they following *me*?" said Mrs. Culp. Her voice was high-pitched and panicky. "I really don't know where Ken went. Maybe we should just stop. I'll tell them I don't know where he is, and then they'll leave us alone."

Steele adjusted his visor mirror so he could see her. She was turned sideways in her seat, looking back. Her hands were clasped together, as if she was praying. "It won't help talk to them, Mrs. Culp. The fact that they are still following us tells me they probably weren't trying to find your husband after all. They know we won't lead them to him. But if that's so, I have to ask myself why they would want you so badly. What aren't you telling us, Mrs. Culp?" He watched for her response in the mirror. She looked confused.

"Me? I don't know anything. What do they want?"

"You tell me."

"Honestly, Mr. Steele, I don't know."

She seemed to be telling the truth. But if she didn't know anything about her husband's disappearance, why had they lured her to Crueltown? It didn't make any sense.

"They're getting closer," said Rudd.

Steele could see he was right. "Not much I can do about it in this traffic. But let's see how bad they want us." He darted out into the left lane and hit the gas. The Ford picked up speed quickly, but moving that fast in the heavy Pacific Coast Highway evening traffic meant he had to keep a close watch on every car they came up on to be sure they didn't make an unexpected move. Luckily, most of them saw the Ford's very bright halogen driving lights closing fast behind them and stayed out of his way.

"We're coming to Wilmington," said Rudd. "You gonna stay on PCH?"

"For now."

"There's a deserted stretch of this road before we get to the 710 freeway," said Rudd. "They may try something there."

"I was thinking the same thing," said Steele. "But there's an industrial area there. I know the streets. Hopefully, they don't."

"Think you can lose them?"

"I'm going to try. There's a shortcut the truckers use to keep from getting weighed."

Just before they got to the shortcut, they came up on a white Mercedes convertible that made a sudden lane change, pulling right in front of them. Steele had to brake hard to keep from smashing into it. The squealing of his tires startled the very-blonde older woman in the Mercedes, so she reacted instinctively by giving him the middle-fingered LA salute. Steele darted around her in the right lane and accelerated away.

"Jesus, that was too close," said Rudd, waving his middle finger back at the woman. "And that Beemer was right behind us. I thought it was gonna smash into the back of us. They must have just about as gooda brakes as you do."

Steele stayed in the right lane, ready to duck into the industrial area when the shortcut street came up. As usual, there was a bit of the evening fog coming in off of the Long Beach harbor. Steele's bright driving lights boring through the fog made an eerie effect.

The BMW came up close behind and stayed there.

Steele pushed the accelerator to the floor and yelled, "Hang on everybody."

Mrs. Culp reached forward to grab Steele's shoulder. "Please slow down. You're scaring me."

Rudd reached over and pried her hand off. "Just sit back and make sure your seat belt is tight, Mrs. Culp. Steele knows what he's doing." But then he mumbled to himself, "I hope."

Steele let off the gas just enough to make sure the BMW was right on his tail, then he hit the brakes and jerked the steering wheel hard right. It put the car into a four-wheel slide, and when it was lined up with the side street that led into the industrial area, he feathered the gas pedal just enough to give the tires a bit of traction. As the tires bit, the car darted onto the side street, coming much too close to the huge front grill of a big semi-truck that was just pulling up to the stop sign.

Mrs. Culp shrieked, "Oh my God." She closed her eyes and put her hands over her face.

As soon as Steele got the car straightened out, he accelerated away down the dark street. The truck driver leaned on his air horn, but the sound quickly faded as they sped away into the darkness.

Rudd looked back. "It worked. They missed the turn. Ha! They almost smashed into that damned truck."

Steele put the car into a drifting turn again to get around the next corner. The tires howled, but the heavy-duty suspension held steady. One more turn, this time just grazing the outside curb, and they were on a straight street, picking up speed. He swerved to get around another semi, and then the street was dark ahead. He pushed the car even faster, trying to make it out of the industrial area before the BMW could recover and come looking for them.

"I think you lost them," said Rudd. "Now if we can just get back to the main street before they--"

Suddenly, there were bright lights coming out of the fog right in front of them. Steele managed to miss the oncoming car, but as it shot past, he saw it was the silver BMW.

"Damn," said Rudd. "How did they find us so quick?"

In the mirror, Steele saw the BMW make a tire-smoking U-turn, and soon it was gaining on them again.

"Here they come," said Rudd. "Boy, that car is fast!"

Steele heard a pop, and a spider's web of cracks appeared in the back window.

"Get down," yelled Steele.

"What was that?" screamed Mrs. Culp.

"They're shooting," shouted Rudd. "I guess we're gonna get to test that bullet-proof glass you had installed."

"It's holding so far," said Steele. "Stay down, Mrs. Culp. You too, Rudd."

The sound of several metallic pings came from the rear of the car, followed by the whine of bullets glancing off of the pavement.

"They're still shooting," said Rudd. "I think they're trying to hit our tires."

Steele couldn't see Mrs. Culp anymore. He said, "Are you all right, Mrs. Culp?"

She only whimpered in response.

"There's enough Kevlar in the trunk to stop their bullets," said

Steele, "but I don't know how long that window will hold."

"Man oh man," whimpered Rudd, scrunching down in the seat to make himself as small a target as possible. "If anybody here knows how to pray, this would be a good time."

Steele heard Mrs. Culp whisper to herself: "Dear God, just let me live through this and I'll change. I really will."

More bullets hit the rear window, and Steele began to swerve back and forth. He heard another ping as a shot hit the trunk lid, and then a loud crack as yet another shot hit the glass.

"The back window's still holding," said Rudd. "But what if they get up next to us? Are these side-windows bullet proof?" He tapped on the glass.

"Only a couple of layers of polycarbonate," said Steele. They'll hold for the first shot, but that's all."

"That's reassuring," mumbled Rudd. "Maybe we should tell them to only shoot once." He scrunched down even further, as far as his seat belt would let him.

Steele didn't have time to answer. He was approaching the onramp to the 710 freeway, and he knew he was going too fast to make the turn because the steering felt heavy; it meant one of the front tires had been hit. The double-chambers of the racing tires would keep them partially inflated for a while, but if the outside chamber became completely deflated, he wasn't sure they would stay on the rims under really hard braking.

Time to test them, he decided. He hit the brakes hard, and the rear end immediately broke loose. It meant at least one of the rear tires was also partially flat. He corrected the slide, but realized he was going to hit the curb anyhow. He steered into it to make sure they hit straight on. They bounced over the curb, slid sideways, clipped a sign pole, and scraped the concrete ramp barrier, but somehow Steele managed to get the car straightened out in time to enter the freeway. By some miracle, they were not hit by any of the cars in the fast-moving stream of late-afternoon traffic.

Steele saw an opening in the traffic in the middle lane and hit the gas to dive into it. The engine responded, but the car felt unstable; it was tending to pull to the left, and that meant the tire on that side was deflating fast and might come apart.

"Doesn't this freeway come to an end soon?" shouted Rudd.

"It dead ends out by the Queen Mary parking lot," said Steele, but I plan to get off before then. Are they still back there?"

Rudd peeked over the top of his seat. "Yeah, they're right behind us. It looks like they've stopped shooting."

"Too many witnesses on the freeway," said Steele.

Steele had to work hard to keep the car straight. He moved into the right lane to make sure the BMW couldn't come up next to them to keep him from taking an exit.

"What're you gonna to do?" said Rudd. "Shouldn't I be calling the police?"

"Go ahead and make the call if you want to, but we'll be there before the operator figures out where we are."

"We'll be where?"

"We've got tires going down. I'm going to try to make it to the Long Beach police station. It's not far off the freeway. Is Mrs. Culp all right?"

Rudd looked back. "She's lying down on the seat. Are you all right Mrs. Culp?"

She murmured something.

"I think she's crying," said Rudd. "Or praying. Or both."

"Good," said Steele. "Tell her to keep on praying. We can use all the help we can get." He saw the downtown Long Beach exit coming up and got ready to take it. With partially-flat tires, it wasn't going to be easy.

The driver of the BMW seemed to sense what he was about to do and came up fast. Before Steele could take evasive action, the BMW smashed into his back bumper, throwing them sideways. Steele fought to correct the slide. "Hold on," he yelled.

Mrs. Culp's praying got louder.

Steele barely had time to get the car straightened out before the BMW hit them again, and this time they didn't back off. They were pushing, hard. Steele knew they were trying to spin him out, or push him into the guardrail. He hit the gas and tried to keep the car straight as he approached the exit. The BMW broke contact and swerved into the next lane, clipping the rear end of the white SUV that was next to Steele's car. There were several surprised-looking women inside it. The SUV's driver failed to let off the gas, and it hit the side of Steele's car. She over-corrected and swung her car back to the left, smacking into the side of a shiny new red pickup truck. The resulting series of collisions and spin outs was the last thing Steele saw in his rear-view mirror as he dived off the freeway onto the Broadway Street exit.

But before he could make it down onto the surface street, the BMW came roaring up from behind and again smashed into his rear bumper. Steele managed to keep the Ford straight, but then the shooting started again. The rear window finally couldn't take any more hits and blew in, scattering fragments of glass everywhere inside the car. Mrs. Culp was screaming non-stop now, and even Rudd let out a scared yelp as he frantically tried to brush the glass out of his hair.

"Keep your heads down," yelled Steele. "We're almost there."

He pushed the accelerator to the floor. He was trying hard to keep the car straight, but it was wandering back and forth on the curved off-ramp, hitting first one side wall and then the other. Steele hoped it hadn't bent the fenders in to the point they would cut into the front tires.

Finally, they made it down to the surface street. Steele knew the police station was only two blocks ahead. All he had to do was keep the BMW behind him until he got there.

"Here they come again," yelled Rudd.

With Steele's car crippled, the BMW soon made up the distance. They came up alongside and a Hispanic-looking man in the passenger seat seemed to be laughing as he pointed a large revolver right at Steele's face. Steele hit the brakes just as the man squeezed off a shot. From the sharp metallic pop, it sounded as if the shot had hit the door post. Too close.

The BMW slowed, and the man had his revolver out the window, getting ready to fire again, but Steele slammed the accelerator to the floor and his car shot forward. Steele heard the shot, but didn't hear it hit anything.

Mrs. Culp's screaming got *much* louder.

Steele saw the light turn red at the next intersection, but he didn't let up on the gas. A red convertible sports car with two bikini-clad girls in it moved out into the middle of the intersection, waiting to turn left. As Steele shot past them, missing the front of their car by inches, they shouted and waved cheerfully.

In the rearview mirror, Steele saw the BMW swerve to miss the girls' car, and then accelerate to come again.

The parking lot of the Long Beach police station was coming up on the right. Steele aimed for the entrance, hoping his tires would hold together long enough to make it.

Rudd looked up just in time to see the arm of the wooden guard gate coming at them. He yelled, "Oh, no!" and put both hands against the dash.

The guard's eyes got very wide as Steele blew through the gate, turning it into flying splinters. The moment they were through the gate, Steele hit the brakes, but it felt like both rear tires were now flat. It made his car skid to the side where it glanced off of a parked black and white cruiser and then into the side of a shiny black unmarked police car. Steele's car pushed the black car several yards sideways until it hit a motorcycle that fell over onto another motorcycle. Steele's car finally came to a stop, but the row of police motorcycles continued to fall over, each one knocking over the next, every one of them eventually going down like a line of noisy metal dominoes.

Steele switched off the engine and said, "Well, here we are." He calmly rolled down his window and waited for the police to come.

The cop from the guard gate came running up, his gun out. "Stay where you are!" he yelled. "Keep your hands where I can see them."

Steele raised his hands. "You don't have to be afraid of us," he said cheerfully. "Just a little mishap. I can explain everything."

The guard was screaming into his radio. "Get me some help out here. Somebody just crashed into the Lieutenant's car. And they knocked over all the motorcycles too."

Soon, a large number of policemen came running out of the station. They surrounded the car, pointing their guns.

Steele smiled and said, "Good evening, fellas. Sorry about the mess."

The police held their ground until a man in a suit arrived, out of breath. He put both hands on Steele's windowsill and said, "What the hell's the matter with you? That's my car you just ruined." He was looking at the smashed-in shiny black car, grimacing as if he was in pain.

"We were being chased," said Steele. "If you ask the guard, he will tell you that a silver BMW sped away as we came in. They were shooting at us. As you can see, they shot out my rear window. You'll also find several bullet holes in the trunk."

The man glanced at the back of the car, and then scowled at Steele. "Yeah, I can see that. But for Christ's sake, did you have to take it out on *my* car? It was brand new."

"Sorry," said Steele. "Would you mind telling your men to lower their guns. We have a very frightened woman in here."

The man leaned in to look at Mrs. Culp who was still lying on the back seat, whimpering. "What's the matter with her?".

"She's praying," said Rudd. He leaned across Steele and stuck out his hand to the policeman. "I'm John Rudd, crack reporter for the Independent, and when I write my story about this in tomorrow's paper, I'll be sure to tell them what a great job you and your men are doing out here in Long Beach."

The man shook his head and turned away. "Put these people in the detention cell until I can figure out what the hell happened here."

"Right, chief. On what charge?"

"I don't care. Just lock 'em up. Book 'em for . . ." He turned to look at his smashed-in car. "How about destroying public property. For starters."

# Chapter 2

*T*he buzzing of a cell phone was like a warning, part of the dream in which a young boy in rags was leading the way into bombed-out ruins. A map of Baghdad was spread out on the blood-stained table. It showed where all the IEDs were hidden.

As the cell phone continued to buzz, Steele stared up into the darkness. He had hoped the war dreams would end after he left Iraq. They hadn't.

He shook off the remnants of the dream and felt for the phone. He clicked it on and mumbled, "This better be a wrong number."

The response might have been a cough, or more likely, a suppressed laugh.

"You sound sleepy, Steele. Didn't wake you, did I?"

It was Rudd. Why the hell would he be calling in the middle of the night? "Very humorous, Rudd. Why would you think I'd be asleep at . . ." Steele snapped on his bedside light and tried to focus on the clock. "Four AM?"

Rudd chuckled again. "Yeah, well, you'll be happy I woke you when you hear what I just picked up on the police scanner. I was trying to help you find your missing Vegas guy, and I heard some squawk about a body they found out at Crueltown. Next to the west fence. How about that, Steele? West side of Crueltown? Same place as somebody led Mrs. Culp last week. That get your interest? Or do you think it's just a coincidence."

It did get Steele's attention. Crueltown again. And Steele didn't believe in coincidences. "What makes you think it's him?"

"Call it reporter's instinct."

Steele swung his feet out of bed and reached for his pants. "Reporter's instinct, eh? What was it really?"

"Well, soon as I heard the report on the scanner, I called my contact at county sheriff's dispatch. She'd heard some radio chatter from the cops on the scene. They said the stiff was an older guy, gray hair. Not only that, they said he was a big guy. Doesn't that sound like your missing man?"

"More likely it's just another old transient. They find dead transients out there all the time."

"Yeah, I know they find a lot of bodies out at Crueltown, but hey, when somebody dies inside there, don't they usually just throw 'em over the fence? This guy was in the trunk of a car."

Steele cradled the cell phone with his shoulder as he strapped his prosthetic foot to his lower leg. The little Beretta automatic and the pen gun were still in place. Expecting more trouble, he'd left them there since the car chase in Long Beach. But there had been no further sign of the men who had attacked them. Mrs. Culp had gone back to Las Vegas. He had advised her to go to the casino for protection, but she hadn't, and for some reason, she wasn't returning his calls.

The police hadn't found the BMW, which didn't surprise Steele. Despite the apparent disappearance of their attackers, Steele knew the car chase wouldn't be the end of it: somebody had been trying to kill him, and they had been willing to do it in front of witnesses. Sooner or later, they would try again.

His car had been repaired, and the insurance company had begrudgingly paid for all the damage before canceling his policy. The Long Beach police department's charge of destroying public property had been dropped, and it was as if the whole incident had never happened.

"Hey, Steele, are you still there? Am I right, or am I right?"

"So you put two and two together, and figured it had to be the old guy my client is looking for."

"Well, why not? It could be, couldn't it? Maybe he was out there at Crueltown trying to buy drugs and got himself killed. And get this, my contact said the cops on the radio were all jabbering about something that was burned into the stiff's forehead. A warning of some kind."

"A warning?"

That's what she said."

"Burned? Like what? Like a tattoo?"

"She said burned. That's all she knew. C'mon, Steele, aren't my hunches usually right on? Let's go take a look."

"All right, I'll meet you there in half an hour." Steele clicked off the phone, and as he finished dressing, he thought about what Rudd had said. Why would somebody go to the trouble of burning some kind of warning into the forehead of a body? And what kind of warning would fit on a forehead? A word? A symbol?

He went to his closet and got out an inconspicuous-looking tan Harris tweed jacket. He slipped it on as he went into his office. He sat down at the desk and turned on the lamp to look up Monroe's number at the Golden Palace Casino in Las Vegas. He punched in the number, and while it rang, he turned on the computer and scanned through his old emails. He found the email from Monroe and printed out the attachment that provided the missing man's description.

"Yeah? Whatta ya want?"

Monroe always sounded a little pissed off. "Mr. Monroe? This is Drew Steele calling from LA. I may have something for you."

"You found him already?"

"Not sure yet. Could your employee have been into drugs?"

"Are you kidding? You think we'd put a drug freak in charge of the count? Culp was as an old man, about as straight'n narrow as they come. With a plain-as-mud wife. Two kids already grown up and left the nest. Does that sound like a guy who would go in for drugs?"

"It doesn't, but the police here found a body of a large older man in an area known as a place to buy drugs. I'm heading there now to check it out, but if it's Culp, I'm going to need some way to make a positive identification."

"I sent you the pictures. Didn't you get 'em?"

Steele moved aside the overnight delivery envelope, and picked up the two photos. "I'm looking at them now, but from these head-and-shoulder shots he could be Joe Anybody. Ever see a dead body, Mr. Monroe? Even the relatives have a hard time identifying the deceased."

"All right, you go check it out. If you think it might be Culp, call me back and I'll fly down there to identify him myself. Did they find the money?"

"No report of any money. The body was found in the trunk of a car. If he had any money, the killer wouldn't be likely to leave it behind."

"No, I guess not. Well, call me back in . . . what, a couple of hours?"

"You won't be asleep?"

"We're on Vegas time here, Steele. I sleep in the daytime."

# Chapter 3

As he drove over the bridge to the harbor, Steele saw one of the huge Hong Kong container ships being unloaded at the far side of the ship channel. The crane was in the process of lowering one of the large metal containers onto a waiting flat-bed truck. A line of empty trucks stretched for half a mile around the periphery of the gigantic parking lot, waiting for their turn to be loaded.

Steele thought about those containers being filled and loaded onto that ship by Chinese laborers back in the Hong Kong harbor. The last time he was there, he'd spent a lot of time down at the harbor watching the busy activity. He liked wandering the streets near the harbor, exploring the dockside shops, many of which were filled to overflowing with strange looking, but apparently edible, root vegetables that emanated an amazing diversity of exotically indescribable odors. He had enjoyed the trip, despite the sad way that case had turned out.

It would be fairly warm in southern China this time of year. Maybe he should take another trip there, this time for pleasure. If not there, he should at least take a trip somewhere, as soon as he was done with this case, as soon as he found the elusive Mr. Kenneth Culp.

Steele took the printout of Culp's description out of his pocket and turned on the overhead light to read as he drove. Sixty-three years old, six foot one, two hundred and forty pounds. A big guy. If Culp really was the man in the car's trunk, it would be a tight fit.

The summary sent by Monroe said Culp had been reported missing by his wife when he didn't come home from work at the usual time. In his original phone call, Monroe had said they thought a good chunk of the casino's money was gone too. They were still checking it out. That made it seem like a straightforward case: guy up and disappears along with an unknown amount of money. Happens every day. Rudd suspected he had run off with a younger woman, and with an older man like Culp, it did often turn out to be some kind of mid-life crisis: failed aspirations, trouble with the wife, tired of his job, or just dissatisfied with life in general. Usually a younger woman was involved. But when Steele had suggested they check to see if any of Culp's female fellow employees were also missing, Monroe had sent back a terse email to say none were, and besides, that wouldn't be like Culp.

Steele turned off the overhead light and put the printout back in his pocket. Maybe this wasn't the usual mid-life crisis thing after all.

As he approached Crueltown, Steele saw the police red and blue lights flashing vaguely through the thick smog. As he got closer, he saw several squad cars lined up next to the Crueltown fence. He recognized the last car in the line as Captain Pruett's unmarked black Buick. Steele was mildly amused. Pretty early in the morning for Pruett. Maybe they'd roused him out of bed for this one.

Steele parked a short distance from the police cars and got out. As he locked his car door, a young sheriff's deputy approached him. The deputy cautiously looked him over, keeping his flashlight's beam in Steele's face. "Can't stop here, sir. Police investigation."

Steele showed his private investigator's license. "I got a call. Is Pruett in charge here?"

"Yes, sir. Did Captain Pruett call you?"

"I'd better talk to him. I'm supposed to identify the man. They haven't taken the body away yet, have they?"

"No, not yet. Well, uh, if Captain Pruett okayed it, I guess I can let you by. They're over there by the fence." He pointed with his flashlight toward a group of men standing behind a car.

Steele recognized Pruett even from that distance. He was dressed in his usual worn-out suit, a charcoal pin-striper that might have fit him twenty years earlier. He was shining a bright light into the trunk of a new-looking Mercedes. But it wasn't Culp's car: Monroe's email had described the missing man's car as an older Honda hatchback. The Mercedes would probably turn out to be stolen.

When Steele got closer, he saw that the dead man in the carpeted trunk was curled up in the fetal position, crammed in tight. A blue tarp was under him, partially wrapped around his legs. There were no apparent injuries to the man's body, and it didn't look like there was any blood on the tarp. The lack of blood indicated the man had been killed somewhere else and dumped into the trunk afterward. And more than one person was involved because it would take at least two strong men to put that big body in there. Could it be a professional killing? If so, there would be a small hole in the side of the man's head. A pro would pride himself in doing the job with a single shot from a small caliber weapon.

Steele leaned over Pruett's shoulder. "Was it a pro hit?"

Pruett turned to shine his flashlight in Steele's eyes. "Steele. Who let you in here?"

Steele held up his hand to ward off the light. "I got a call. This may be a man I've been looking for."

"So you're up and around now. I heard you got torn up pretty bad over there in Iraq. One of those IED bombs, wasn't it?"

"I'm fine now. Can I look this guy over?"

"You're gonna have to wait 'til we send him down to the morgue. We haven't finished here yet."

"Bet you won't find a thing," said Steele. "Dinner at Monte's says the car is clean."

"You're probably right about that. Car's clean as a whistle up front. Trunk looks pretty clean too, but we'll know more when we get this guy out. I'll take the free dinner anyhow. Give me a call later." Pruett turned away to shine his light back into the trunk.

Even from where he was standing, Steele could see that there were some dark marks on the body's forehead. Was that the message Rudd had mentioned?

Steele took a moment to memorize the car's license number, then he put his hand on Pruett's shoulder. "What about that warning on his forehead?"

Pruett turned back to face him, scowling. "What do you know about that?"

"The warning may have been meant for my client."

"Listen, Steele, if you know anything about this you'd better tell me right now."

"Like I said, it may be a guy I've been looking for."

"Yeah? Well, maybe you can tell us why somebody would want to burn a couple of words onto this stiff's forehead. Where is it we're supposed to keep out of? Crueltown?"

Steele shrugged. "Let me in on this and I'll tell you everything I know. We can work together."

"I've heard that one before. If you know somethin', you'd better tell me. This is the third body we've found out here since Christmas. It means somethin's goin' on inside Crueltown. You've been inside the fence. What's going on in there? Some kind of drug war?"

Steele shrugged. "I don't know any more than you do. I haven't been in there since I went in after Furtado."

It was the truth. Steele hadn't set foot inside the Crueltown fence since the Furtado drug ring had kidnapped the mayor's little daughter to try to ransom her to get back a huge heroin cache the police had seized. The kidnapping of a kid was about the only thing that would take Steele inside that fence, but his job had been to find her and he did. Too bad she was already dead.

Pruett took Steele's arm and walked him away from the car. "I can't let you roll the guy over to ID him until we're done here. We haven't even dusted for prints yet. But the coroner's on his way so we should have this guy packaged up and out of here pretty soon. After they get him checked into the morgue, you can tell the guys down there I said it was all right for you to give him the once over."

# Chapter 4

*B*y the time Steele got back to his car, Rudd was there, leaning up against it. His face looked tired and his wrinkled and baggy old brown suit looked like he'd slept in it. Steele suspected Rudd often slept fully dressed, probably dozing next to the police scanner, ready to jump up and bolt out the door to be well ahead of any other news reporters if he caught wind of a late-night LA crime.

"Careful, you'll scratch the paint," said Steele, unlocking the door.

Rudd turned to pat the Ford's fender. "You'd have a hell of a time figuring out which scratch was mine. When are you gonna get a new car, Steele?"

"This car is fine."

"Seems like you should've made the insurance company replace it instead of just patching it up after our Long Beach adventure. Hey, I know you've put a lot of special stuff into this car, but it's gotta be . . . what, four years old? It'll be a classic soon."

"Then it won't be inconspicuous anymore and I'll have to get a different one."

Rudd shrugged and pointed toward the line of police cars. "They wouldn't let me in. What did you find out? Is it your man?"

"From what I could see, it might be. Gray hair, and about the right height and weight."

"See there. Didn't I tell you?" Rudd tapped the side of his head. "Reporter's instinct."

"Maybe I should give up investigating and just go on your instincts."

"You could do worse. Well, whatta ya think? Is there a story in this for me?"

"Not likely. A casino employee goes missing and turns up dead. Your rag won't print that unless he got abducted by aliens."

"Don't make fun of the independents, Steele. Without us all you'd get is the sanitized, big-brother version of corporate-controlled news. And besides, what about that warning that was burned into his forehead? That's not your normal missing persons deal."

"That's true. An odd touch. They wouldn't let me get a close look, but I'm guessing the words were 'Keep Out.' What do you make of that?"

Rudd thought about it, scratching his chin. "Keep out? Sounds like a sign on a fence. Keep out of where? Crueltown?"

"Could be. I guess that's what we're going to have to find out, isn't it?"

"We? Does that mean you're going to let me in on this one?"

"I could use your help on something. Want to follow me back to my place?"

"Sure. Hey, we could sit out by the pool and talk about it. Maybe some good-looking girls will be out there having an early-morning swim."

"Not likely. Follow me. I'm going to take the harbor route back."

"I'll be right behind you."

As Steele turned back to the south, he saw Rudd's headlights swing around to follow him. It would be nice if Rudd *would* meet a new woman, somebody kind and gentle who would take care of him, at least until he got back on his feet. Since Rudd's divorce, he'd been hitting the bottle a little too hard and haunting the downtown bars where he seemed to have a knack of meeting some of the strangest women in LA. Even worse, lately Rudd had been pestering him to come along on those bar-hopping outings, trying to convince him that since Loren had run off to Paris to study art he should try to find some new female companionship.

Steele turned up the police scanner, trying to catch any mention of them finding a body in a car trunk. There was nothing but the usual freeway pile ups and police pursuits.

As he drove back toward the harbor, Steele thought about how the big man's body had been stuffed into the trunk of that Mercedes. It would take more than one strong man to do that. And the lack of blood on the blue tarp showed he'd been dead for some time before the killers threw him in there. So why did they bother to put a tarp under him? It was as if they wanted to protect the car. But why would they do that if the car was stolen?

After he was through the toll gates and starting up over the long arching bridge that spanned the west ship channel, Steele saw that they had almost finished unloading the big Hong Kong container ship. The port was shrouded in the usual smog mixed with fog, but the bright phosphor lights from the crane operator's cabin high above the ship were bright enough to penetrate the murky night. The crane was rapidly lifting the containers off the ship and lowering them onto the waiting flat-bed trucks. A short distance away, another container ship was tied up, still fully loaded, waiting its turn. They would be unloading that one for the rest of the night and most of the morning.

Steele drove the rest of the way over the bridge thinking about ships and far-away places. It was definitely time for another trip abroad, but maybe not the Far East this time. What about Paris? He hadn't been there in years. Maybe he should surprise Loren, let her take him to the Louvre and explain which of the paintings were great and which ones weren't. She'd like that. But on second thought, maybe she wouldn't be so happy if he showed up on her doorstep unexpectedly. She might be involved with somebody else by now. Lately her emails had been mentioning one particular art professor that seemed to have taken a great fancy to "her work."

At his sprawling hillside condo complex overlooking the Pacific, Steele pulled up to the front gate. When the guard came out of the glassed-in guard shack, Steele rolled down his window. "There's a guy behind me in an old Dodge. Name's Rudd. Big guy. Thinning hair. Give him a visitor's pass when he gets here?"

The guard wrote down the information and waved him in without smiling. After the last round of home-invasion robberies in the surrounding neighborhood of expensive homes, the guards had begun to take their jobs much more seriously.

Steele parked in the upper-canyon parking structure and hurried to his condo unit. Inside, he turned off the alarm system and went upstairs to his office to check his email. He scanned through the list of messages. Nothing regarding the Culp case. And nothing from Loren.

He clicked on the icon of the international clock at the bottom of the computer screen and selected Paris. It was mid-afternoon there. Maybe Loren would be home from class by now. Should he call her? He glanced at her picture on the desk and decided to take a chance. He punched in her number on the desk phone's autodialer. No answer. When her answering machine came on, he left a brief message saying he was thinking about coming to Paris for a visit. Maybe as soon as his current case was finished. Would she be free?

He was just hanging up when he heard Rudd's knock on the door. He went downstairs to let him in. As soon as Steele opened the door, Rudd said, "Let's hit the pool."

"At six AM? No self-respecting woman would be out there at this time of day."

Rudd grinned. "I'm not looking for a self-respecting woman. I'm looking for . . . the other kind."

Steele ignored that comment. "I thought you said you wanted to help on this case. We've got work to do. I need a license number."

"The car the body was found in?"

"That's right. It was a fairly-new Mercedes Turbo Diesel. California plates. I'll write down the number for you."

"Why bother checking it out? It had to be stolen, didn't it?"

"I'm sure it was, but somebody put a tarp in the trunk before they threw the body in there."

Rudd frowned. "They didn't want to get the trunk messed up? That's odd, if the car really was stolen."

"It could mean the thief knew the owner of the car."

"What? You're saying the thief felt sorry for the car's owner? If I put that kind of thing in my story nobody would believe it, not in LA."

"What other reason can you think of for being so careful? Pruett said the interior of the car was also clean."

"Hmm. Okay, so you want me to call the DMV to find out who the owner is. I'm not sure I can ask Kate for another favor."

"Try."

"Well, maybe she'll talk to me. But the last time I was with her, she kind of said she never wanted to see me again."

"Use your charm on her."

"Actually, I may have used too much charm on her last time. Besides, can't you do it yourself online? You know, get on your fancy computer and go to one of those pay-for-info sites?"

"Not so easy to get info on a California plate since they passed the California Citizen's Privacy Act. That ten-thousand dollar fine makes even the online outfits think twice. Besides, that method takes time. I need the info right away."

"So you want me to be the one who gets the big fine?"

"Just make the call, Rudd."

"All right, all right, but she won't be into work for a couple of hours. You could use the time to make me breakfast. I'm starving. And then maybe we could go down to the pool to see if any of those non-self-respecting women are out there."

"I'll put some toast in the toaster. Then we should head for the morgue."

Rudd frowned. "Forget the toast. If I know you, all you've got is that healthy whole wheat stuff. And probably no jam either."

While Rudd went out to see if anyone was at the pool, Steele went up to his office and got back on the computer to check his crime news-alert service. After he put in his password, he searched for the latest reports. There was nothing much of interest during the past twelve hours, only two car chases and a shooting in Pico Rivera. Most of the alerts were about some Hollywood starlet who'd smashed her car into the front of a 7-11 store. The most current alert, only seventeen minutes old, said the starlet claimed to be only stoned on pot, definitely not drunk.

Rudd was soon back from the pool. "Nobody out there except some guy swimming laps. I asked him if he knew any hot girls in this complex, but he ignored me." He leaned over Steele's shoulder to look at the computer screen. "Anything new?"

Steele signed off the computer and stood up. "Nothing about the body at Crueltown. We'd better get going. I want to get to the morgue before they start processing the body."

"Don't you ever slow down?" complained Rudd. "And what about that breakfast? I'm really hungry."

"As I said, there's plenty of wheat bread. Help yourself."

Rudd turned up his nose. "Forget that healthy stuff. Hey, I know, let's stop on the way and get us some donuts."

"Donuts for breakfast?"

"Sure, why not? Breakfast of champions, or anyone with real taste buds."

They started for the door, but Rudd stopped and snapped his fingers. "Hey, that gives me an idea. Remember that old movie 'Breakfast at Tiffany's' where Audrey Hepburn eats her donut while she window-shops at Tiffany's? When I write my story about this case, I'll call it breakfast at the morgue."

# Chapter 5

*O*n the way to the morgue, Rudd spotted a donut shop and insisted Steele stop.

Steele waited in the car, listening to the police scanner, while Rudd ran in to buy "his favorite," the baker's dozen bag of assorted chocolate-covered and surprise-filled donuts.

The rest of the way downtown, Rudd munched on his donuts and rambled on about a girl he'd met at a plastic bar out in West Hollywood a few nights before. "She had really nice red hair," he said, "and it was almost her real hair color too, I'm sure of it. She had this cute way of tilting her head to the side every time I asked her a question. I'm sure I wrote down her number, but when I got home I went through every pocket and couldn't find it. Hey, Steele, how about we go back out there tonight? Maybe she'll be there again."

Steele shook his head. "Not tonight. How about trying your friend Kate at the DMV now about that license plate number."

Rudd looked up her phone number in his little black book and punched it in on his cell phone. He spoke to someone, then quickly hung up. "She's not there yet. They said she'll be in soon."

When they reached the imposing gray stone county building that housed the morgue, Steele parked in an official business space and led the way to the short flight of stairs that led up to the unloading dock.

As Steele used his sideways method of getting up the stairs, Rudd took Steele's elbow to help him.

Steele pulled his arm away and stopped to look at him. "What the hell do you think you're doing?"

Rudd quickly jerked his hand back. "Oh, sorry. I forgot. It was just . . . I mean, I know you don't need any help, but you always seem to have trouble with stairs. I thought maybe your legs were hurting you, or your foot, or I mean, where you used to have a foot. I . . . Aw, hell, you know what I mean."

"I can get up stairs fine. It just takes me a little longer than it used to."

Rudd nodded. "Right. Sorry, I wasn't thinking."

Steele made it up the last few steps and went into the building. He hurried as fast as he could down the long hallway to the morgue's intake room. The sound of his uneven steps echoed off the walls reminded him of how his odd gait must look to others: like a cripple. He hated that, but there was nothing he could do about it. Although the prosthetic foot had a flexible joint in the middle, the real problem was with his reconstructed knees: after many surgeries, they had finally become somewhat stable, but they were still both stiff, forcing him into an unnatural walking motion that was quite noticeable.

Rudd stayed close, but kept his hands to himself. "Jeez, Steele, doesn't this place give you the creeps? I used to hang out here on Saturday nights. You know, looking for offbeat stories. But eventually it got to me. After a while you get pretty sick of seeing them roll teenagers in here all shot up like they'd been in a war or something."

Steele didn't reply, but he'd spent enough nights in the morgue to know what Rudd said was true. South Central LA *was* a lot like a war zone when the gang wars heated up, and quite a few of the gang kid participants in the turf wars ended up at the morgue. It made him think once again about taking that trip abroad. LA was a great place to be in the detective business, but it was also a place you had to get away from now and then.

They found Ed Kelly busy working on a new arrival, a dirty-looking man with a long ragged beard. The body was still clothed, lying on it's back on the stainless steel table. The bright overhead light made the old man on the table look as stark and pale as a fake body from an old monster movie.

Kelly looked up from his task. "Hey, guys, what brings you down here so bright and early?"

"We just love to watch you work," said Rudd.

"Always glad to have admirers. But you might want to stand back a ways from this one. They found him camped out under some cardboard in the river channel. From the smell, I'd say he's been dead for . . . uh, three days, maybe four. I'd better get this one tagged and bagged and into the fridge quick." He used a pair of electric scissors to efficiently cut away the many layers of filthy clothes, revealing the man's bloated belly that sagged to one side. The smell of decaying flesh filled the room.

"Yuck," said Rudd. He turned away and fanned his hand in front of his face.

"We're looking for a body the homicide division sent in this morning," said Steele. "Pruett said I could take a look at him."

"The old guy they found out at Crueltown? The one with the forehead thing?"

"That's him."

"Drawer six." Kelly nodded toward the cold storage room. "I'll try to get to him before lunch."

They found locker six and Steele opened the door. The familiar smell of death came out, mixed with another strong odor.

"Damn," said Rudd, turning away and wrinkling up his nose. "What's that smell?"

"You know what it is," said Steele, "you just don't associate it with this place. Normally you'd like that smell."

Rudd turned back and sniffed the air again. "Burned meat? Steak?"

"That's right. Captain Pruett said the words had been *burned* into his forehead."

"Oh, Jesus," said Rudd. "You mean his skin got like . . . cooked?"

"Burned human flesh smells pretty much the same as any other animal's burned flesh," said Steele, sliding out the drawer. He folded back the plastic sheet. The two words on the man's forehead were small, but they stood out clearly, one word above the other: "Keep Out." It had been carefully done, impossible to ignore and easy to read even after death had contorted the man's features.

Rudd peered over Steele's shoulder. "Man, look at that, 'Keep Out' burned right into his skin. Looks deep too. Damn, that's horrible. I hope the guy wasn't still alive when they did that."

"Maybe Kelly can tell us about that when he does the autopsy."

Steele took out the two photos Monroe had sent him. Despite the bloating, Steele could tell it was the same man, the same sharply-pointed nose and thick curly eyebrows.

Rudd looked at the photos. "Looks like mug shots. Had your man been in jail?"

"These are probably copies of the photos the casino provides to the Nevada Gaming Commission. They're required of all key gaming personnel."

"So he's a casino boss?"

"Middle-management. He was a member of the count team at the Golden Palace Casino." Steele pulled down the plastic sheet to look at the clothes the body was dressed in. The man's conservative dark suit was fairly new, but not expensive. His white shirt was dirty around the collar, as if he'd worn it some days without having it washed.

"The Golden Palace? Hey, I been to that casino. They've got it all fixed up like a sultan's royal palace."

"No longer. They went into bankruptcy and got bought out. Their web site says the casino and the hotel are both undergoing a complete renovation to modernize it." Steele pulled the plastic sheet further down. There was mud on the man's pant legs, and his shoes and socks were missing. Had he tried to run away from the killers?

"So this guy was the one who got to count the casino's money, all those coins people shove into the slot machines?"

"No, that's done by machine. The count team counts the paper money. The take from the gambling tables."

"Ah, I guess somebody has to count it. Hey, wouldn't that be somethin', handling all that money?"

"I expect it gets pretty boring after a while," said Steele, pulling the sheet back up over the man's chest. "Like sorting dirty pieces of paper, over and over." He moved to the other side of the drawer to look at the side of the man's head. "Come look at this. There's a small bullet hole in his temple."

Rudd came to his side. "A pro hit?"

"Looks like it."

"You're not sure it was pros? Why not?"

"The single shot to the head makes it seem that way, but I'm wondering why pros would leave the body in a car."

"Hey, that's right. They could have dumped the body at Crueltown and then got rid of the car somewhere else."

Steele pushed the drawer closed. "I'd better call my client in Las Vegas. I'm pretty sure this is his man."

They went back out into the examining room.

Kelly was finishing up the prep on the old transient. He looked up at them, wiping his hands on his filthy rubber apron. "Was that your guy?"

"Yes, I think so," said Steele. "My client will come in to identify the body. When do you think you'll be starting the autopsy?"

"In a couple of hours. Hey, what about those words on his forehead? Pretty weird.

"It is," agreed Steele. "Very."

"Weird is a good word," said Rudd. "Weird sells. My readers are gonna love this one."

# Chapter 6

*B*ack out in the car, Steele called the casino.

Monroe answered on the first ring. "Yeah?"

"I'm here at the LA county morgue, Mr. Monroe. I think we've found Culp. You said you wanted to identify him personally?"

"Okay, I'll fly down. Text-message me the address of the morgue. I'll meet you there in three hours." He hung up.

"He's coming here," said Steele. "Three hours."

"Okay," said Rudd, "what do we do until then? Hey, I know a great little Italian restaurant near here. How about we go there for a snack? They've got the greatest spaghetti and meatballs you ever had, with all the garlic bread you can eat for free."

"Won't your friend at the DMV be at work by now?"

"Oh, yeah. I'll call her."

While Steele sent Monroe the morgue's address along with the link to a Google map of the location, Rudd called his lady friend on his own cell phone. When he was finished, he turned to Steele, grinning. "What a sweet gal. Wants me to meet her tonight for a drink. And here I thought she was still mad at me about that last time."

"Did you get the information?"

"Yeah. Car's registered to a woman out in Marina del Rey. Pretty swanky address." He tore the sheet out of his little notebook and handed it to Steele.

"Swanky? Now there's a word you don't hear much anymore."

Rudd shrugged. "It's what I think of every time I see a Marina del Rey address. You know, sea breezes, sunsets, gin and tonic out on the veranda"

Steele glanced at the paper. "Jenny Dainty? Is that her real name?"

"Kate said that's what it says on the registration."

Steele shook his head. "Only in LA."

On the way out to Marina del Rey, Rudd rattled on about his friend at the DMV, about what a great talker she was, about how you didn't need a key to wind her up.

Steele imagined them together, both talking a mile a minute. If she was as much of a talker as Rudd was, maybe they would spend more of their time talking and less time drinking. It might get Rudd out of the bar-hopping, romance-hoping game, at least for a while.

"Hey," said Rudd, pointing, "there's a burger joint. Let's stop."

"We've got to see this Jenny Dainty and get back to the morgue in three hours. My client is on his way from Vegas."

Rudd let out a low whistle. "How could he get here from Vegas that fast? What's he got, a magic carpet?"

"I expect he has a corporate jet. And he must have had the plane's crew standing by. It makes me wonder why identifying a dead casino employee is so important to him. What's the hurry? Culp isn't going anywhere."

"Hmm. Well, speaking of being in a hurry, are you sure we don't have time to stop for a burger? I could just run in and grab a few. I've hardly had anything to eat all day."

Steele glanced at him. "It wouldn't hurt you to have something healthy to eat once in a while. It wouldn't hurt your waistline either."

Rudd sucked in his breath and looked down at his protruding belly. "Hey, I'm a big guy. You can't expect me to eat the kind of food a skinny person like you eats. I've always been big. It's my hormones. I hardly eat a thing and I still put on weight."

Steele didn't comment. Maybe if Rudd really did get hooked up with the lady from the DMV she'd take pity on him and cook him some real food once in awhile.

He handed his smartphone to Rudd. "Let's check out this Jenny Dainty. Try Googling her."

Rudd typed for a moment and then waited. "Hey, I got some hits. Aha, should have known. She's an actress. She plays somebody on that soap opera 'Loves of Our Lives.' Let me see what else I can find out about her." He typed in something. "Oops, wait a minute. She's not on that show anymore. This soap-opera fan site says they killed her off. Just recently. Her character was supposed to have been mistakenly poisoned instead of her best friend who was fooling around with a Saudi prince." He held the phone up in front of Steele to show him the picture of the actress lying in a golden casket. "Pretty cute girl, eh? So our Miss Jenny Dainty is probably out of work. Hey, maybe she was in on it."

Steele glanced at him. "A soap-opera actress?"

"Well, maybe she, uh, got somebody to steal her car so she could collect the insurance."

"Not likely an actress would know how to do that, but let's see what she has to say about it. If she's out of work, it could mean somebody noticed her car wasn't being moved very often. Maybe it was just an easy target."

The Marina del Rey address turned out to be a new-looking three-story apartment complex right next to the marina. Steele parked in the underground parking garage and they went around to the front. The front door to the building was locked, but the mailboxes all had intercom buttons.

Rudd found her name on one of the second-floor mailboxes. "Shall I ring her?"

Steele shook his head. "Let's not alert her. I want to see her reaction when we show up at her door." He punched in a third-floor number. When a voice answered, he said, "UPS. Got a package for your neighbor. Nobody home. Buzz me in, could you? I'll just leave it inside the door down here."

When the door buzzed open, they hurried to the elevator and went up to Jenny Dainty's apartment.

She opened the door right away. "Yes?" She looked surprised, but Steele could tell she wasn't scared at the unexpected knock on her door. She was a blonde, about as small and thin as her name would imply, dressed in white shorts and a tight-fitting blue sleeveless top.

Steele showed her his ID.

She glanced at it and then looked at it closer. "Drew Steele? Is that your real name? Like in those old Civil War detective novels?"

"That was my great-great grandfather. Same name."

"No kidding? He was a real person? And you're a detective too?"

"Runs in the family. Did you report your car stolen, Miss Dainty? A Mercedes Turbo Diesel?"

"Oh yes. Did you find it already?" She smiled and seemed relieved.

If she was hiding anything about the car, Steele couldn't detect it. "Yes, but I'm afraid you won't be able to get it back just yet. It was used in a crime."

She frowned. "Uh oh, I was afraid of that. Our garage doesn't have a gate and I was afraid some gang kids might have taken it to . . . to do whatever they do. Drive-bys or something."

"It was something like that," said Steele. "Can we come in?"

"Oh, sure." She stood back and gestured toward a semicircle of four director's chairs that faced a floor-to-ceiling window that overlooked the marina. Those chairs and an old glass and chrome coffee table were the only furniture in the room. She obviously wasn't rolling in money. Outside her window, rows of small sailboats bobbed and swayed in the wind.

Rudd stepped forward and took her hand. He did a little bow and said, "John Rudd, ma'am. Nice to meet you."

As Steele moved stiffly toward the chairs, she noticed and said, "Oh, did you hurt your leg?"

"Yes," said Steele, "but it's almost better now."

Once they were seated, Steele said, "We aren't quite sure of the details yet. About how your car was used in this crime, I mean. Did you report it as soon as you noticed it was gone?"

"Let's see, I called it in on . . . Tuesday morning. But it might have been gone the day before. I hadn't been out for a few days."

Rudd picked up a magazine from the coffee table and leafed through it as if he wasn't interested in the conversation.

Steele took out his smartphone and used the stylus to enter a note about the possible date of the theft. Culp's body hadn't deteriorated very much, but the car might have been stolen some time before he had been killed. "And you have no idea who might have taken it?"

She looked surprised. "Why no. I mean, it wasn't gang kids?"

"It might have been. The police are still investigating."

"But . . . aren't you the police?"

"No ma'am. I'm a private investigator. I'm working with the police on this case, for a private client."

"Oh . . . I see."

She looked concerned, but Steele still couldn't detect any attempt at deception. He was sure she didn't know who had stolen her car. But there was something she wasn't saying. "You were going to say something else?"

"Oh no, only . . . well, it might have been my fault."

"Your fault?" Steele waited while she searched for the words.

Rudd was secretly watching her over the top of his magazine.

"It's only that I . . . well, I didn't tell the police this, but I hid a spare key under the front bumper. You know, inside one of those little magnetic metal boxes. I have a bad habit of putting my keys in that little tray between the seats while I gather up my things. Then I get out and forget to pick them up before I close the door. I locked myself out . . . well, several times, and with my apartment key on the same key ring . . . The locksmith who came out to unlock my car charged me quite a lot."

Rudd lowered his magazine. "Under the bumper. That's the first place car thieves look. Saves them the trouble of pulling the lock."

She looked down at her bare feet. "Yes, I should of known better."

"No harm done," said Steele. "Your car doesn't seem to have been damaged at all. In fact, the thieves seem to have been very careful with it. By the way, did you have anything in the trunk? Tools? Tarps? Anything like that?"

"No nothing. Thank goodness for that anyhow. There was nothing they could steal."

"Is it possible it was stolen by somebody who knows you?"

She looked surprised. "Knows me? You mean it might have been somebody who . . . like maybe somebody who lives here?"

"You said you hadn't driven it for a few days. Maybe somebody noticed."

"Well, I haven't lived here very long. I know the girl who lives next door, slightly. Her balcony is right next to mine, but other than that I don't really know anybody in this building."

"All right, ma'am, I'll try to find out when they're going to release your car and let you know."

"I hope they don't have to keep it too long. I've been going to auditions, trying to find work."

Rudd lowered his magazine. "You're an actress, aren't you? Haven't I seen you on TV?"

"Well, I was on TV, but only for a little while. It was a short-term part on a morning soap opera. Probably not anything you've ever seen."

Rudd put down the magazine and put a surprised look on his face. "Now wait a minute. Weren't you on 'Loves of our Lives'?"

"You watched that?"

"Sure, never missed it. You were great. I felt terrible when they killed you off."

She looked at him skeptically, as if she wasn't sure if he was kidding her or not. "They did it out of the blue. I'm not sure why. Maybe they wanted somebody older. Now I'm making the rounds of auditions for something else. In fact, I've got one this morning. I hope they bring my car back soon. The cost of taking cabs is killing me."

Rudd stood up smiling. "Well, if you're ready now, we can drop you off. Can't we, Steele?"

Steele nodded.

"Oh, that would be so nice of you. Just let me grab my costume. I'm trying out for a Halloween TV special. For next fall. A witch's assistant."

"I can't imagine anyone as pretty as you could be a witch's assistant, Miss Dainty," said Rudd. He did his odd little bow again.

She smiled at him and touched his hand. "Well, what a nice thing to say, Mr. Rudd. But I'm not even sure what they're looking for. I hope I find something soon. The rent's due. By the way, it makes me feel . . . funny when you call me Miss Dainty. It's like you're talking to my mother or something. Just call me Jenny, okay?" She turned to smile at Steele. "You too, Mr. Steele." She hurried out of the room.

While they waited for her, Rudd opened the sliding glass door and stepped out onto the balcony. He gestured for Steele to come out. "How would this be, Steele? You should move into a place like this. Maybe some girls live here who have a sailboat. We could get to know them. You know, they could take us out sailing."

Steele didn't reply. They stood there leaning against the railing, looking at the hundreds of docked sailboats. The docks were deserted and there was only one boat moving in the channel that led out to the open ocean. "I wonder how often anybody actually takes a sailboat out."

"Yeah," said Rudd, "it must be costing them a fortune to keep 'em docked here waiting for that rare sail."

Steele looked back to be sure Jenny hadn't come into the room.

"Speaking of money, hasn't it struck you as a bit surprising that a young unemployed actress could afford a new Mercedes turbo diesel?"

Rudd shrugged. "Maybe, but I don't think she knows anything. It was just chance her car was taken. You know, that key hidden under the bumper thing. Made it an easy grab."

"There's something she's not saying, but I agree she doesn't know who took it. But I'm still bothered by the fact that whoever stole her car took very good care of it, even going to the trouble of putting a tarp under the body. She said she didn't have a tarp in the car. Why would they be so careful with the car if they didn't know the owner?"

"Maybe they used the tarp to carry him. Maybe it was around him before they put him in."

"It didn't look like that. It seemed to have been carefully spread out in the trunk before they threw him in."

Rudd was about to respond when Jenny came back. She was dressed in a low-cut black dress and she was carrying a wide-brimmed black hat. "What do you think?" she asked, giving them a wicked smile as she turned in a circle. "Do I look like a witch?"

"Naw," said Rudd. "You're much too pretty to be a witch."

"Actually, the part is for a witch's apprentice. This is the only black dress I have. Last night I sewed some tassels on the bottom. Do you think it looks anything like a witch's apprentice outfit?"

"Of course it does," said Rudd. "I'm sure you'll get the part. How could they not choose you?"

# Chapter 7

As Steele drove away from her apartment building, Jenny leaned forward from the back seat to read him an address from her Daytimer. It was in Hollywood, on Gower.

Rudd punched in the address on the GPS.

Jenny showed them the casting call flyer. "See, it says there are three open parts. A witch's apprentice and two goblins. Maybe I should have tried to be a goblin. What do you think, Mr. Steele?"

Steele glanced at the flyer, but Rudd grabbed it and read it. "No, no, you're much too beautiful to be a goblin," he said. "You're a witch's apprentice if I ever saw one."

She laughed. "Well, I don't know about that, Mr. Rudd, but it's sweet of you to say so."

As they drove to the location, Jenny cheerfully told them about all of the parts she'd tried out for in the last few weeks: a nurse on an emergency room TV show, a movie role about a girl who gets chased through the desert by a mummy, even a non-speaking part about a bank teller who gets tied up and gagged while a bank robber tells her all about his sad life. "No luck on any of them," she said with a shrug, "but I haven't heard back yet about the one where I'd get to be chased by the mummy. I think they're still looking for funding."

They arrived at her audition location and she hopped out. She leaned against Steele's window sill. "Thanks again for dropping me off. Should I call you if . . if I think of anything else? About the car, I mean."

Steele handed her his card.

She seemed about to say something else, but then she shrugged and ducked down to wave good-bye to Rudd. "See you, Mr. Rudd." She turned and hurried toward the building.

Rudd leaned across Steele to call after her. "John. You can call me John."

She turned back to wave again, and then went into the building.

"Hey, she's somethin'," said Rudd grinning at Steele. "I sure hope she gets the part. I bet she's a great actress."

Steele pulled back into traffic and headed for the morgue. He wasn't sure about the great actress part, but she did have a quality that might come across well on the screen. "She is more . . . unpretentious than most actresses I've met," he said.

Rudd shrugged. "Yeah, well, that's good, isn't it? Maybe she should look for . . . I don't know, maybe a girl-next-door part. She'd be good at that. I'd love to see her in a movie. We could say we met her before she made it big."

Steele drove on in silence, but Rudd wasn't willing to let it go. He looked at Steele. "Well, what do you think? Interested? You should be. She took to you right away. It was obvious by the way she looked at you. But I'm not surprised. You look like the movie hero type, tall, blonde, and you've got what they call those rugged good looks. Have you ever thought about going into the movies? That scar on your chin could be a problem, but I think it gives you . . . character. I bet she'd go out with you if you asked her. You should call her up. That's what I think. Maybe she has a friend."

Steele didn't resply, but he had to agree that Jenny did seem like a likable young woman. And she was, as Rudd had suggested, very attractive. Maybe too attractive, and too personable, not to be hooked up with somebody.

When they got back to the morgue, they found Kelly already working on Culp's body. Kelly glanced up as Steele and Rudd came in. He waved them over. "Hi, guys, welcome to my afternoon slice and dice session. Ya know, I get all sorts of weird things in here, but this is a first. Never seen words burned into a stiff's forehead before. Any idea what it means? Keep out of what?"

"Yeah," said Rudd, leaning over the body to look closer at the two words, "and who is it that's supposed to keep out of . . . wherever it is?"

"Maybe it's warning everybody to keep out," said Kelly. "Captain

Pruett said they found this one out at Crueltown. Maybe it's just a warning for everybody to stay away from there, including the cops."

Steele doubted the message was for the police. It was well known that the police were not allowed to go inside Crueltown so there was no need to warn them to stay out. But Rudd had a good point: who was the message intended for? Someone had gone to a lot of trouble to put that message on Culp's forehead. Maybe the message was not so much to warn people away, but to call attention to this particular body, to make sure it didn't get overlooked as just another dead transient.

Under the powerful lights of the examining table, Steele could see why the two words were so clear: the flesh at the edges of wounds had been burned black, outlining the letters. "How was it done?" he asked. "Can you tell?"

Kelly used a magnifying glass to examine each of the letters. "Not sure. Maybe a wood-burning tool, or a soldering iron. Very carefully done. Very clear."

Rudd said, "Maybe they practiced first."

Kelly looked surprised. "Christ, let's hope not. I don't want to see any more like him coming in here."

"Was he already dead when it was done?" asked Steele.

"Don't think so. See the discoloration around the edges of the letters? It's the body's response to the tissue damage."

"Jesus," said Rudd, "still alive and somebody does that to you." He shuddered. "I don't even want to think about it."

# Chapter 8

"*I*s that him?" They all turned around to see who had spoken. It was a broad-shouldered man standing in the shadows by the door. He was wearing a dark, expensive-looking suit, but no tie.

Steele went to him. "Mr. Monroe?"

"Yeah. You must be Steele." He leaned to look around Steele. "Is that Culp on the table?"

Steele turned back to Kelly. "I asked Mr. Monroe to come here to see if he could make a positive identification of the body. Is that all right?"

Kelly shrugged. "Sure."

Monroe went to the examining table and took a quick look. "That's him alright. But what the hell is that on his forehead?"

"Words," offered Rudd. "Burned in. It says 'Keep Out.'"

Monroe looked at Rudd for a long moment. "I can see what it says." He turned back to Steele. "But what's it supposed to mean?"

"It doesn't mean anything to you?" asked Steele.

"Me? Why the hell would it mean anything to me? Keep out of what?"

"We don't know," said Steele. "Apparently, somebody used his body to send a message. You don't think it could be a message for you? Or for someone at the casino?"

"I can't imagine who. What kind of person would do that to a body? Just to send a message?"

"It was done while he was still alive," said Rudd. "Kelly said so."

Monroe stared at him. Then he shook his head and took Steele by the arm to lead him away from the examining table. "This is too bizarre, Steele. Culp was just an old guy who did his job and didn't make trouble. I doubt he even got noticed by most people. And now this? Murdered, with words burned onto him? What's it all about?"

"I don't know," said Steele. "We were hoping you could tell us." Steele watched Monroe's reaction. He seemed genuinely surprised and upset. If the message was meant for someone at the casino, Monroe didn't know who or why.

Monroe shook his head and glanced back toward the body on the examining table. "It's so weird to see something like that on Culp's forehead. You have to imagine what he was like. About as straight-laced as they come. Been with the casino for years and years. Nobody would have ever expected him to steal, let alone get murdered. Okay, maybe he was doing something nobody knew about, but to end up dead like this? With his body used for a message board? It doesn't make sense."

"Maybe we should step outside," suggested Steele. He led Monroe out into the hallway and away from the morgue door before speaking. "Frankly, Mr. Monroe, this man's murder could be less complicated than it seems. Culp might have needed money badly. That's usually what leads a man to steal from his employer. He might have been in some kind of trouble."

"His wife says no debts."

"Maybe he had medical problems."

"Not according to his wife, if we can believe her."

"Do you believe her?"

"No reason not to. We can't find anything funny on either one of them. They had a normal-sized mortgage on their so-so house, but other than that, no big bills that we can find out about. No criminal contacts either."

"Did he gamble?"

"Nope. We keep a close eye on that kind of thing. Far as we know, he didn't gamble at all, except for a small-time employee's poker game. A weekly thing, nickel-and-dime stuff"

"Could he have had a drug problem?"

"Culp? Not a chance."

"I want you think about what you saw in there, Mr. Monroe. Think about that message on his forehead. Could it be related in any way to something going on at the casino?"

"I don't see how. Why do you say that?"

"When someone disappears and is found dead, the murder is almost always related to the disappearance. Let's start at the beginning. Something caused him to suddenly disappear. You say he was stealing money from the casino. Therefore, it's logical to assume he left because he was about to be found out."

"Yeah, we'd pretty much pinned down the shortages to the morning count. His shift."

"So that's why he disappeared."

"Okay, but why did he end up dead?"

"It was probably related to the money. Others may have been involved in the theft."

"So you think they had a falling out."

"Not an uncommon occurrence when stolen money is involved."

"Okay, then, that's your job. Find out about that, and find out who killed him."

"My job is finished, Mr. Monroe. I was hired to find him."

"Yeah, but there's obviously more to this now. Aren't you curious? I am. Those words on his forehead are gonna keep me awake nights."

"I am curious, but in my work I see a lot of curious things. This is a murder case now. It is no longer about the disappearance of an employee. At this point, my further involvement might be seen by the police as interference in an ongoing criminal case."

"The hell with that. What they don't know won't hurt 'em. Listen, Steele, this is important to me . . . to us. We have to know why Culp was here in LA, and why he was killed."

"Who is us?"

"Uh, corporate."

"You're saying your superiors want to me continue to investigate? They told you that before you flew down here?"

"Yeah, they want to know more about what Culp was up to. Don't know why. Maybe they're afraid somebody is trying to cause the casino trouble."

"Somebody?"

Monroe shook a cigarette out of a crumpled pack. "I don't know. They tell me what to do and I follow orders. They said to get you to stay with this, so that's what I'm hiring you to do."

"You can't smoke in a public building in California, Mr. Monroe. If

I was to continue my investigation, I would need to know more about what you are referring to. Have there been threats against the casino?"

Monroe tried to stuff the cigarette back into the pack, broke it, and threw it to the floor. "Not that I know of. All I know is this whole thing has the higher-ups real nervous."

"That type of in-depth investigation you are referring to could take time."

Monroe, leaned close and lightly tapped Steel's chest with his fist. "Listen, Steele, I'll let you in on a little secret. It sounds to me like money is no object."

"Sounds to you?"

"Fact is, the big-shots from corporate won't even tell me what they're worried about. I'll try to get you more info when I can. Why don't you just take their money and do the best you can? They said I'm authorized to double your normal fee, no matter how much it is. Hell, why don't we triple it? They can afford it. And when they hear about those two words on Culp's forehead, they'll pay. I'm sure of it."

"You told me you were the head of security, but now you're saying you are only a middle man."

"Of course I'm a middle man. Even the top bosses at a casino are middlemen when you get bought out by somebody new."

"I read you'd been bought out. Was it a Las Vegas company?"

"No, an Atlantic City outfit called the Omnivexx Corporation. Don't know much about them, but most everybody at the casino is grateful they bought the place out of bankruptcy. They seem willing to put some money into it to bring it back to what it used to be. They left middle management pretty much in place, but they sent a couple of overseers to make the most important decisions. We're pretty much expected to do whatever they tell us to do. It beats me why the overseers think Culp's disappearance is such a big deal. As far as anybody knew, Culp was just an old guy who'd been around the casino for a long time. I'm told he started out as a slot keyman thirty-some years ago, back when the Golden Palace was one of the hottest properties on the strip. He worked his way up from the bottom and got put on the morning count team a couple of years ago. He kept his nose clean and did what he was told. We made him count supervisor last summer when another old guy retired."

Steele thought about what Monroe was saying. If Culp was such a low-profile employee, why would the new managers from the buyout corporation be so concerned about his disappearance? "Tell me this, Mr. Monroe, you said the overseers from the Omnivexx Corporation thought Culp's disappearance was a *big deal*, to use your words. Did they ask about him before they found out he had been murdered?"

"You bet. They called me as soon as word got out he hadn't showed up for work."

"How did they find out about it?"

"Not sure. But rumors fly around a casino pretty quick. When Culp didn't show up for his shift, my second-in-command called me immediately. Maybe he told other people too."

"Did Culp report to you?"

"That's right. All count teams are considered security so they're under me. The state doesn't want them supervised by the gambling bosses. You can probably guess why."

"They don't want any possibility of collusion between gaming and accounting."

"Exactly. The state wants to make sure the count is right so they get their full cut."

Steele was still troubled about why a New Jersey corporation would be so concerned about one middle-management employee. Maybe Culp was more than he appeared to be. "Tell me this, Mr. Monroe, could Culp have been involved in something bigger? Maybe he had a secret life."

"That would really surprise me. You can't imagine how boring Culp was. No disrespect to the dead intended."

Steele nodded and continued. "If a person disappears voluntarily, it's because they are in some kind of trouble. But when a person is murdered, it usually involves strong emotions, love, hate, fear, disappointment, resentment. That kind of thing. But this does not appear to be that kind of murder. The way he was killed was more . . . systematic. It might have been a professional killing."

That seemed to catch Monroe off guard. "A pro killing? Culp? You've got to be kidding. Man, if he was leading that kind of mysterious other life, he sure the hell knew how to keep it a secret. Everybody at the casino just saw him as a nice old guy."

"Stealing from an employer is often an indication the thief was in desperate trouble. Take a moment to think about it, Mr. Monroe. What kind of trouble could he have been in?"

But Monroe didn't take any time to think. He shook his head. "No idea at all. I've been in casino security for nineteen years and I can usually spot the bad apples. Culp looked to me like your regular, run-of-the mill middle manager. Like I said, a low-profile guy. Mostly he kept to himself. I can guarantee you he'd never once been in trouble as long as he'd been at the casino. I dug out his supervisor's evaluations as soon as he disappeared. Spotless. Everybody liked him, said he did his job well. And I contacted my friends at the Las Vegas police department too. They checked their records thoroughly. Nothing there either."

"Nevertheless, Mr. Monroe, there had to be something going on. If he was stealing, something motivated him to do it. And something made him leave Las Vegas and come to LA. Find that out and you'll probably find out why he was murdered."

"Sounds like you're getting curious now, aren't you, Steele. You're going to take the job, right? Triple fees, like I said."

Steele thought about it. Triple fees. It would be a very lucrative case. He didn't really need the money, but the fact that they were willing to pay so much simply for information was enough to arouse his curiosity. Besides, that trip to Paris would be expensive. This case might provide just about enough money to pay for a side trip to the Riviera, even if Loren wanted to stay in one of the best hotels on the *Promenade des Anglais*. "My expenses might be high on this one. I have no clear starting point."

"Hell, money's no issue for them. Just keep good records and fax your expenses to me. I'll email you the fax number."

"All right. I'll see what I can do."

Monroe smoothed down the front of Steele's tweed jacket, as if he had mussed it. "Great. I was told you're the very best, so do your best. If you have any questions, you have my number."

"All right. Let's start with the day Culp disappeared. Did anything unusual happen that day?"

"Not as far as I know. They say he put in his shift and just left, like normal. The next day, when Culp didn't show up, they called me and I asked around to find out if anybody'd seen him. Nobody had, but one of the other people on the count team said his wife had called the night before wondering where he was. So I called his house real quick and found out he never came home that night. His wife was real worried. She said she'd been calling everybody she knew to try to find him."

"So it wasn't normal behavior for him? He was not the type to stay out all night?"

"Apparently not. I asked his wife the same thing and she said he always came straight home from work."

"Did you ask her if any of his clothes were missing?"

Monroe scratched the back of his neck. "Didn't think of that. Do you want me to call her back and ask her? Or maybe you should talk to her."

"I will. Just a few more questions. When she found out he was missing, do you know if his wife called the police?"

"She didn't. I asked her that right away. She said she wasn't ready to do that yet. She wanted to give him a little time. She hoped he'd turn up soon."

"That might mean she knew why he disappeared, even if she didn't know where he was."

"Maybe, but I'm pretty sure she didn't know in advance he was gonna take off. She was really upset about it."

"Maybe she was upset for some other reason. You said you contacted Las Vegas police. What did they say?"

"They said they couldn't act until somebody filed a missing-persons report. As far as I know, she never filed one. Next thing I knew, you were calling to say you'd already found him. Dead."

"And when you told the people from Omnivexx that I'd found him, they said to keep me on the case?"

"Yeah. I got a call from the top guy. He said they'd checked you out and I should fly down here and convince you to stay on the job. And now that I've done that, I'd better get back to the casino."

"Before you go, Mr. Monroe, have you ever heard of the place they call Crueltown?"

"Crueltown? What's that?"

"It's where they found the body. It's out by the LA harbor."

Monroe raised his eyebrows. "Crueltown? Okay, I'll bite. Why do they call it that?"

"If you knew the place, you'd understand how it got that name. It's a couple of square miles of low-lying polluted land that nobody wants to claim. It used to be a small oil refinery, but they went bankrupt and left a swampy mess. The feds said it had to be cleaned up before anybody else could occupy the land, but the estimated cleanup cost was in the millions. For a while, an outfit called the Mobile Home Recycling Corporation took it over, promising to do something about the pollution. They used it as a place to temporarily park worn-out mobile homes, a convenient drop-off location until the old wrecks could be fixed up enough to make the trip down to Mexico for resale. But they never did any cleanup and eventually OSCA found out they were mostly using it as a dumping ground. They shut them down and the trailer-recycling company immediately declared bankruptcy to avoid prosecution."

"So that's Crueltown? Why cruel?"

"Because of the people who hide in there. A lot of crime goes on inside Crueltown. Drugs and prostitution. And a lot of transients land there, mostly illegals from across the border. The old trailers are gradually sinking into the muck, but that doesn't stop people from living in them. A few years after the trailer-recycling company left, the local authorities noticed quite a few people coming and going so they put up a tall chain-link fence around the whole place and posted keep-out signs. Of course that didn't keep them out. They just cut holes in the fence. A free place to live in LA draws people like flies to garbage. Smells pretty much like garbage in there too."

"No sewers, I suppose."

"Not even any electricity or running water. In the last few years, it's become known as a place to set up drug deals. The word on the street is that some big-time dealers are operating out of there now, people with Mexican connections."

"So why don't the cops shut it down?"

"That's also tied to the toxic-waste designation. The city of Wilmington found out how much the clean up would cost and declared Crueltown to be just barely outside their city limits. They even went so far as to move their official town border a half-mile away, just in case. Then the city councils of the other surrounding cities voted unanimously that the area was definitely not within their city limits either. But just in case somebody could prove it was, they all voted to forfeit the property to the LA Harbor Commission. The Harbor Commission said no way, and that's when the court battles began. The cities have all ordered their police to stay away just to make sure their city doesn't get forced into some kind of legal jurisdiction over it."

"I get it," said Monroe. "You end up with unknown numbers of homeless squatters and dopers and other criminals in there. No rent, no landlord, and no police. Crueltown probably doesn't do much for the tourist business in that area."

"That part of the harbor district is seldom visited by anybody. The whole area is low-lying and swampy. And it's downwind of the refineries so that area is always smoky and smells like burnt oil. Sometimes it gets hard to breathe out there."

"Sounds like this Crueltown is a pretty scary place."

"It is."

"You've been in there?"

"Twice. The last time I was lucky to make it back out alive. A kidnapping case."

Monroe gestured toward the door to the morgue. "So, do you think that's what the words, 'Keep Out,' refer to? Keep out of Crueltown?"

"That would be the obvious interpretation. Maybe too obvious."

"Well, if you end up having to go inside that place it sounds like you may earn your triple fees. But I guess that's what you get paid for. Let's hope it works out better than that job you did in Iraq."

That brought Steele up short. "What do you know about that?"

"All I know is what one of the bosses from Omnivexx said. I told you they'd checked you out. He said you had top credentials as an investigator and did some kind of private contractor work for the U.S. Embassy over there. In Baghdad."

"Do you know the source of their information?"

"They didn't say. Why, is it supposed to be a secret or something?"

"Not really." Steele tried to say it casually, but it *was* supposed to be secret. Top secret. How could a casino corporation have even learned he was in Iraq, let alone that he had been a private contractor in Baghdad?

"They said you got wounded by one of those roadside bombs. IEDs, isn't that what they call them? I noticed you've got a deep scar on your chin and you walk with a limp. What happened over there?"

Steele involuntarily started to reach up to touch the still-painful scar, but stopped himself. "It's nothing to worry about. My injuries have pretty much healed. I think I'd better start my investigation in Las Vegas. I want to try to find out why Culp started stealing the casino's money in the first place. I'll drive over later today."

"Good idea. I'll hold a suite for you. Come to my office when you get there." Monroe glanced at his watch. "Got to get back. See you later today." He hurried away down the echoing hallway.

Steele watched him go, wondering if Monroe's corporate bosses were telling him everything they knew about Culp's disappearance. Paying a high-priced LA detective to follow up on a murder of a casino employee didn't seem like something big corporations would normally do. What made them think Culp would head for LA? And why had they been so interested in the disappearance of one middle-management employee in the first place? A Las Vegas Strip casino would have thousands of employees. Was it something about this particular employee? Or were they just nervous about the possibility of employees stealing? It couldn't just be the money they'd lost. Maybe they were worried Culp was involved in some kind of an inside conspiracy. If so, why hadn't they hired a Las Vegas detective to investigate? Or used their own security department? Didn't they trust them? And why would they tell Monroe they were willing to pay a Los Angeles detective more than his already-high fees to find Culp's killers? A lot of things about this case didn't add up.

# Chapter 9

$S$teele went back inside the morgue. Kelly was giving Rudd a lecture about how to properly examine stomach contents. Rudd was looking a little pale.

Using a long pair of forceps, Kelly held up a bloody piece of sagging plastic. "Hey, come here, Steele. Whatta ya think this is?"

"Looks like a condom."

"Right on. But now tell me what it might be doing in this guy's stomach."

"Some kind of gay thing?" guessed Rudd.

"Gay thing?" Kelly laughed. "Whatta ya think he got carried away and swallowed it?" He shook the thing in Rudd's face.

Rudd ducked away. "Damn it, Kelly, keep that away from me."

Kelly turned back to Steele. "Well, you got a guess?"

"Drug trafficking," said Steele.

Kelly nodded. "Bingo. A way to carry drugs across the Mexican border. "He pushed his glasses up on top of his head and looked closely at the condom. "And it's busted. You know what that means."

"Overdose."

"Right. I find these things all the time." He went back to probing inside the body. "I'll tell you guys a funny story. When I first started in this business, when I was just an innocent young intern, they told me there was a condom-eating fad going on. That's why we kept on finding condoms in the stiffs' stomachs. Finally, somebody took pity on me and let me in on the secret. It was the condoms in their stomachs that was killin' 'em. Mules, they call 'em. Kids carrying condoms full of heroin in their stomachs to sneak the stuff across the

Mexican border. Damn thing springs a leak and oops, kid falls over dead at the airport, or on a bus. We open up the stomach and find a deflated condom."

Steele leaned over the open cavity of Culp's stomach as Kelly probed around. "I doubt this man died of a drug overdose, but will you be checking to see if there were drugs in his system?"

"Yeah. I'll ask for a toxicology report. I agree that it doesn't look like the typical drug overdose thing. He's been beat up pretty bad and, that's a bullet hole in the side of his head."

"Small caliber?" asked Steele.

"I haven't got to diggin' it out yet, but it probably was. Looks like a pro job. Those guys take pride in doing it quick and easy. No mess."

Rudd came back to stand next to Steele. "So, you gonna get that bullet out of his head next?"

"Yeah. Soon as I bag up the stomach and bowel contents. You want to stick around for that?"

Rudd shook his head and backed away with his hand over his mouth.

"When you're done, can I get a copy of your report?" asked Steele.

"You know better than that," said Kelly. "I could lose my job."

"I could get you a ticket to a Lakers game. They're playing Phoenix tomorrow."

Kelly didn't answer. He was focusing on his work.

"Have you ever sat down close to the court? How about second row? Right behind Nicholson."

Kelly looked up. "You must have a pretty nice expense account on this case."

Steele waited.

"Well, I might accidentally leave a copy lying around here tonight. It happens."

"If you could accidentally email it to me, I'll have them hold the tickets at the box office for you."

Kelly shrugged. "It could happen." He used the scalpel to make a long curving slice to open up the man's intestines and the room immediately filled up with the odor.

"Christ! Can't we get out of here now?" said Rudd from the doorway.

Steele followed Rudd out into the hallway.

Rudd waved his hand in front of his face. "Geez, the smell in there. How does he get used to it? He acts like he's cutting up something for lunch."

"He's been doing it for a lot of years," said Steele. He headed for the parking lot with Rudd close behind. They got back into Steele's car, but before he could pull out of the parking place, they had to wait for one of the large black police morgue vans to finish backing up to the loading dock.

"So, what do you think?" asked Rudd. "What was that thing doing in his stomach anyhow?"

"It's possible somebody forced it down his throat knowing it would be found in an autopsy."

Rudd let out a low whistle. "Really? Why would they do that?"

"Hard to say. The simplest answer would be to make the police think he was a drug carrier."

"I get it. So they'd think he died from a burst drug balloon."

"I suspect they might notice the bullet hole in his head first."

"Oh, that's right. So why did they bother with the fake drug balloon?"

"Maybe they wanted somebody to think he was mixed up in some kind of drug business."

"Somebody? You mean the police?"

"Maybe the police. Maybe somebody else."

"Ah, so you think it was another message. First the words burned into his forehead, and then a second message hidden in his gut."

"I'm just speculating. It could mean something else altogether."

"Man, that is weird," said Rudd. "Using the poor guy's body to send messages."

Steele backed out of the parking space and headed for the street. Rudd was right, it was weird, but more important, it didn't fit the pattern. Professional killers prided themselves on their neatness. Using a dead man to send messages was not their usual M.O. Maybe there was a drug connection. That would lead back to Crueltown, the most notorious drug haven in LA. Maybe there was something going on in there. Something big. The last time he'd been inside Crueltown, it was to try to find the mayor's daughter. That one turned out to be drug-related. Some of Furtado's men had tried to ransom her to get back a huge cache of heroin that had been confiscated by the LA police. At first they tried the usual method to get it back: bribing the police. When that didn't work, they got desperate and kidnapped the girl. The mayor hired Steele to try to find the girl and he did, inside Crueltown. But she was already dead. He managed to trick Furtado into meeting him to pick up the fake ransom money and Furtado ended up being convicted and put way for life for his role in the girl's murder. Later, the rest of the gang had been rounded up. So who was operating inside Crueltown now? A different drug ring? Culp's body had been found next to the Crueltown fence, but that could be just a diversion. Or was it another message?

"What are you thinking about?" asked Rudd.

"Just trying to put it all together. The killers used Culp's body to send two messages, the words on his forehead and the condom in his stomach. Why two messages?"

"Yeah, why would they send messages to say the murder has something to do with drugs, but stay away? Maybe there's some kind of drug war going on inside Crueltown."

"Maybe."

Rudd snapped his fingers. "Yeah, I bet that's it. It's a drug war. One gang kills the guy and uses his body to send a message to the competition."

"But what would a man like Culp have to do with drug gangs?" said Steele.

"Anybody can get hooked on drugs. He was probably an addict. That's why he stole the money. He gets in over his head because of his drug habit, and pow, his drug dealer offs him."

"Not likely. Monroe said Culp lived a very straight life."

"It happens to the best of 'em," said Rudd with a shrug. "So, what do we do next?"

"I want to start in Las Vegas. I need to find out if he really stole the casino's money, and if he did, how and why. I'll give you money for a cab to go back out to Palos Verdes so you can pick up your car."

Rudd shook his head. "Oh no you don't. I'm on this story to the end. This kind of weird murder sells newspapers. I called in the first installment this morning. I called it the warning-on-the-forehead murder. I told my boss I was gonna to do another one of my day-in-the-life-of-a-private-eye stories and he gave me the go-ahead. From here on, I'm sticking with you and filing episodes as we find clues, like

I did when you traced those kidnappers to Crueltown."

"This is different, Rudd. That time, your stories were supposed to make the kidnappers think I was focusing on the Tijuana area, just like the police were."

"I know, I know. You used me and my newspaper to trick 'em. It's okay. Did you see me complaining? It made for a great story. So why can't I do the same thing again this time?"

"I don't want the killers to know I'm even on this case. Besides, after your stories about the case came out, every reporter in town was trying to figure out who your mysterious detective X was. I got dozens of calls asking if I was Mr. X."

"Well, they never found out, did they?"

"I'll drop you at your office. Or you can call a cab."

"No way. I'm going with you. I need this story. Besides, I love Vegas. It's been ages since I've been there. Tell you what. So far I haven't written anything about you being involved. I only called in a preliminary story about another murder victim found out at Crueltown. I didn't know what the warning was then so all I said in the story was that it was an unknown man with some kind of warning burned into his forehead. So I can wait until the case is over and done with before I file the story of how Detective X solved the mystery. But I'll write it up like we're still hot on the killer's trail. How 'bout this, after you've caught the killer, I'll file weekly episodes, like we're getting closer and closer to finding the killers every week. It'll be great. C'mon, Steele, I haven't had a big story since the last one we did together. My public demands a sequel."

Steele thought about it. It was hard to predict where this case was heading. Rudd's stories might be useful at some point. "Would you be willing to write that this time it's a new detective X, a Las Vegas detective?"

"Sure, whatever you say."

"Then lets get on the road." Steele pulled out into the heavy morning traffic on Mission Road. "I hope you brought your toothbrush."

"I bet they sell toothbrushes in Vegas. Did you bring yours?"

"I always carry everything I might need in the trunk."

Rudd smiled. "Do you really? Hey, I've got to write that down." He pulled his notebook out of his pocket and whispered as he wrote:

"Detective X always carries a packed suitcase in the trunk of his . . . let's see, his brand new S4 Audi convertible, the one with the 4.2 Liter V-8 and the 6 Speed Manual."

Steele frowned at him.

"Well," said Rudd with a shrug, "what do you want me to write? That my hotshot Detective X drives a beat-up, plain white, four-year-old Ford Crown Victoria? I mean I know it's a Police Interceptor, and I know you had all kinds of special engine and suspension stuff put into it, but it's still not a . . . a Beemer or anything."

Steele decided he wasn't going to talk Rudd out of glorifying his Detective X. His readers undoubtedly wouldn't be much interested in his stories if he told the truth how boring and repetitive most detective work was.

As he headed for the freeway, he tried to imagine what had led a long-time casino employee like Culp to his death in LA. What had at first seemed like a simple case of an employee ducking out with some of his company's money had turned strange and complex. If Monroe could be believed, Culp was not the kind of man who would be likely to be involved with drugs.

As he thought about it, Steele had to admit the unusual nature of the case made it especially interesting. But there was also an unusually strong feeling of danger associated with this one. Loren would have had something to say about that. She always said it was the danger that had attracted him to detective business in the first place. And then when he had told her he was heading for an assignment in Iraq, she was both worried and irritated. It had led to an argument that ended abruptly when she said she had finally realized his attraction to danger was more powerful than his attraction to her.

Afterward, he had tried to assure her that it wasn't true, but she wasn't willing to wait and see. She said this time she wasn't going to wait for him. She said she was tired of waiting for the phone call that would say he was in the hospital again--or that he was dead.

Soon after he arrived in Iraq, he got a terse letter saying she was going to Paris to study art. It was something she'd always wanted to do. He didn't hear from her after that and he was sure she was gone for good. But then she'd showed up unexpectedly in Berlin to sit for long hours next to his hospital bed. While he recuperated from the many surgeries they had done to rebuild his shattered legs, she'd made several trips from Paris to be with him. But when he told her he would go back into the detective business as soon as he could, she walked out again and didn't come back. Her parting shot was that he was addicted to danger and always would be.

# Chapter 10

$A$s they inched their way along in the heavy pre-lunch-hour traffic, Rudd fiddled with the GPS. "Hey, look here, Steele. This thing says to take Valley Boulevard all the way over to the 710."

Steele glanced at the LCD readout. "It gets confused." He joined the line of cars in the left lane to access the eastbound 10 freeway, still thinking about beginnings and endings: what could have started Culp on his journey from long-time casino employee and quiet family man to that car trunk next to the Crueltown fence? What brought him to LA in the first place? The chain of events, whatever they were, must have started at the casino. First he would have to find out why Culp needed the money. Except for love triangles, most murders had something to do with money. Would it be the same this time?

Steele's cell phone buzzed. He looked at the number on the screen, but didn't recognize it. He clicked it on. "Yes?"

"Oh, hi. This is Jenny. Uh, Jenny Dainty."

"Hello, Jenny. Did you get the job?"

"I got a callback, so I still have a shot at it."

Rudd waved his hand in front of Steele's face. "It's Jenny? Say hi for me."

Steele ignored him. "But that's not why you called."

"No, I . . . well, I have a confession to make."

"You might know who stole your car."

"Well, maybe. That is, I . . . sort of forgot to tell you it isn't really my car."

"It's registered in your name, Jenny."

"Yes, but it was sort of . . . a gift. From an old . . . uh, boyfriend, I guess you'd call him. I was going to give it back to the guy, but I had all these auditions."

"So you think this old boyfriend might have taken it back?"

"He could have. He had a key."

"And?"

"And what?"

"There's something else, isn't there, Jenny? Maybe something about why you were going to give that very expensive car back to him."

"Yes. I found out what he was doing with it. After he disappeared, I didn't hear from him for a couple of weeks. Then he called to say he was going to have to go away for a while, but I should keep the car. At first he wouldn't tell me where he was going, but finally he admitted he was in trouble and might have to spend time in prison."

"Did it have something to do with drugs?"

"Yes. How did you know?"

"Just a guess. Go on."

"Well, he wasn't into anything big. At least that's what he said. He said he was only a burro. Do you know what that is?"

"Someone who carries drugs across the border."

"That's right. He finally admitted he'd been using the car to bring drugs across the border from Mexico. His connection down there in Tijuana would hide the drugs in the frame of his car and they paid him to drive it back across the border. He said when he got out of prison he'd have to buy a different car so he wanted to give the Mercedes to me. I told him I didn't want his drug-carrying car, and I didn't want to have anything more to do with him. But he said it wasn't the car's fault and I should accept his parting gift. He said he'd sign over the title to me. And he did. I got the registration notice in the mail a few week's later."

"You never saw him again?"

"No. As far as I know, he's still in prison. I really was going to give the car back to him, but I didn't know where he was."

"All right, Jenny. Thanks for telling me."

"But, Mr. Steele, what if he's out of prison? What if he took the car and used it to smuggle drugs again? There might be drugs still hidden in it somewhere. Won't the police find them?"

"They have no reason to think the car was used to smuggle drugs. I doubt they would look inside the frame."

"Should I tell them? I've been worrying about it since you left."

"It's up to you, Jenny, but you don't really know it was him that stole your car. You might want to wait until they return your car and search it yourself."

"When they bring it back, would you mind coming over and helping me look? I wouldn't know what to look for."

"I wouldn't mind getting a closer look at the car. Call me back when the police return it to you. And when you get it back, you might want to have the locks changed on it right away."

"You don't think I should give it back to him?"

"It's registered in your name so it's legally yours. You might want to sell it. It's worth a lot of money."

"Oh, that's a good idea. I sure could use the money right now. Well . . ."

"Is there something else, Jenny?"

"I was just going to say . . . what I mean is, some friends have invited me out for a sail tonight. They're going to have a barbecue on the boat. You could come along. I mean, if you're interested in that kind of thing."

"I'm afraid we're just heading out of town."

"Oh, some other time then."

"I'll expect your call as soon as you get your car back."

"Oh, yes, for sure. Well, until then . . . then."

As soon as Steele clicked off the cell phone, Rudd was ready with questions. "What was that all about? Why did you say you were afraid we were just heading out of town? Did she invite us over?"

"A barbecue. On a boat."

"And you turned her down? For a party on a boat? Let me out." He reached for the door handle.

"We have a murder case to investigate, remember?"

"But can't it wait for one night?"

"I'm afraid not."

"Damn. I've never been to a party on a boat." Rudd brooded for a few minutes, staring straight ahead. Then he turned back to Steele. "What was all that talk about smuggling drugs across the border?"

"The car was a gift from an old boyfriend. She's afraid it might have been used to carry drugs."

"Ah ha! So that's the connection to that drug-carrying condom in Culp's stomach."

"Maybe."

Rudd shook his head and looked out the window. "I can't believe you turned down the chance for a barbecue on a boat. And with such a pretty girl. I bet she has a cute girl friend too. Heck." He turned up the police scanner and wouldn't look at Steele.

Once they were past Victorville, the chatter on the police scanner died down and Rudd got bored. He played with the GPS for a while, searching for shortcuts through the desert, but the screen kept on insisting they should just stay on Interstate 15 all the way to Las Vegas. Soon he was asleep, his head against the window.

That time of day, the traffic was light on the interstate so Steele left the cruise control at 79 all the way through Victorville and Barstow while he thought about what Monroe had said. Despite the fact that Monroe was the head of security at the Golden Palace casino, he didn't seem to know much about the Omnivexx Corporation, the company that had taken over the casino. He'd described them simply as a big Atlantic City company. Did that mean they owned other casino's in Atlantic City?

Steele picked up his smartphone and Googled Omnivexx. There was only one hit, a listing on the Atlantic City chamber of commerce site. The brief description said Omnivexx was a privately-held New Jersey corporation with offices in downtown Atlantic City. Were they involved with one of the Atlantic City Casinos? If so, why was there was so little information about the company on Google? He would have to have his information-search agency do a more complete search on them.

As he passed the little desert town of Baker with it's many signs proclaiming the dubious distinction of being the home of the world's tallest thermometer, he tried to think how a New Jersey corporation could have found out he'd been in Iraq. That was classified information. The Director would have to be informed. It could indicate there'd been some kind of leak about the Hopeful Horizons operation. Steele made a mental note to call him, but not until he learned more about Omnivexx.

The traffic was fairly light the rest of the way to Las Vegas. As they started down the hill toward the town, Steele turned up the police scanner. That caused Rudd to stir. He sat up rubbing his eyes with the backs of his hands. "Are we there yet?"

"Just coming into town now."

"Good, my back is killing me. I'm ready to get out of this car. Hey, I know, let's go hit the slots."

Steele glanced at him. "I thought you wanted to tag along with my investigation, to write a story about it."

"Time enough for all that later. Hey, this is Vegas, right? Lights, action, girls. Did you know there are more single gals in this town than in any other city in America? I read it on the internet."

Steele got into the right lane and turned off on Flamingo. "I'm heading for the casino."

Rudd looked surprised. "You mean it? Great. I thought you'd be all work and no play here."

"I have to check in with Monroe."

"Oh, you mean the Golden Palace Casino. I should have known. All work and no play for Detective Steele. Okay, but the Golden Palace has slots too. We get to try a few of them out, right?"

"Maybe later."

"Maybe later? Here I am in Vegas with some loose change burning a hole in my pocket, and all you can say is maybe later?"

Steele parked in the parking structure and they found their way to the corporate offices on the top floor of the casino. A quick-eyed guard manned a desk in the waiting area near the elevator.

Steele asked for Mr. Monroe and the guard told them to have a seat.

After five minutes, an attractive, dark-haired young woman in a stern blue pantsuit came out and led them back to Monroe's office. She left them standing there by the door while Monroe finished a phone call. The office was huge with a floor-to-ceiling window that commanded a view of Las Vegas Boulevard. Two cranes were working on each side of yet another new high-rise casino that was going up across the street.

Monroe hung up the phone and came around the large desk to shake Steele's hand.

Steele gestured toward Rudd. "You remember my associate, John Rudd."

Rudd stepped forward and stuck out his hand, but Monroe didn't shake it. He looked at Rudd oddly. "That's not your real name, is it?"

Rudd's smile faded. "It isn't?"

Monroe pointed toward a couple of chairs and went back behind his desk. "When I put in my approval for your fee, the controller recognized your name. Turns out he's a big fan of those Civil War-era Drew Steele mysteries. Long lost relative of yours? He had the same name as you, and the same . . . uh, profession."

Rudd and Steele sat down.

Steele said, "My great-great grandfather."

Monroe stared at him for a long moment, as if he suspected his leg was being pulled. Then he looked at Rudd. "And I suppose the newspaper reporter named John Rudd in those stories was your great grandfather too?"

"Sure was," said Rudd grinning. "They say I look a lot like him."

Monroe shook his head, frowning. "So, Steele, did that morgue guy tell you anything else about Culp's death?"

"I'm expecting an email tonight with the results of the autopsy and the toxicology report. I'll let you know if it tells us anything new. In the meantime, I'd like to talk to Culp's fellow count-team employees."

"I've already talked to all of them. They don't know anything."

"Still, I'd like to ask them a few questions."

Monroe shrugged. "All right, I'll arrange it. But it'll have to be tomorrow. They're on the early morning shift."

"Are they still on the count team?"

"Are you kidding? Until this investigation is completed, they're doing office work."

"So you think they were in on it?"

"Not really. At least we don't think they took any money. We spent quite a bit of time . . . you might say . . .interviewing them. They seemed as surprised as anybody that Culp was stealing money. In fact, they swore there was no way he could have done it without them knowing."

Steele nodded. "I'll talk to them in the morning then. In the meantime, I'd like to look at the tapes."

Monroe lifted his eyebrows. "The video tapes of the count?"

"Yes. I'd like to see all the video you have of Culp's shift. Especially the last few days before he disappeared."

"What do you expect to see?"

"I'm not sure. Right now, I'm just looking for a thread, a place to begin. You still have the videotapes, don't you?"

Monroe nodded. "Sure. You seem to know a lot about how things work in a casino. Ever work in one?"

"I spent some time in a small casino. A case in Reno."

"Then you probably know we're required to keep all surveillance tapes for thirty days."

"A minimum of thirty days. So, can I see them right away?"

"It's not something we ordinarily allow outsiders to see."

Steele waited.

"But I suppose you can look at them if you want to. I doubt you'll spot anything we didn't."

"So you've looked at them closely?"

"I did, but what's more important is that they were analyzed by people who're supposed to know what to look for. We were sure some money was being skimmed off of the count because the hold tallies just weren't right for the morning count. There were some tables that were supposed to have had good action the night before, but they always came up a bit short. And it kept on happening. Whatever was going on had been going on for quite a while, but we couldn't pin it down. Since Culp disappeared, the tallies have come right back up again. It proves he was the one doing it, but we still don't know how. We looked at the tapes of his shift over and over again. We didn't see anything suspicious."

"I suppose the gaming commission is still investigating."

Monroe shrugged. "I'm not at liberty to get into that. They do their investigation, we do ours. You can look at the tapes if you want to, but I think you're wasting your time. There's nothing on them."

"Nevertheless, I'd like to see them."

Monroe shrugged. "Suit yourself. I'll have somebody take you down to the surveillance room." He glanced at Rudd. "But you'll have to go alone."

Steele turned to put his hand on Rudd's shoulder. "Rudd would probably like to spend some time exploring the casino anyhow. Isn't that right?"

Rudd reached into his pocket to jingle his change. "Yeah. I'd better check out your slot machines, Mr. Monroe. Make sure they're operating correctly."

For the first time, Monroe smiled. "I'm sure you'll find them satisfactory." He turned back to Steele. "I'll have them hold a two-bedroom suite for you tonight. Or maybe a couple of nights?"

Steele said, "I'm not sure how long we'll be here. I also want to talk to Culp's family."

Monroe frowned. "I'm afraid you're on your own there. I spoke to his wife on the phone. She was just leaving for LA to get his body. I guess one of her son lives down there and he's meeting her."

"I've already talked to Mrs. Culp. She claims not to know anything about her husband's disappearance. But you say her son works in LA? She didn't mention that. Is that why you thought Culp might end up there? Is that why you hired me instead of a Las Vegas detective?"

"Like I said before, it was the big bosses that said to hire you, not me. Maybe they knew one of Culp's sons lived in LA, maybe not. Me, I'm just the middle man."

"So you didn't know about the son in LA?"

Monroe shook his head. "Nope. Culp was pretty closed mouthed. I don't think anybody around here knew him very well."

Steele thought about that. How would Omnivexx, an Atlantic City company, know so much about Culp? Maybe Culp was more than just another mid-level employee. "You said *one* of her sons? There's more than one?"

"Yeah, her other son works at a casino downtown. You want to talk to him?"

"Yes. Today, if possible."

"Okay, I'll find out what time he's on duty."

He picked up his phone and called somebody named Rachel, telling her to come take Steele down to the surveillance room.

Rachel turned out to be the young woman who had led them into Monroe's office. She accompanied them to the elevator without a word and responded only with "Uh huh" to Rudd's friendly question about whether she liked working in a casino, and "No" when he asked if she ever gambled. She led Steele off the elevator on the third floor, coldly telling Rudd to wait for Steele in the coffee shop downstairs.

Rudd held the elevator doors open. "Actually, I think I'll go down and check out the slots. Come find me there, Steele."

Without a word, Rachel led Steele to an unmarked door. She knocked and after a few moments a wiry young man in a colorful Led

Zeppelin T-shirt opened it and peeked out.

Rachel said, "Did Mr. Monroe call you?"

"Yeah." The young man sized Steele up. "Is this the guy?"

"Yes. This is Mr. Steele. You are to show him the tapes of the morning count. Culp's shift."

"Okay, whatever you say. C'mon in, Steele. I'm Gary." The young man stood back, avoiding eye contact with Steele.

Steele went in and Gary quickly closed the door. The large room was completely dark except for the glow of dozens of small TV monitors along one wall that showed a variety of shots of the casino's gambling floor. Another young man sat in front of a bank of consoles, closely watching the TV screens. He had his hand on a joystick and he was using it to pan the camera to follow a man in a Hawaiian shirt and plaid shorts who was casually walking between the rows of slot machines.

Gary pointed toward the back of the room. "Over there. There's a VCR set up for reviewing."

He led Steele to a worn steel desk and pointed to a stack of VCR tapes. "I laid out the tapes. Past ten days." He picked up a tape and pushed it into the slot. "Uh, what is it you're looking for? Something to do with Culp's disappearing?"

"I'm not sure yet," said Steele, sitting down at the desk.

Gary slid a remote control toward Steele. "Here's a flipper. Have fun."

Steele waited until Gary had gone back to watching the gambling-floor TV monitors, then he pressed the eject button and looked at the label on the videotape. The date was hand-printed: January 26th, ten days before Culp had disappeared. The labels on the other tapes indicated they were of the days that followed. The last tape was labeled February 5th, Culp's last day on the job before he had gone missing. Steele took out his smartphone and entered the dates. Then he pushed the January 26th tape back into the VCR.

At first there was nothing but static on the TV screen. Then the picture came on, showing an empty room with a gray, Formica-topped table in the center. Three chairs were around the table, two on the far side, one on the left. The view was from overhead, apparently from a stationary camera mounted high on a wall.

Seconds later, the count team entered the room, Culp first,

followed by a middle-aged, rather stout woman, and a very-tall bald man. Culp wore the usual dark suit of management; the other two wore the standard countroom dress of short-sleeved, pocketless white shirts and plain pocketless black pants. All three seated themselves. Culp sat at the head of the table, filling out a paper form. The other two just sat there facing the camera, hands folded on the table, chatting amiably, obviously waiting for something.

Steele noticed a pair of earphones plugged into the front of the VCR and put them on. The sound was weak, but he could hear the muted voices of the count team echoing off of the unadorned walls of the room. He turned the sound all the way up but was still barely able to make out what they were saying. They were discussing the weather, kids, a high-school basketball game.

Steele focused on Culp and was surprised to see that he looked even older in life than he had in the morgue. He was stoop-shouldered, with a tired, and maybe a little worried, look on his face. Steele found it strange to watch a man calmly carrying out his job after seeing him lying naked on his back in the morgue. He couldn't help but look at Culp's forehead, remembering the strangeness of those two words burned into it.

The count team turned when two uniformed guards came into the room pushing a heavy-looking cart stacked high with metal drop boxes. As soon as the guards left, the count team started a routine they obviously knew well. The tall man's job was to go to the cart to get one of the drop boxes. He brought a box labeled "B1" back to the table and the woman used a key from around her neck to open it. Then she dumped the box's contents onto the table. The tall man took the empty box back to the cart and got the next box, labeled "B2." He placed it at the far end of the table, in plain sight. Then all three of them began to sort the pile of bills into loose stacks. Steele leaned closer to the screen to watch Culp's movements. His job was to stack the one-hundred-dollar bills. He carefully stacked them right in front of himself, never moving any of the bills anywhere close to the edge of the table. The others did the same, stacking the lower denominations of bills in front of themselves.

When all the bills were stacked, the woman counted her stacks, calling out the amounts while Culp wrote them down on a printed paper form. Then she pushed the bills to the tall man who recounted the same stack and reported the amount. Culp also wrote down that amount. The stacks of bills were then pushed to Culp who placed them in a wooden rack that stood next to the table. The stack of hundred-dollar bills in front of Culp was counted last. He pushed them to the woman who counted them and then to the tall man who recounted them before pushing them back to Culp who wrote down the total count and put the bills into the rack. When all the bills were off the table, they opened the next box, dumped it on the table, and the tall man went to get another box off the cart to start the procedure all over again.

They worked efficiently, but all three looked totally bored. Steele knew the repetitive nature of the job was part of the security plan: with an unchanging routine, and the money in plain sight at all times, any unusual movements could easily be spotted.

Steele stopped the tape and took out a small notebook. He drew a quick diagram of the room, noting the positions of the camera, the table, the rack, and the cart. He noted the fact that the camera provided an unobstructed view of the money at all times. Then he sat back to think about it. The procedure was very similar to what he had seen in Reno. The most vulnerable point was when the bills were first dumped onto the table. Until that moment, no one knew how much money had been stuffed down through the hole in a gaming table to end up in that particular drop box. Even when the money was on the count table, it was hard to estimate how much was there. If that particular gaming table had been populated with small-time players all through the previous night, there might be a large number of low-denomination bills that wouldn't add up to much. On the other hand, if some high-rollers had spent the previous night gambling at that table, the same sized pile of bills could represent a lot more money.

Steele stared at his drawing of the count room. Was there any way Culp could have used some kind of slight of hand to stash some of those hundreds while he was counting them? Steele put the tape back in and watched them count a few more boxes. Then he stopped the tape and again looked at his drawing. The camera was positioned perfectly. The unwavering camera-view meant there was absolutely no possibility for any one of the three to steal any of the money. The boxes on the cart were locked. The woman had the only key, and besides, the cart and all of the boxes were in plain sight at all times.

Then, when the box was brought to the table and dumped, it was not only in full view of the camera, it was always in full view of all three people. If there was to be any stealing going on, they would all have to be in on it. And they would have to somehow hide it from the camera. Once the money was counted and placed in the rack, it had been accounted for. Even if Culp had intentionally written down the wrong numbers, the tape could be rerun to carefully listen to the amounts that were being called out. Then, those amounts could be compared with the numbers Culp had written down. Monroe said the tapes had been carefully scrutinized by experts and Steele was sure they would have done that kind of comparison. Nevertheless, Monroe seemed very sure Culp had been stealing money from the count. But how?

Steele pushed the tape back in and after he had watched the entire tape, he put in the next one and sat back to watch the count team carry out the exact same process over again. There was so little variance from tape to tape, Steele was sure anyone who reviewed them would soon be as bored as the count team. But after Culp disappeared, the casino's security people must have watched the tapes very carefully. If Cult was stealing money, how could they have missed it?

Steele paused the tape and stared up into the darkness of the quiet room to think. If Culp had somehow gotten a large amount of money out of that count room, it would have been in large bills. It was his job to count the 100s. But how could he have stolen even a few of them under the close scrutiny of that TV camera? Even if the other two members of the count team were in on it, how could they take even a single bill without it being obvious to anybody watching the videotape?

Steele restarted the tape and watched the three people carry out their robot-like tasks over and over again: the bills from the drop box were emptied onto the table to be sorted and stacked and logged, then the next box was retrieved to start it all over again. What was he missing? Maybe Monroe was right; maybe he *was* wasting his time even looking at the tapes.

Steele put in a new videotape and as he watched it, he thought about what others would have been looking for as they watched this tape. They would be looking for money being taken off of the table. Maybe he should look for something else.

He found the slow-motion button and watched the three people slowly carry out their counting task. There was no way the camera could have missed anything unusual. But what if there hadn't been a camera? What if only the other two count people were watching Culp? Steele continued to watch the count in slow motion, but this time, instead of looking for money being taken off the table, he watched for any kind of *opportunity* Culp might have had to take money off of the table.

Then he saw it. After the tall man emptied the box labeled "C1" onto the table and started to take it back to the cart, the woman turned to say something to him. At that moment, neither of them was watching Culp. Steele ran back the tape and restarted it in regular motion. He listened carefully to what she was saying as she turned away from Culp. "I bet craps table two will have a lot in it. I saw a crowd there last night."

She was breaking the boredom by speculating about how much money the next box would have in it, and she was facing away from Culp as she did it. If Culp wanted to take money off of the table, he could have done it at that moment and the other two would have never noticed. But at the moment, Culp didn't move. He sat quietly with both hands on the table.

Steele got up and went to find Gary. The young man was leaning close to a TV monitor that was showing a busy craps table. Steele cleared his throat and Gary turned, smiling. "All done?"

"No, I'd like to see every tape of the morning count you have."

The young man looked surprised. "Well, uh, I'll have to see if I can find them. You want . . . all of them?"

"Mr. Monroe said I could see as many of them as I wanted. Is there a problem?"

Gary shook his head. "No, I didn't say that. I'll . . . uh, get 'em."

Steele returned to his seat in front of the VCR and waited.

Gary soon came with a stack of videotapes so tall he had to hold them against his chest to keep them balanced. He dumped them on the desk. "This is all we've got. Thirty days worth."

Steele looked up at him. "Thirty days. The exact number of days the state gaming commission requires you to keep the tapes?"

Gary shrugged. "We tape over the old ones."

He turned to leave, but Steele caught him by the arm. "One more thing, Gary. I assume somebody watches the count live."

"Sure, gaming regulations require it. In case something goes wrong with the VCR."

"And can you tell me who watches the morning count, the one Culp is in charge of?"

Gary shrugged. "Actually, that's me. It's my shift so I have to watch it every morning. Pretty boring stuff, isn't it?"

Steele released his arm. "That's all I needed to know. Thank you, Gary."

The young man frowned and walked away.

Steele put the tape with the earliest date into the machine and played it, listening to what the woman was saying whenever she turned away from Culp. Halfway through the next tape he heard what he was looking for. Her words were exactly the same as they were on an earlier tape. She said, "I bet craps two will have a lot in it. I saw a crowd there last night." Neither she nor the tall man were looking at Culp at that moment. Something had been cut out of the tape and video from an old tape had been spliced in to replace it. The routine was so exact, the tape could be altered and nobody would ever see it. The only way to tell it had been edited was to listen to the woman's words. Steele ran the tape back and looked at it again. The splice was undetectable: whoever had done the editing knew what they were doing.

Steele turned to look for Gary. He was not at his station.

Steele picked up the two videotapes that showed the duplication and went to the other surveillance person who was concentrating on a TV screen. He was manipulating a joy stick to follow a nervous-looking man in a LA Dodgers baseball hat who was hovering near one of the blackjack tables.

"Where did Gary go?" asked Steele.

"Oh, he had to go to the bathroom," the man said without looking away from the TV screen. "He'll be back soon."

"I wouldn't count on it," said Steele, heading for the door.

# Chapter 11

*U*pstairs at the executive offices, Steele didn't wait to be announced. He barged into Monroe's office and found him on the phone. Steele pulled the two video tapes out of his jacket and held them up.

Monroe immediately hung up. "You found something?"

"I would suggest putting a clock on the wall behind your count teams."

"Why? What did you see?"

Steele put the two tapes on Monroe's desk. "Somebody has been editing the tapes. Have your people listen to the words the woman is saying anytime the man goes to the cart to get another drop box. At that point, neither of them is watching Culp and it must have been at that moment he was pulling one hundred dollar bills out of the count. Have your people listen to the audio carefully and they'll find exact duplicates in the words she is saying and how she says it. It means somebody has patched in video from an earlier tape to cover up whatever Culp was doing at that moment."

Monroe frowned. "But my people looked for any kind of glitch in the tapes to make sure they hadn't been altered."

"Somebody must have downloaded the tapes to a digital editing system. That way, they could create new modified video and then copy it back to overwrite the entire tape."

"So Culp really was stealing money out of the count. The sneaky old bastard."

"Yes, but it required the help of whoever had control of the videotapes. That person must have been doing the editing. You might want to talk to a young man named Gary, if you can find him."

Monroe jumped to his feet. "Gary? I've been suspicious of that little prick all along." He snatched up the phone and punched in a single number. He shouted, "Gary has probably run off, just like I said he would. Get somebody out looking for him. Now!" Monroe slammed down the phone and turned back to Steele. "If he's still in this town, we'll find him. Damn it to hell, if you were able to figure out the videotapes had been edited, what's wrong with my people? They've been looking at those tapes since the day Culp disappeared."

"Culp and Gary were counting on how boring it is to look at these tapes. Your people probably just fast forwarded through them looking for any sign of stealing."

"I don't give a shit if it's the most boring job in the world, they were supposed to examine them with a fine-toothed comb. Damn it to hell!" Monroe turned and walked to the window. Without looking back, he said, "So Culp really did it. Everybody said it wasn't like him, but in my gut, I knew it had to be him. There were just too many low counts on his shift." He turned back to Steele. "What about the other two people on the count team? They must have been in on it too."

"I don't think so. The tapes only seem to be edited when their attention is elsewhere. But if they turn up missing tomorrow, you'll know."

Monroe came back to his desk and picked up the phone. "I'm not gonna give them a chance to make a break for it. I'll pull them in now."

Steele held up his hand to stop him. "If you really want to know if they were in on it, I'd give them some rope. See what they do now that Gary has run off."

Monroe thought about it for a few seconds before finally hanging up the phone. "All right, but I'm gonna get somebody out to their homes to keep an eye on 'em. What's next for you? Back to LA?"

"No, I still want to talk to those two count people in the morning, assuming they show up. And I want to talk to Culp's son."

"Right. He works in one of the downtown casinos. He's a pit boss. I wrote down the info for you." He handed the piece of paper to Steele.

Steele glanced at the paper. "James Vinelli? His name's not Culp?"

"Nope. He isn't Culp's real son. His wife's kid, by a previous marriage. She rolled into town quite a few years ago with two young boys in tow. Got a job here as a cocktail waitress. I guess she met Culp on the job and things went the way they usually go. Anyhow, before long they were married. From that point on, far as we know, it was your usual married bliss thing, even though she was a lot younger than him. She quit carryin' drinks and stayed home to raise the boys."

"So her name was Vinelli before he married Culp. And the two boys kept that name."

"Right."

"Do you know what shift he's on?"

"Day shift. He'll be there . . ." Monroe glanced at his watch. "For another couple of hours. But if he finds out you're working for me he may not be very eager to talk to you."

"He knows you?"

"Yeah. He used to work here. Got laid off, shortly after Omnivexx took over."

Steele didn't reply, but on his way to the elevator he thought about a case he'd been involved in several years before. It had ended badly when a laid-off employee came back with a gun. Did this case have something to do with the son's firing? Maybe Culp suspected he was about to get laid off too. But Culp must have been close to retirement anyhow. It just didn't seem likely Culp's stealing could be for revenge. Something else must have happened, something so significant it made him start stealing after a lifetime of honest employment at the casino.

The racket in the slot area was intense, with wailing sirens, constant beeping, and the clatter of coins dropping into metal drays that Steele knew had been specifically designed to make as much noise as possible. Nearby, a mechanical chorus inside another slot machine cried out, "Wheel of Fortune" every few seconds.

Steele found Rudd playing a slot machine that had a colorful picture of Elvis on the front. He was so engrossed in watching the spinning images, he didn't even see Steele come up behind him. When three guitar symbols lined up on the center line, Rudd shouted, "Yes!" and punched the air as quarters began to drop into the tray.

When the machine finally finished it's weird, cartoon-like version of Elvis singing "All Shook Up," he tapped Rudd on the shoulder and said, "Winning?"

Rudd turned. "Oh, hi, Steele. Did you see that? One more guitar on the center line and I would've won a thousand bucks."

"So you turned your pocket change into a tray full of quarters?"

"I sure did. Well, I did have to hit the ATM machine, but only once. Except for that, I'm almost ahead."

Steele smiled at the concept of *almost ahead*. "Well, while you're still almost ahead why don't we go do some work."

Rudd scooped his quarters into a plastic cup. "Sure. Where we going?"

"Downtown. I want to talk to Culp's stepson. He works down there."

Rudd jiggled his cup full of quarters. "At a casino? Hey, I hear the slots are looser down there."

"Well, then we'd better get down there before the casinos all go broke."

As Steele led the way toward the parking structure with Rudd following, counting his quarters. When they were in the car, Rudd said, "No, really. A guy at my newspaper came to Vegas a while back and wrote an article about all the different places that have slots. He said the airport slots were the worst, along with the ones in the Safeway stores. But he said the ones downtown are really good."

As they merged into the heavy Las Vegas Boulevard traffic and inched their way toward downtown, Rudd asked. "So, did you see anything on the surveillance tapes?"

"Yes. I think Culp was pulling money out of the count and a young surveillance employee named Gary was editing the videotapes to hide it. Gary disappeared soon after I started looking at the tapes."

"No, kidding? So Culp *was* stealing, and he had help. How much did they get away with?"

"Hard to say. It depends on how long they'd been doing it. If he was taking one-hundred dollar bills, it could be thousands every day.

"Thousands? A day? That'd beef up his salary a bit. But why don't they know exactly? Can't they do an audit or something?"

"No one knows how much is in the drop boxes until they count them, not even the dealers."

"Uh, what's a drop box?"

Steele glanced at him. "Did you ever play blackjack?"

"Once. Lost forty bucks and went back to the slots."

"Well, when you bought chips from the dealer, he pushed your forty bucks down through a hole in the table. The bills fall into a metal box under there."

"I get it, the drop box."

"Right. Until the morning count is complete, no one knows how much is in each drop box. If Culp stole some of the hundred-dollar bills before they were officially counted, no one would ever know for sure how much was gone."

"So why did they suspect him?"

"Monroe thought Culp's morning counts of the busiest tables were always coming out too low. But with the videotapes not showing anything, he wasn't sure until Culp disappeared."

Rudd let out a low whistle. "Wow. Hundred-dollar bills. And no way to detect it. But why are we going downtown to see his son?"

"Culp had two sons. They were Mrs. Culp's kids. One of them works in LA. It seems she forgot to tell us that, didn't she? I'm still sure she knows more than she told us. For one thing, she didn't tell us her name used to be Vinelli. Her sons kept that name. I'm hoping this son can shed some light on what his step-father was up to."

During the rest of the ride downtown, Rudd busied himself counting his slot winnings. Steele used the time to think about why a man like Culp, with a secure middle-management position in a casino and nearing retirement, would risk it all to steal. And he must have recruited Gary to help him. It's always riskier to get someone else involved. Why would someone like Culp feel he had to take such risks? Why did he need the money so desperately? Gambling losses? If so, nobody at the casino knew about it. Blackmail? Was someone forcing him to steal? But what would a man like Culp have done to make him vulnerable to blackmail? And if he had secrets, who would he want to keep them from, his wife?

Many of the streets in downtown Las Vegas were undergoing repairs, but Steele was finally able to make his way to the casino where Culp's son worked. He pulled into the self-parking garage.

"Hey," said Rudd, "why not use the valet service? Are you sure you want to walk all that way?"

"I don't want the valets snooping into all the special devices in this car."

"Suit yourself," said Rudd, "but you've been doing a lot of walking today."

"Don't mother-hen me," said Steele. "What did I tell you about that?"

Rudd shrugged. "Forget I said a word." He folded his arms and stared out the window sullenly.

Steele parked the car and looked at Rudd. "I know you mean well, John, but the more walking I do, the stronger my legs will get."

Rudd nodded toward Steele's leg. "I get it. But doesn't it hurt where it . . . you know, straps onto your leg? I know I'm not supposed to ask, but . . . doesn't it? Tell me the truth."

Steele hesitated, bur finally decided Rudd had a right to know. He had been a good friend, both before and after he had gone to Iraq, and he was the only one who cared enough to ask for details. "It does hurt a bit, but to tell the truth, my knees hurt more. I lost a lot of cartilage out of both knees, so I need to strengthen the muscles of my legs to compensate.

Rudd nodded with a grim smile. "I get it." He paused, and then added, "Thanks for telling me."

Steele opened his door. "Are you ready to go, old man? I'll race you to the elevator."

Rudd grinned. "So we're actually going to take the elevator instead of walking down five flights? And who're you callin' old man?"

They took the elevator down to the casino. It was a small casino with only a few gaming tables, but there were a lot of slot machines crammed into the confined space. The floor was littered with torn coin wrappers, and as usual, the slot noise was deafening. The place was fairly crowded with rows and rows of people perched on their stools, all leaning forward, all intensely interested in their machine's spinning symbols.

Rudd seemed to be irresistibly drawn to the racket. "I think I'll just go check out their slots," he said over his shoulder. "Come get me when you're ready."

Steele called after him. "Do me a favor and sit at a slot machine where you can watch the pit."

Rudd stopped and turned back. "What's a pit?"

"It's over there, said Steele, pointing. "That circle of blackjack and craps tables. The bosses hang out in the middle."

"You want me to watch them? Why? You expecting trouble?"

"No, but when I ask to talk to Culp's son, I want you to keep an eye on the other employees. See if anybody's watching him."

"Got it." Rudd headed for a slot machine on the end of the row.

Steele waited until Rudd was seated in front of the machine before heading toward the pit. He asked a guard which one was James Vinelli and the guard pointed out a tall, dark-haired man in a light-colored suit who was leaning against a podium near the busy craps table. He was talking to a woman dealer who seemed to be complaining about something.

Steele waited until the woman left before he approached. Then he leaned across the thick velvet rope that separated the customers from the employees and said, "Excuse me, Mr. Vinelli, I'm sorry to bother you at a time like this, but can I talk to you for a few minutes?"

Vinelli sized him up. "What about?"

"My name is Drew Steele. I've been hired by the Golden Palace to investigate your father's death."

Vinelli stared at him for several moments before replying. "He wasn't my real father. But I suppose you already know that."

Steele nodded.

"So why'd they hire you? To find the money?"

"My investigation is not about money, Mr. Vinelli. I'm trying to find out who killed your father, and why."

"It's always about the money. Don't let 'em kid you."

"Nevertheless, I am trying to find out what happened to your stepfather."

"All right. Not your fault who hired you, I guess." Before Steele could reply, he added, "But we can't talk here. Let's go to the coffee shop."

He said something to the other pit boss, and then he led the way to the restaurant. He stopped at the entrance to wait for Steele. "Somethin' the matter with your legs?" he asked.

"An injury. Gradually getting better."

Vinelli shrugged and led the way to a small table in the back of the coffee shop. The table had a reserved sign on it. The waitress hurried over. "You want some coffee, Mr. Vinelli?"

He looked at Steele. "You want coffee? Somethin' to eat?"

Steele shook his head, wondering why Vinelli seemed so casual and unconcerned. His father's body had only been identified that morning. Didn't he care? Or was he hiding his feelings?

Vinelli waved the waitress away. "So, Steele, you're what? Some kind of private detective?"

Steele realized Vinelli's mother hadn't mentioned her trip to LA. That was odd. "That's right."

"Don't remember ever seeing you around here."

"I'm from Los Angeles."

Vinelli nodded. "I get it. That's where he was found. So, what're you doing here in Vegas?"

"I'm trying to find out why he left here to go to LA. Do you have any ideas?"

"Me? I haven't even seen him in months. Not since, hell, let's see, not since last summer I guess."

"You weren't close?"

"That's putting it mildly. We were . . . well, that doesn't matter now, does it?"

Steele watched Vinelli closely. He seemed calm, but he was constantly glancing toward the door. Was he expecting someone? Or was he afraid someone would see him talking to a stranger?

"Maybe you could tell me something about him," said Steele.

Vinelli shrugged. "He was, well, most people would call him . . . quiet. Or moody."

"Did he have any friends I could talk to?"

"Not that I ever knew of. A real loner. Except for Craig. He and Craig used to be close I guess, until he moved to LA."

"Craig?"

"My kid brother."

"And he lives in LA?"

"Yeah, runs a poker joint down there. In Gardena."

"So you're all in the gaming business."

"Yeah, have been since we came to Vegas. We all worked at the Golden Palace at one time. "'Til the new managers came in and started getting rid of the old employees."

"The Omnivexx Corporation?"

"Yeah, that's right. After the bankruptcy, they brought in new people at the top and right away they started laying off anybody who wasn't . . . you know . . ."

"Cooperative?"

"That's one word for it. Willing to lay down and be run over is what I'd call it. They brought in new rules, new ways to cut tips, increased security. They made it pretty clear it was their way or the highway. Craig was one of the first to get sacked."

"Why?"

"Let's just say business is business and . . . ah, well, Craig's got a big mouth."

"Did you get fired too?

"It wasn't long before they did a general layoff and my name was on the list."

"Your stepfather couldn't prevent it?"

"Couldn't or didn't."

"You sound bitter."

"Naw, not at him anyhow. There are . . . other issues involved."

"Other issues?"

Vinelli shrugged. "Aw, hell, it doesn't matter now. Who knows if he could have done anything anyhow. If they wanted to get rid of us, they'd get it done somehow."

"But your stepfather stayed."

"He claimed he had to stay because he had a plan to get us all back together there, get us back our jobs."

"A plan?"

"Yeah, something to do with the bankruptcy, but apparently nothing ever came of it."

"But as I understand it, Omnivexx bought the casino after it went into bankruptcy. The people I talked to there seem grateful that they did."

Vinelli shrugged. "Well, if anybody thought different, they'd keep their mouths shut, wouldn't they?"

"Are you saying your stepfather objected to their takeover?"

Vinelli hesitated. "You might say that."

Steele waited, but Vinelli didn't seem willing to say more. Steele decided to probe a little deeper. "Why would he object? Isn't Omnivexx a reputable Atlantic City corporation? It sounds like just the kind of company the Golden Palace needed, someone to pay off the bills and fix up the place."

Vinelli looked away. After a few moments, he turned back to Steele. "All I really know is he had some kind of plan. He went downtown to talk to the bankruptcy judge. He and my mother had some arguments about it, but they did their arguing behind closed doors. Far as I know, nothing ever came of it. Doesn't matter to me. After I got this job down here I didn't much care what happened out there at the Palace. I like the people here better anyhow. Here we get together when we're away from work. Family picnics, deer hunting in the fall, things like that. And the boss has a houseboat on the lake we get to use. You wouldn't catch any of that Golden Palace bunch letting their employees use any damn houseboat, would you?"

"I don't know much about the management at the Golden Palace, Mr. Vinelli. But I have to ask you, do you think the . . . situation at the Golden Palace had anything to do with your father's death?"

"I'm not saying that. But ten to one they think he stole some of their money, don't they? That's the way they think over there. Guy disappears, he must be a thief."

"What do you think? Is it possible he might have stolen money from the casino?"

"Are you kidding? He'd never steal a dime from anybody. Let me tell you a story, Steele. One time when I was a kid I swiped a few bucks. I wanted to go to this pony ride they had set up in the park, but he said I'd already spent my allowance so tough luck. Long story short, I took the money out of my mother's purse. Later, he found out about it and was really pissed. Called me a little thief and came at me with his belt. I told him to go ahead and hit me, told him I didn't give a shit, he wasn't my real father anyhow. Know what he did? He broke down and cried. Stood right there in front of me and cried like a baby. Cruelest thing he could do to me, like I'd let him down. I'd of damn sure rather he did hit me."

"Sounds like he was a compassionate man."

Vinelli looked up. "You'd think so wouldn't you?"

Steele was about to ask more, but Vinelli said, "Hey, old family stories aren't gonna help you figure out who killed him, are they?"

"Any information you give me might be helpful"

"Yeah, maybe. But that's about all I can tell you anyhow. I gotta get back to work." He stood up.

"I'd like to also talk to your brother. Can you tell me how to find him?"

Vinelli sat back down. "Craig? Why do you want to talk to him?"

"Same reason I'm talking to you. Maybe he knows more about your stepfather's plan to bring you all back together at the Golden

Palace."

"He might. But he may not be so . . . cooperative, to use your word. Like I said, before, he's . . . Well, I guess that's your problem. You'll find him at the Four Aces Club, on Gardena Boulevard."

"All right, I'll go see him when I get back to LA. You'll tell him to expect me?"

Vinelli stood up again. "If I happen to talk to him. Sometimes he's hard to track down."

"Won't he be coming to the funeral?"

"Maybe."

"Maybe?"

"You never know about Craig. Like I said, sometimes he's hard to track down." He turned to go, but hesitated and turned back. "They said the old man was murdered. Shot."

"That's right."

"Hard to believe."

"I imagine."

"Maybe . . . if you . . . I mean if you find out why, or anything."

"I'll let you know."

"If he was into something bad, it would be hard on my mother. She--"

"I understand."

Vinelli nodded thoughtfully. "Yeah. Well, good luck."

After Vinelli left the café, Steele stayed there, thinking. Vinelli had been relatively forthcoming, but there were clearly some things he wasn't saying. What was Culp's plan to get them all back together at the Golden Palace? And what were the behind-closed-doors arguments about? Vinelli didn't seem to know much about it, or wasn't willing to say. It sounded as if he had cut off ties with his stepfather after he'd left the Golden Palace. But Vinelli was sure his stepfather couldn't be a thief, even though the evidence was clear that he had been stealing money from the casino. Something wasn't right. If Vinelli was telling the truth and Culp was a man who insisted on honesty, why would he suddenly start doing something so out of character? Such things rarely happened: either a man had the personality of a thief, always looking for opportunity, or he didn't. Something must have happened to change Culp, something so important, or so threatening, he felt he *had to* steal.

# Chapter 12

*S*teele found Rudd still glued to the same slot machine where he'd left him. His cup of quarters was almost empty. Steele tapped him on the shoulder. "Run of bad luck?"

Rudd was so intent on watching the symbols on the slot's screen roll to a stop, he didn't even turn around. When they finally stopped, he slapped his knee in disgust. "Damn! I keep missing it by one." He turned to Steele. "Did you see that? I think these things are fixed. They make it look like you're about to hit, and then it doesn't."

Steele smiled and put his hand on his old friend's shoulder. "I'm afraid the programming inside these machines isn't that sophisticated. They're manufactured to be random and the state gaming commission makes sure they stay that way."

"So you say, but it sure seems like they keep egging me on." He slid off the stool and shook his nearly-empty cup of quarters. "Hey, I've got a few quarters left. I'll buy you a sandwich."

"Maybe later. Let's go back to the Golden Palace and check into our room. I've got to make some calls."

"Right. Hey, we'll be on their tab. We can order room service."

As they headed for the parking structure, Rudd said, "Did you find out anything from his son?"

"Only that he doesn't believe Culp would ever steal."

"But you're sure he did."

"All the evidence points that way."

"Hey, maybe he was in on it too. A father and son team."

"Not very likely. Both he and his brother used to work at the Golden Palace, but they got fired after the buyout by Omnivexx. He says he hardly ever talked to his stepfather. I think he was telling the truth."

"They all worked there? Are you sure they weren't all in it together?"

"I don't think so. The other son works at a poker club in LA now. And Vinelli seems content with his job here. But I've been wondering if Culp might have started stealing after they got laid off."

"Revenge?"

"Maybe, but from what I've learned about him so far, it would be very out of character. I think something else was going on."

"Like what?"

"I don't know yet. What happened after I went to the café with Vinelli? Anybody notice?"

"Nobody seemed to. That other guy inside that pit place got on the phone and talked to somebody, but only for a minute. Do you think that means anything?"

"Hard to say."

Rudd dumped his remaining quarters into his hand and stared at them. "I've had it with these downtown machines. They're too tight, no matter what anybody says."

When they got back to the Golden Palace, Steele asked at the Complementary Guests check-in desk for the key to their suite. The man behind the counter was very friendly, and very curious. "We haven't had you in one of our top-floor suites before, have we, Mr. Steele? Will you be staying with us long?"

"Hard to say."

"Well, you be sure to let me know if I can do anything for you. We take good care of our special guests here at the Golden Palace."

As they headed for the elevator, Rudd chuckled. "He must have heard that Monroe personally approved your suite. He thinks you're a whale, a big out-of-town-bettor. That means we can order anything we want from room service and you can just sign for it."

Steele didn't comment. He was still thinking about James Vinelli's attitude about his stepfather. Culp had been married to his mother's since he was very young so they must have had something of a father-son relationship. That story about stealing money showed he could be hurt by his stepfather's opinion. What had happened to change their relationship?

The suite was larger and fancier than Steele would have expected. It had deep carpets, a wet bar, a desk, and a large beige sofa that was big enough to sleep on. Steele took the top-floor suite as yet another indication of how important the management viewed his investigation.

Rudd went to stand in front of the floor-to-ceiling window. "Wow, come look at this view, Steele. We're almost as high as the Mirage Hotel over there. And look at all the people down there in front of Treasure Island. They must be getting ready for the afternoon battle of the pirates against the Sirens. Hey, maybe we should go down and watch it too."

Steele didn't reply; he was on the phone calling his answering service to get his phone messages. There were a few prospective clients calling, nothing pressing. There was no return phone call from Loren.

Rudd settled on sandwiches, French fries, and beer from room service, and as soon as the food arrived, he parked himself in front of the huge TV.

Steele ate his sandwich at the desk while he got his laptop set up. The first email he sent was to ask his information-search service for a whatever data they could find about the Omnivexx Corporation. He also asked for a full-scale search for information about Mrs. Kenneth Culp, aka Vinelli, and about James Vinelli of Las Vegas and Craig Vinelli, currently employed by the Four Aces Poker Club in Gardena.

When his email finished downloading, he found a brief message from Kelly with the autopsy and toxicology reports attached. He quickly called the ticket scalper in LA to arrange for a second-row seat at the Lakers game.

As soon as he hung up, Rudd turned down the volume on the TV and came over to the desk. "Got something?"

"The autopsy report from Kelly."

"What's it say?"

Steele opened the first attachment, the autopsy report. "It says Culp died from trauma to the brain. A single bullet."

"So it *was* the bullet that killed him."

"Right, but it says there was also other serious trauma, mostly to the body."

"Uh oh," said Rudd. "Why would they beat an old man like

Culp?"

Steele thought about that. Why would they beat him up if they were going to kill him anyhow? "They must have been trying to get some information out of him."

"Like what?"

"Hard to say, but whatever they were after, they probably got it. A man like Culp would not be prepared to resist pain very long."

Rudd tapped the laptop's screen. But it says *extensive, repeated* trauma to stomach and to the back. It looks like he resisted for quite a while."

Steele reread that part of the report. It said there was blunt force trauma to both the upper and lower back resulting in extensive muscle damage. Steele pointed to the screen. "Muscle necrosis and rhabomyolysis, indication of renal damage, bleeding of the spleen."

"Holy shit," said Rudd. "Sounds like they beat him half to death."

"I'm afraid so," said Steele. "He was probably unconscious when they shot him."

"Well, thank goodness for that. Maybe he was out cold when they burned those words into his forehead. too"

"Very likely. It's clear that they were trying to get something out of him, something he didn't want to tell them."

"Maybe they were after the money he stole," suggested Rudd.

"I doubt if he would be willing to take that kind of punishment over mere money."

"Why not?" said Rudd. "I saw on TV that some old lady got dragged down the street rather than give up her money to a purse snatcher."

"She was probably just reacting instinctively. Culp couldn't have accumulated all that much money. Certainly not enough to die for. You remember when I went to Iraq?"

"Yeah, you took that job at the embassy. You said you couldn't tell me what it was all about."

Steele thought about how much he could say. Rudd knew he had been in Iraq, but he didn't know why. The cover story was that Steele had been hired by a private company to investigate security leaks among employees at the U.S. embassy in Baghdad.

Rudd sat back in his chair and crossed his legs. "Well? Are you going to tell me or not?"

Steele decided to describe it as hearsay. "When I was in Iraq, I heard about certain . . . special forces that were to go undercover in Baghdad. Before they were sent out, they underwent anti-interrogation training. If captured, they were told to freely give up any information the enemy wanted, unless it would compromise their unit. They were taught how to deal with pain, both psychological and physical. Some of them *were* captured and some were beaten to death because they wouldn't reveal the identities of their undercover comrades."

Rudd thought about that. "So you're saying Culp might have been protecting someone. Who? His family?"

"Possibly. A story his stepson told me makes me think Culp had a very strong sense of personal values. And I think he cared quite a bit about his stepsons."

"So he was protecting them? From what?"

"Maybe they *were* trying to get him to tell where the money was," said Steele somberly. "Maybe he left the money with his son in LA and was willing to take a beating rather than tell his killers that."

"Jesus," said Rudd, "it all sounds pretty gruesome. Are there really people who would beat an old man half to death just to find out what he did with a few thousand bucks?"

"Plenty of people. Remember that drug-carrying condom that was in his stomach? Violence is business as usual in the heroin business."

Rudd shook his head. "So what does the report say about drugs? Were there drugs in Culp's system?"

Steele downloaded the toxicology report and scanned through it. "Pretty much what I expected. A trace amount of heroin in his system. Not enough to kill him, just enough to show up in his blood. Also, Kelly's report says the body had no needle tracks so he wasn't an addict."

"So you still think that condom was a plant?"

"Yes. This report proves his killers had access to heroin, and they were willing to give him a little of it to make the ruse about the condom more convincing."

"So he *was* killed by drug dealers."

"By somebody who had access to heroin, at least. But the question still remains, how would a man like Culp get involved with drug dealers?"

"What about his stepson? You said he works in LA."

"Right. It seems likely he went to LA to see his stepson Craig. But why would his stepson introduce him to drug dealers?"

"Well," said Rudd, "the autopsy shows he wasn't shooting up heroin, but he might have been into other kinds of drugs."

"I don't think so," said Steele. "Think about this, something drove him to steal from the casino. What else do drug dealers have besides drugs?"

Rudd thought about it for several seconds. Then he snapped his fingers. "Money!"

"Right. Culp was driven by the need for money. If he needed money badly enough to start stealing from his long-time employer, it seems likely he went to LA to search for more."

"He went to some drug dealers for a loan? You'd have to be pretty crazy to do something like that."

"Or very desperate. Or maybe he didn't know they were drug dealers. Culp was undoubtedly very naïve about such things. Maybe he just saw them as people with money."

"Okay," said Rudd, "let's say you're right and the killers went to all the trouble to feed him a condom and some heroin before they killed him. Why? Just to make the police think it was a drug killing?"

"That would be the obvious reason, but what would the police think when they found out he was an old man with a family and a good job?"

"They'd think it was just another old guy gone bad because of drugs. Threw away job and family because of a drug habit."

"Maybe that's what the police will think, but I don't. I think it's another message, like those words burned into his forehead."

"Another message? For who?"

"That's what I'm trying to figure out."

"Well, I guess that's why you're the famous detective and the cops are . . . well, just cops."

"They're smarter than the cops they portray on TV."

"You give the police too much credit. Give them a dead body with a single bullet to the brain and heroin in his system and they'll write up the report as a drug deal gone bad every time. They'll file it and go on to the next case."

"Maybe, but Pruett sometimes gets his teeth into a murder case."

Rudd went back to watching the TV, but it left Steele wondered if Rudd was right. Maybe the police *would* think it was one of the drug-related killings that were becoming all too common in LA. The killers had gone to a lot of trouble to tie Culp's death to drugs; if it really did have something to do with drugs, why would they call attention to that fact? Culp's body had been found next to the Crueltown fence. That would also make the police suspect the murder had something to do with drugs. But did it? Also, somebody had tried to lure Culp's wife there. Why? What did it all have to do with Crueltown?

Rudd turned toward Steele. "What about the car?"

"What about it?"

"Why did they leave the body in the trunk of a car?"

Rudd had a point. If the killers were trying to convince the police the murder had something to do with Crueltown and drugs, why leave the body in the trunk of a stolen Mercedes? Why not just dump the body out by the fence? The police found a lot of drug overdose cases there, and quite a few murder victims also. And it meant the killers would have had to arrange for another car, a getaway car. Or did they just go inside Crueltown after they parked the car? But wouldn't that also be too obvious? Even if they were sure the police wouldn't go in after them, why leave such a valuable car? A chop shop would give them at least a thousand dollars for it, and if they got rid of the car they wouldn't have to worry about the police finding a stray fingerprint or an overlooked hair that would carry their DNA. The car was a loose end, something that didn't seem to fit the otherwise neat, apparently-professional killing.

Steele's thoughts were interrupted by a knock at the door. He got up and went to look through the peephole. He was surprised to see Monroe's assistant waiting out in the hall. But she wasn't wearing the severe suit she had been wearing earlier; instead, she had on tight-fitting jeans and an almost-transparent lavender blouse.

He opened the door. "Good evening, Miss . . ."

"Hill, Rachel Hill. Can I come in?"

"Of course, Miss Hill. Come in."

"It's just Rachel." She squeezed by him and Rudd jumped up to greet her, his napkin still tucked into the top of his shirt.

"You remember my associate, John Rudd?" said Steele.

"Yeah." She turned back to Steele. "I thought I'd drop by to make sure you were comfortable."

"We sure are," said Rudd, "real comfy. We got room service to bring up beer and sandwiches and this big-screen TV is great."

"There are also TVs in the bedrooms," she said dryly.

"Yeah, I noticed that. But look at how big this TV is. The ball game is on. The Dodgers are up in the ninth and--"

"In the bedroom," she repeated.

For a moment, Rudd looked puzzled. Then he got it. "Oh, uh, right. Maybe I'll just go watch the TV in my bedroom for awhile. More comfortable in there anyhow." He picked up his bottle of beer and hurried into the bedroom, closing the door behind himself.

Rachel turned off the TV and pointed toward the sofa. "Can we talk?"

Steele followed her to the sofa.

She sat down and leaned back. "Aren't you wondering why I'm here?"

"I expect you'll tell me when you're ready."

"I didn't have to come. My job ends at five, officially."

"I noticed that you'd changed out of your work clothes."

She kicked off her shoes. "Maybe I just wanted to drop by to see if you needed anything."

"I can't think of anything."

"Maybe I'm just showing you how friendly we are to our out-of-town guests."

"Maybe you could get to what you want, Miss Hill."

She sat up straight and frowned at him. "So we're back to Miss Hill, are we? All right, Mister Steele, I'll admit that my boss wanted me to find out what you learned downtown, but I didn't have to come here tonight. I could have used the phone, you know."

"Listen, Rachel, let's call a truce. We're both after the same thing, trying to find out why Culp disappeared and why he was killed. As soon as I met you, I could tell you were a competent, professional employee, dedicated to your work. I will, of course, tell your boss everything I find out, as soon as it is appropriate to do so."

For the first time, she smiled and moved closer to touch his hand. "So I don't have to pry it out of you using my feminine wiles?"

"You are a very attractive woman." He took her hand in his and she smiled in response. "I'm sure Rudd would be glad to tell you whatever you want to know."

She frowned and punched him lightly in the chest. "I think we may have to be friends, Steele. I like your sense of humor." She stood up. "Don't you have anything to drink around here?"

Steele nodded toward the cabinet next to the refrigerator. "I haven't looked in there, but I'm sure you know what's available."

She went to the cabinet and took out a small bottle of Scotch. She held it up to read the attached card. "If opened, this will be charged to your room. Well, too bad, I'm opening it. I'm sure you can afford it."

"I'll just tell your boss you drank it. He can take it out of your salary."

She came back with the bottle, along with two glasses and ice." You'll do no such thing. He doesn't know I'm here."

"Really?"

"Not unless he's got somebody watching me. He might do that. He's a bit paranoid."

"Why?"

She poured the Scotch. "So, are you going to use your masculine wiles to pry information out of me?" She picked up her drink and waited for him to do the same.

Steele picked up his glass and touched hers with it. "I thought we were going to call a truce. Share what we know."

She sipped her drink. "All right, you first."

Steele put his glass back down on the coffee table. "Vinelli wasn't much help. And he doesn't have a very high opinion of this casino."

"I can't blame him for that. It was before my time, but I heard they didn't fit in."

"He blames the buyout. The new management."

She nodded. "I've heard that a lot. Nobody likes the people from Omnivexx very much, but they're trying to bring the place back to profitability. Maybe people should take the long-term view. If Omnivexx is successful, they'll create more jobs in the end."

"Spoken like a faithful employee."

"Don't give me trouble, Steele. It's true that they laid off a lot of the old-timers, but maybe the old-timers were keeping this place from moving into the new Vegas economy. The town is booming, but this casino wasn't."

"What do you really know about the Omnivexx Group?"

"It's a holding company. From New Jersey. I heard they also have gaming interests in Atlantic City."

"Who are the principals?"

"Beats me. Fact is, we hardly ever see anybody from Omnivexx. They've got two overseers that fly in from back east for weekly meetings with top management. My boss has nicknames for 'em, but don't tell him I told you. He calls 'em haircut and suit, short for hundred-dollar haircut--that's the little one who thinks he's quite the Romeo--and thousand-dollar suit--he's the serious one. I think he's the real boss."

"So Monroe meets with them weekly."

"Nope. Like I said, only the top people get to meet with them. Gaming management only. None of the hotel or security people are allowed into those meetings." She paused to take another drink. "You aren't drinking your Scotch."

"I'm thinking. From what I've heard, most buyouts on the strip are for tear-downs. Make a big show by knocking it down with explosives and put up a megacasino in its place."

"That's true, but they promised not to do that, at least not until they gave us a chance to make a go of it."

Steele wondered if they really planned to do that. If they wanted to build up the Golden Palace to compete with the newer casinos, why hadn't they expanded the gaming floor or added more rooms? They'd done some renovations, but they were only surface changes, new carpets and new furniture.

"Uh oh, that sent you off," said Rachel. "What are you thinking, that they had something to do with Culp's death?'

"Is that what you think?"

"Don't play psychiatrist with me, Steele. I ask a question and you come back with another question. I know people are talking about it. They're saying the mysterious Omnivexx Corporation comes in and Culp starts stealing money. Next thing you know, he disappears and ends up dead in LA. A lot of the employees here love to speculate, but I think it's just a coincidence. People are pissed at Omnivexx because some of their friends got laid off after the buyout. So they start rumors."

"My job is to investigate. I don't rule anything out."

She shrugged. "I guess I don't really know what Omnivexx is up to, but I don't think they had anything to do with Culp's disappearance."

"So why do you think he disappeared?"

"There you go again, using your masculine wiles to get information out of me."

"I'm sure you have an opinion."

"So now you think I'm opinionated."

"I think you've thought about it a great deal, enough to have an opinion."

"Yeah, well, I guess I think pretty much what everybody else thinks. Culp had been stealing money and he knew my boss was onto him. So he took off."

"And his murder?"

"Who knows? Maybe others were in on it with him and they . . . I don't know, had a falling out or something. Or maybe somebody killed him to get the money he stole."

"Those are both good possibilities."

She stared at him for several seconds, then said, "But you think there's more to it than that, don't you?"

"I don't really know."

"Honestly? Now who doesn't have an opinion?"

"In my job it's best not to come to conclusions too soon."

"I guess so." She refilled her drink and sipped at it, gazing at him over the top of her glass. "So, are going to invite me to stay tonight?"

Her question took Steele off guard. Not because he didn't expect it, but because of the blunt, out-of-the-blue way she'd said it. She was smiling, but only a little as she waited for his answer.

"Let's talk a little more, Rachel."

"Why talk? Either you're up for it or you aren't." She took a sip of her drink and looked away. She wasn't smiling.

"Then I'm not," said Steele.

She looked back at him, frowning. "Uh oh, I came on too strong, didn't I? I have a bad habit of doing that. Not about sex. I'm not very . . . I mean, it's not something I do very often. I mean . . . well, you know what I mean."

"You mean this is not like you."

She laughed and seemed to relax a little. "That's putting it mildly. Truth is, I don't even have a . . . social life. My life is my job, and that's no exaggeration. I've got a nice little apartment over on Charleston, but I hardly need it. I end up working so many nights my cat thinks she belongs to my next door neighbor." She took another sip of her whiskey. "What was I saying?"

"You were saying you sometimes come on too strong."

"Oh, right. What I meant was, I like to get to the point. I can't stand it when people say this and say that, never getting around to the point. So, I felt an attraction to you and I said so. There's no need for you to be embarrassed. It's just me."

"I'm not embarrassed."

"So if I started taking my clothes off, you wouldn't call your friend Rudd for help?"

That made him laugh. She was quite different from anybody he'd met for a while. Refreshingly straight forward. He had to admit he was also tired of the games people played, especially the coy games many women played. Rachel might be a lot of things, but she was certainly not coy. "Well, Rachel, if you're going to start ripping your clothes off, I guess we'd better head for the bedroom before Rudd comes out to get another beer."

In the bedroom, Steele closed the door, and by the time he turned around, she was already out of her clothes. She'd hopped into bed, but she hadn't pulled the sheet up. She had a beautiful body and she was clearly not embarrassed about letting him see it. She propped up a couple of pillows behind her head and watched his every move as he undressed.

He took off his shirt and then sat on the bed and faced away from her as he took off his pants. He slid the prosthetic foot with its attached pistol under the bed. When he turned to face her, she sat forward, startled. "Oh my God, what happened to your foot?"

"An accident."

She stared at his lower leg as if she couldn't believe what she was seeing. "I never would have suspected. You hide it well."

"It's not a secret. I just don't want to focus on it. It happened. I've moved on."

She sat up and ran her finger along the scars around his knee. "And what about these scars? Did you get them at the same time? In Iraq?"

"That's right. An explosion. There's a metal plate in there, and a lot of screws to hold it in place." She continued to gently trace the scars with her finger.

He tried to read what was in her eyes, but he saw no sign of horror, or even pity, only sadness. "Did Monroe tell you I'd been over there?"

She looked up at him. "It was in a report about you. I saw it on his desk. Were you a soldier?"

"No. I was doing a job over there." He watched her as she touched each of the terrible scars, as if counting them. "Not a very romantic subject," he suggested.

"But it is," she said quietly. "It's very . . . personal. I bet not many people know about these scars, and your . . . foot. I have a feeling you don't let people get very close."

"Not usually." He lay down next to her and touched her hair.

She closed her eyes.

He let his hand drift down to her cheek, then to her neck, then to her shoulders.

She took his hand and kissed it. "Let's not hurry, shall we?" she whispered. "I want to feel . . . everything."

# Chapter 13

*S*ometime in the middle of the night, Steele felt her sit up. There was just enough light to see that she was staring at him.

"Are you still awake?" she whispered.

"Yes."

"What are you thinking about?"

"Nothing in particular. Just remembering."

"Iraq?"

"I think about Iraq sometimes, among other things."

She lay back down and snuggled up close to him. "Can you tell me about it? Iraq, I mean?"

"I'd rather not," he said.

She didn't reply so he just held her close, feeling the coolness of her slim, naked body against him. He hadn't realized how long it had been since he'd felt that. Not since . . . since that last night with Loren, the night before he left for Iraq.

Neither of them spoke, but after a while, he detected a bit of moisture on Rachel's cheek. "Have you been missing someone?" he whispered.

She hesitated, then said, "No. I mean, not really."

He waited.

"It's . . . it's been quite a while. He was killed. Over . . . there."

"In Iraq?"

"Yes."

Steele thought about her reading that report on her boss's desk. "Is that why you came to see me tonight? Because you knew I'd been in Iraq?"

"No, it was . . . I mean, it wasn't the only reason I came. I was . . . curious about you."

"And about Iraq."

She pushed slightly away from him. "You don't have to tell me if you don't want to. It doesn't matter anyhow."

After a few more minutes, he said, "What do you want to know?"

"Forget it. It doesn't matter."

"What do you want to know?" he repeated

She moved closer, again clinging to him. "I don't know why I can't just forget it. It's been almost three years."

"What was his name?"

"Jeffery. Jeff. He never liked me calling him Jeffery. He joined the reserves. This was back in Ohio. He didn't think it meant anything about being patriotic or anything like that. It just gave him some extra money for a few hours on weekends and they said they would pay for his college education."

"But his unit got called up."

"Yes. He tried to convince me it would only be for a few months and then things would be back to normal. But they sent him to Iraq and he didn't come back."

"A roadside bomb?"

"That's what his mother said. She didn't want to talk about it. Told me not to call her anymore."

"I'm sorry, Rachel."

"It's okay. Like I said, it was a long time ago. The problem is I never had anybody to talk to about it. My girl friends at college thought the whole war was stupid. They couldn't understand why we went over there in the first place."

She was quiet for several minutes. Then she said, "Was it really as bad over there as they say?"

Steele tried to think how to answer her question. He'd never talked to anybody about it, wasn't allowed to say much about his mission over there even if he wanted to. "War is . . . chaotic," he began. "In the midst of chaos, people can be . . ." He wasn't sure he wanted to go on.

"Please tell me."

"Well, you can imagine some of it. From what you see on the news. But they don't show what it's really like. They show the aftermath of some of the suicide bombings, the carnage in the street, but what they don't show, can't show, is the fear that is part of daily life. The people who had money, or connections, left the country early on. Those who were left lived in constant fear. In such chaos and violence, everyone's focus was on trying to survive."

She sat up and took his hand. "And the soldiers? Are they afraid too? I mean, what do you think it was like for Jeff? Was he afraid?"

"Everybody was afraid, but only if they had to go outside of the Green Zone. The Green Zone was a relatively safe area in the middle of Baghdad, well protected. It's strange, inside the zone, life was boring for the soldiers. I used to watch them kill time by playing cards. They watched mindless American movies on TV until they were sick of them. They were totally bored, at least until it was time for them to get ready for a mission. They always got more and more agitated as the time to go out approached. You could feel it. They got quiet and moody. Outside of the Green Zone, the streets of Baghdad were the most frightening place in the world and those young men knew it. They knew they would be targets the moment they stepped out onto the street."

She didn't say anything for a while and he thought maybe he shouldn't have said anything. Then, she said, "Thank you for telling me that. I've tried so many times to imagine what it was like for him, but there was no way for me to know. He didn't even have time to write to me. He was killed during his first week over there. After it happened, I thought about all the time. It just didn't seem right. Why him? He didn't want to be a soldier and kill people. He didn't care about that country. All he ever wanted to do was go to college."

"There is no right or wrong to it, Rachel. Death is almost random in a place like that."

She thought about that for a while, then she touched his scarred leg again. "Tell me what happened to you."

"There's not much to tell. I was in a convoy, the lead truck. We were in what's called an undercover convoy. Ordinary trucks, as if we were just delivering machinery or something. But somebody knew we were coming. I saw the locals watching us. They knew it was going to happen. I warned the driver, but it was too late. There was an explosion. That's all I remember."

"Another one of those roadside bombs. The same as with Jeff. "

"Yes. "

"Did you think you were going to die?"

"I didn't have time to think about that. After the explosion, I have a few vague images of smoke and fire. Some kids gathering around, poking at me, people yelling. I woke up in an emergency room inside the Green Zone."

"Sounds like you're lucky to be alive."

Steele nodded. "The driver died. He was sitting right next to me. Two men in the other truck were killed in the shootout that followed. Another was dragged away and later executed."

"But they didn't kill you?"

"They must have thought I was already dead. I was pretty . . . messed up."

Rachel stared up at the ceiling. "Thank you for telling me," she whispered. "I've always wondered what it was like for him . . . at that last moment. I guess it was . . . like that."

"Probably."

"Except he didn't make it." She let out a long sigh. "I wish I could just get over it. It's been years, and it wasn't like we were married or anything. I should just move on with my life. Meet new people."

"You haven't been with anybody since?"

"No. I pretty much stayed by myself afterward. As soon as I graduated from college, I was ready to get out of Ohio so I came out here to take a bookkeeping job in the casino's accounting department. I didn't want to get involved with anybody so I just focused on my job."

Steele touched her hair and she took his hand and held it against her cheek.

"But it's hard to be alone, isn't it?" he said quietly.

She shrugged and put her head against his chest. "I don't think about it much. Let's talk about something else."

"The weather?"

She looked up to see if he was joking. When she saw he was, she smiled and pinched him. "I've only been working for Mr. Monroe for a few months, but security is a lot more interesting than bookkeeping. I've been trying really hard to impress him."

"I'm sure your job is very interesting. Gaming security is--"

She put her fingers to his lips. "I didn't mean to get us talking about my job. Just be with me. For tonight, at least, just be with me."

# Chapter 14

*I*t was still dark when Steele was awakened by a noise. He realized Rachel wasn't in bed anymore. He sat up and heard the outer door open and close. He lay back down and stared into the darkness, wondering why she felt the need to leave in the middle of the night. During their love-making, she had been unexpectedly fragile, wanting his assurance that she was desirable, beautiful, smart. She was unsure of herself, but she was direct. He liked that. If she wanted something, she said so. Maybe that was why he'd agreed to let her stay. He was tired of pretense, tired of the games people always seemed compelled to play. After Iraq, pretense seemed absurd. And then the long days and the very long nights in the German hospital after they'd flown him out of Baghdad changed him even more than the attack itself had. The attack made him wary of people, but the repeated surgeries on his legs and the long painful months of rehabilitation also made him impatient. He knew something fundamental inside him had shifted since Iraq. He was less tolerant of people, even though he tried not to be.

As Steele lay there in the dark remembering, he thought about her wanting to know what it was like over there. She was unusual in that, even among those who had lost someone there. Most people didn't even want to think about it; they just wanted it to be over. He realized she was the first person he had talked to about it. In fact, he hadn't really talked to anyone about much of anything since he got back. Mostly, he stayed away from people, except as was required by his job. Like Rachel, he found it more comfortable to bury himself in work. He now enjoyed doing the leg work, running down leads, doing the internet research. He focused on doing his job systematically and thoroughly, always striving for objectivity. It might not make him a very sociable person, but it made him a better detective.

He turned onto his side and realized he could still smell Rachel's vague odor on the pillow, probably some kind of scented soap. He liked the memory of her lying there next to him, but it left him vaguely uncomfortable. Rachel was a nice person, a concerned person, and she had left in the night without making any demands of him. So what was he worried about? Was he afraid it was some kind of first step, that eventually she would come to depend on him, just as Loren had? Loren had left because she knew she would never find the kind of interdependence she wanted with him. She wasn't willing to be second to his job, a job that took him away for weeks, even months at a time. And there was also the danger issue. In the end, Loren said she couldn't let herself care that much about a man who might leave one day and never come back.

Would Rachel be the same? Only time would tell. Maybe she had only wanted to talk to him about Iraq, to be with him as a substitute for her lost Ohio lover. Maybe there would be this one night and that would be the end of it.

As he did most nights, Steele propped himself up against a couple of pillows and used the remote to turn on the TV. Sometimes the TV helped turn off the thoughts and the memories. He flipped through the many channels trying to find something moderately boring. He finally decided on a mildly interesting documentary on the National Geographic channel about Alaskan bears who lived in a city dump. But after watching that documentary for half an hour, he knew he wasn't going to get sleepy. He decided to get up and get some work done.

He showered and dressed and went to his computer to reread Kelly's autopsy report. Strange how boring an autopsy of a human can sound when it's written up in dry, technical language. Almost as if it wasn't about a real person at all, but only a body made up of labeled parts. Kelly hadn't even made a big deal about the bullet found lodged in Culp's brain. It was just a piece of lead that had torn through the brain's tissue resulting in the person's death. The report made it seem no more important than the contents of Culp's bowels or the noticeable enlargement of his left ventricle.

Next, Steele downloaded the reports from the information-search agency. So far, they'd found out little about the Vinelli's that he didn't already know, but the report did say they'd found listings for a number of Vinellis in Chicago. They were checking that out. A second report was about the Omnivexx Corporation. The report said the company had been in business since the seventies and that it was an investment company that owned a chain of restaurants in New Jersey and had once been part owner of an Atlantic City casino. There was nothing else of interest in the report, except that they had found a business-news item about an obscure venture-capital group named Affiliated Capital Partners had recently invested a very large amount of money in Omnivexx. Little was known about Affiliated Capital Partners because it was an off-shore company, headquartered in Bermuda. The report closed with a note saying they would keep digging.

Steele had already closed the report and was reading through his email when Rudd wandered out of his bedroom, still in his undershorts. He yawned and scratched his protruding stomach. "What are you doing up so early? It's barely getting light outside."

"Getting caught up with my email."

"Still can't sleep, eh? More bad dreams about Iraq?"

"Just not sleepy."

Rudd glanced toward Steele's bedroom and lowered his voice: "Is she still in there?"

Steele didn't look up from the computer's screen. "No, she left."

"Interesting gal. Did you . . . I mean, how was--"

"I expect you're hungry. We could go down to the restaurant."

"Right. None of my business anyhow. I didn't hear a thing. Pretty thick walls, I guess."

"Just drop it."

"Right. Dropping it. This is me going to get dressed. Be with you in a minute."

Downstairs in the casino, Rudd expressed his surprise at how many people were there gambling at that time of day. "Look there," he said, pointing, "that craps table is almost full."

"Most of the men need a shave," said Steele. "It means they've been there all night."

They stopped for a moment to watch. The shooter, a huge man

who had to be close to three hundred pounds, threw the dice and shouted, "C'mon, baby. Eight the hard way."

A loud groan went up from the others as he sevened out.

They went on to the restaurant and Steele was grateful to see that it was almost empty. They sat in a booth near the back wall. The tired-looking waitress took their order and it came quickly. Steele picked at his pancakes while Rudd wolfed down an omelet and two orders of sausage *and* pancakes, rambling on about how after breakfast he was going to hit the slots and beat that Elvis machine.

"I'm afraid your slot fortune will have to wait a bit," said Steele. "I've got a job for you."

"Really? What?"

"How would you like to go to a mortuary?"

"A funeral parlor? I don't mind. Actually, I like funerals, long as it's nobody I know. Remember that big funeral we went to for that girl they thought had hung herself? Amazing that guy gave himself away by showing up. I guess after the inquest said it was a suicide he thought he was home free."

"Culp's funeral won't be for a few days yet, but I need you to find out what kind of funeral they're planning, and if possible, who's paying for it."

"I get it. Nose around. Use my reporter skills."

"Exactly. Find out if it's going to be a private family funeral or if the casino is involved. See if anybody there knows anything about Culp. I looked up the address of the only mortuary in the part of town where Culp lived. If the funeral isn't to be there, they might know where it will be. Take my car and check it out." He slid the keys across the table.

Rudd grabbed the keys and stood up. "Will do. I'll call you as soon as I find out anything."

After Rudd left, Steele went up to Monroe's office. The receptionist said he was down on the casino floor somewhere, but she would page him.

After a few minutes, Rachel came out. "Won't you come this way, Mr. Steele?"

She led him back to Monroe's office, acting as formal and unsmiling as she had the day before. But once they were inside Monroe's office, she grabbed his arm and leaned close. "Sorry I left in the middle of the night," she whispered. "I couldn't sleep. I'm not used to . . . you know, sleeping with anybody."

"It's all right. I'm not either."

"Well . . . anyhow, it wasn't because I didn't like it. I mean . . . like you. Like I said, I've been too busy with my job . . . Well, I guess we already talked about that, didn't we?"

"I understand. You had to get home to your cat."

She smiled and patted his chest. "Something like that. Well, anyhow, you should have heard Monroe this morning. He lined up all his security people and read them the riot act about not figuring out what was going on with those videotapes. Demanded to know how some damned LA detective that doesn't know shit about the gambling business could come in here and do their job for them. I've never seen him so pissed."

"Any sign of Gary?"

"Nope. He just flat disappeared. Just like Culp did. Monroe thinks he's still in town though. Hiding out somewhere. He thinks--" She didn't finish her sentence because they heard Monroe outside the door yelling at somebody.

The door flew open and Monroe rushed into the office. "Oh, it's you, Steele. Rachel says you didn't find out much from Vinelli."

Steele glanced at Rachel.

She quickly said, "I told him what you told me last night. When I, uh, saw you in the restaurant."

"That's right," said Steele, "in the restaurant." He turned to Monroe. "Vinelli says he hadn't seen much of his stepfather since--."

"I know, I know, since he and his brother got sacked. Hell, I can see why he'd still be pissed off at us, but it's his own fault. Should have kept his mouth shut when the new management came in. Play along, like his old man did. So, what now?"

"I still want to talk to Culp's co-workers. The count team."

"Oh yeah, them. I've got 'em both doing busy work in the back office 'til we get this thing sorted out. Rachel will take you to 'em. Anything else?"

"I'll be heading back to LA later today. I'll keep you informed about what I find out there."

"Good. The people from corporate are coming in day after tomorrow. I'd like to have something to tell them by then."

"I'll keep you informed."

"Good, good. Okay, Rachel, take him down to interview those two count people. I've got a meeting."

Rachel led Steele out of the office and down the hall. She leaned close to whisper. "All I said was I happened to run into you last night."

"Don't worry about it."

Rachel led him through a large room full of cubicles to a small glassed-in conference room. "You wait here. I'll get them."

Soon, she was back with the two people Steele had seen on the videotapes, the middle-aged, stout woman, and the tall man. Even though they were no longer on the count team, they were still dressed in the pocketless shirts and pants they had been wearing when he'd watched them on the videotapes. They both seemed very nervous.

Rachel introduced them and left the room.

Steele sat across the table from them. He looked them over and that seemed to make them even more nervous. Steele was sure they hadn't been in on Culp's scheme; otherwise, they wouldn't still be there. But their nervousness made him wonder if they knew something. Maybe they had suspected something and kept quiet about it. He decided to take a direct approach. "You know why I'm here?"

The woman shrugged. "About Culp, I guess."

"I suppose a lot of people have been asking you questions."

They both nodded.

"I don't believe you had anything to do with it."

They both seemed relieved, but neither of them spoke.

"But I think you suspected something was going on."

The woman leaned back in her chair and crossed her arms. "We didn't know a thing. If anybody told you we did, they're lying."

"I didn't say you *knew* something was going on, I only said you might have suspected it."

She shook her head. "Nothing was going on. They videotape every count. All you have to do is look at the tapes. You'll see."

"I have looked at the tapes. Culp was stealing hundred-dollar bills right from under your noses."

The woman looked shocked. Then she recovered and shook her head again. "You're crazy. I know people who've looked at those tapes, more than once. They told me there was nothing on them."

Steele took out his small notebook and opened it to the drawing he'd made of the count room. He turned it so they both could see it. He took out his pencil and used it as a pointer. "This is the table where the three of you sat. This square is the cart with the drop boxes on it. I've drawn three circles to represent the three of you. This circle at the end of the table is Culp. This circle is you, ma'am. What happens when your partner here dumps the bills out of a drop box?"

"Nothing. He takes the box back to the cart."

"I know that, but what do you do?"

"I wait for him to come back."

"No, you don't. You turn to look at him and you suggest which box he should bring back next."

"So what?"

"So, neither of you is looking at Culp."

"Are you telling me Culp could have taken money in that brief moment?"

"That's what I'm telling you."

"Ridiculous."

The man leaned forward to look at the drawing. "It's possible," he said.

She looked shocked. "What?"

"All I'm saying is that it's possible." He pointed to Steele's drawing. "Look, I'm over there by the cart, picking out a box to grab. You're looking at me, telling me which box to bring back. Neither of us is paying any attention to what Culp's doing. And the money is already on the table."

She looked panicked. "For Christ's sake, don't say that. They'll can us for sure."

He tapped on Steele's drawing. "It was my fault. I did see an odd thing. I should have said something. You remember that last day he was here? After I dumped out the box, I kind of noticed there were a lot of hundreds in it. Then, when we did the count, there weren't very many. I thought I must have been seeing things."

"You never noticed anything like that before?" asked Steele

"Nope."

The woman pushed the notepad toward Steele in disgust. "So you're trying to tell us Culp really was a thief?"

"The evidence is clear."

"And we were just too dumb to notice."

"I didn't say that."

"Well, he couldn't of grabbed all that much."

"Depends on how long he'd been doing it."

She frowned. "Yeah, well, I've known Culp . . . knew him, I mean, for a long time. He wasn't the type."

"Based on what I've learned, you're right," agreed Steele. "But something drove him to start stealing. Do you have any idea of what that could have been?"

"Haven't a clue," she said, looking away.

"Me neither," said the man.

"Are you sure? It's important."

They both shook their heads.

"Did you notice any change in his behavior."

They looked at each other.

"Tell him," the man said.

She shrugged. "Well, it was kind of hard to tell with him, He never did say much. But he seemed kind of irritable the last few months. Since the buyout, you know. But then a lot of people around here have been kind of jumpy since the new management came in so it's not our fault if we didn't say anything."

Steele thanked them and told them they could go. They both seemed happy to get out of the room.

Steele stayed there, thinking about what they had said about Culp's change in behavior after the buyout. Was that when he started stealing? Or was it after his stepsons got laid off? He would have to ask Monroe when he had first started noticing the light counts.

# Chapter 15

*W*hile Steele waited for Rudd's call, he went back up to the suite to make notes about what he had learned from the two count employees. He was now even more convinced they weren't in on it, but the man had noticed something on Culp's last day. It was important information because it meant Culp knew he was going to have to disappear. He must have grabbed as many hundred-dollar bills as he could on that last day. But why did he think he had to run? Did he think management was on to him? Or was it something else? What happened that day that forced him to sacrifice job and family to go on the run?

He was still entering notes when Rudd called. "You're not going to believe this one, Steele. I'm here at that mortuary and they thought I came for a job. Seems they put the word out they were going to need a bunch of temporary help for a big funeral. Ushers, car parkers, all kinds of jobs. I played along and the guy hired me on the spot. So guess who the big funeral is for."

"Culp."

"Yep, Mrs. Culp called them up this morning and said, 'Spare no expense. We're going to show this hick town what a real funeral should look like.'"

"Did you ask who was paying for it?"

"What, you mean it might not be his wife?"

"I don't know where she would get that kind of money. Is Mrs. Culp there?"

"Not yet. The mortuary guy said she's on her way. She's bringing the body in from LA."

"Stay put. I'll take a cab and be there soon."

"That's it? I find out the most important clue yet and all you say is 'stay put.' At least you could say good going or something."

"Good going. I'll be there as quick as I can. Keep nosing around."

Steele clicked off the phone and packed up his computer and his traveling kit. Then he hurried down to the front entrance and hailed a cab. He gave the driver the address of the mortuary and sat back to think about what Rudd had told him. Why would Culp's wife want to make a big show of his funeral? And how could she afford it? Even if Culp gave her some of the money he'd been stealing, why would she blow it on a big funeral that would only call attention to her finances.

At the mortuary, Rudd hurried out to greet him. "She just arrived. In that car." He pointed to a black Rolls Royce parked near the side entrance. "They followed the hearse in. She was all in black, with a big guy in a dark suit."

"Where is she now?"

"Inside. Talking to the funeral director. Both of 'em."

Steele told Rudd to wait outside while he went in to find her. The chapel was empty, but he heard voices coming from another room down the hall. A man with a loud voice was saying he didn't want any cheap shortcuts. "Out here in the suburbs, I know you're used to old people and stillborn babies, but I want you to make this like a downtown affair. This man was a top casino executive and his funeral should prove it."

"Yes, sir," said a meek voice. "You can count on us."

"I *am* counting on you. Don't you forget it."

Mrs. Culp came out of the room. She was followed by a heavy-set man in a very expensive-looking navy-blue suit. Mrs. Culp spotted Steele and hesitated. The man immediately moved in front of her.

"She doesn't want to talk," said the man.

He seemed threatening, and Steele wondered why. He was sure he didn't know the man.

"I just need to ask Mrs. Culp a few questions."

"I said she doesn't want to talk." The man took Steele's elbow to lead him toward the exit door.

Steele only allowed the man to lead him a few steps away from Mrs. Culp before he stopped. "From the way you're holding my arm you think you can handle me," said Steele calmly, "but you can't."

The man met Steele's eyes. "You think not? You don't seem all that steady on your feet, mister."

Steele twisted his arm out of the man's grip. "My name is Drew Steele. I've been hired by the casino to find out why Mr. Culp was murdered. I need to talk to his wife. She knows me."

There was a sign of recognition in the man's eyes. "Oh, so, you're the big-time LA detective. She told me about you. I thought you were a reporter. Well, what've you found out?"

"And you are?"

"Let's just say I'm a friend of Mrs. Culp."

"I see. Are you paying for his funeral?"

"That's none of your business, Steele. The way I hear it, your job is to find out why he was killed, and that's all."

"Is there a problem, Frank?" Mrs. Culp had come close enough to overhear what they were saying.

"No problem, Rita. I was just getting rid of him."

Steele leaned around the man. "I need to talk to you for a few minutes, Mrs. Culp."

She touched the man's shoulder. "It's all right, Frank, I'll talk to him."

Steele could see the man didn't like that. "You don't have to say anything, Rita. This guy should be back in LA looking for Ken's killer."

"I only have a few questions, Mrs. Culp," said Steele. "I wouldn't bother you at a time like this if I didn't think it was important."

"Just give us a few minutes, Frank. It's no problem." Frank stayed in the hallway while she led Steele into the chapel. They sat in the front pew.

"I'm sorry for your loss," said Steele quietly. "I know this must be hard for you."

She met his eyes. "You said you had a few questions." Her gaze was steady, but nervous. If she'd been crying, there was no indication of it.

"There are some things you didn't tell me the last time we met."

"Things were . . . different then. I didn't think it would turn out like this."

"No, I guess you didn't. I spoke to your son, James. He told me you all used to work at the Golden Palace. I understand that's where you met your husband."

"A long time ago. What did James say?"

"He said he hadn't seen your husband for some time. I got the feeling they weren't close."

She nodded. "James blamed him for . . . for a lot of things."

"He said your husband had a plan to get them all back together again at the Golden Palace."

"Did he say what the plan was?"

"He said he didn't know much about it."

"He didn't, and it probably doesn't matter now." She turned away to stare at the ornate, carved-wood dais on the stage at the front of the chapel. It was where her husband's casket would rest when it was time for the funeral.

"So you don't think it had anything to do with his death?"

She turned back to Steele, her face fixed in a careful non-expression. "How could it?"

"Maybe his plan required money."

She hesitated. "I wouldn't know about that."

"I know there may be things you don't want to talk about," said Steele softly. "It might seem . . . disloyal, but don't you want to find out who killed him? And why?"

"I do. That's the only reason I'm talking to you. But Frank said we should just move on. He says finding out who killed him won't bring him back."

"What about your two sons?"

"What about them?"

"Do you think they might be in danger also?"

Her eyes widened. "Why would they be in danger?"

"James told me your other son, Craig, works in LA. You didn't tell me that."

"Does it matter?"

"It might have helped me understand why your husband came to California."

She shrugged, and turned away. "That's why I didn't tell you. I knew you would be suspicious."

"Of who? Craig?"

She shrugged again.

"But what if he knows something about your husband's plan?

Might that not place him in danger also?"

"I just saw him this morning. In LA. He didn't seem afraid."

Steele waited.

"You think he should be?"

"I don't know enough yet to say, Mrs. Culp. That's why I'm asking you these questions. What was your husband's plan?"

She again stared toward the chapel's stage. "I don't know the details. You'll have to ask Craig."

"I plan to. You can't tell me anything about it?"

"I don't think I can."

"You can't? Or you won't?"

"If that's what you came here to ask me, I'm afraid I have nothing more to say."

"All right, let me ask you this, Mrs. Culp, can you think of anyone who might have wanted to harm your husband?"

"No."

"He had no enemies that you know of?"

"Of course not. We led a quiet life."

"Why do you think he was in LA?"

"I don't know."

"Do you think he went there to see Craig."

"He might have."

"But he didn't tell you?"

"No."

Steele could see this interview was going nowhere. Was she trying to protect her husband's reputation, or was there something else? He decided to try a different tact. "Listen, Mrs. Culp, if my investigation turns up any information about why your husband left the casino, or why he left town, I will tell you first. If I find out anything personal, anything you don't want known, I will honor your wishes and keep it between us. But I do need to know why he was killed, and by who. Is there anything you can tell me about it? Whatever you say will go no further than this room."

She met his eyes and then stared down at her lap. "They say he stole money from the casino." She looked up again. "Is it true?"

"I'm afraid so."

"But that can't be, Mr. Steele. He wouldn't do such a thing. There are a lot of . . . dishonest people in a casino. It attracts people like . . .

like that. But my husband would never stand for it, not even the little pilfering that goes on. For that reason, some of the other employees didn't trust him. They didn't like him because they knew he would turn them in if he thought they were stealing, even if it was small amounts. Now, how can anybody say he would do the same thing? Steal."

For the first time, Steele saw tears well up in her eyes. "I don't know," he said quietly. "From what I've found out so far, I would have to agree that it was completely out of character for him. But the evidence says he did it. Something changed. Can you think of what might have caused that change? You weren't in any debt? Could there have been some kind of threat? To you, or to your sons?"

"No, it wasn't anything like that."

Steele waited but she didn't go on. She knew something. Or suspected something. If it wasn't financial problems, or any kind of threat, what could it be? "You said he might have gone to LA to see your son. Did he do that often?"

She seemed about to say something, but changed her mind and just shook her head.

"Had he ever gone to see him?"

She shrugged. "I don't think so. Craig comes here once in a while, but not very often. Christmas, usually. A family picnic last summer."

Steele studied her sad expression. "Problems? They didn't get along?"

She shrugged again. "Just the usual. You know how families are."

"I know families do sometimes have problems, but could it have anything to do with what happened to your husband? Why would he suddenly decide to go to LA to see your son?"

It seemed like she was about to answer, but then she sighed and looked toward the chapel door. Steele turned to look back. Frank was still there, arms folded, leaning up against the doorjamb, watching them.

"I don't think any of this is going to help your investigation, Mr. Steele. Frank thinks maybe Ken was just in the wrong place at the wrong time. He says Los Angeles is a dangerous city."

She glanced at Frank again and in response he did a little jerk of his head to indicate she should come. When she didn't immediately get up to leave, he frowned and tapped his watch.

She nodded and turned back to Steele. "I guess I'd better be going."

"You often refer to what Frank thinks, Mrs. Culp. He seems very close to the . . . situation."

"He's been very helpful since . . . since Ken disappeared."

Steele again glanced toward the chapel door. Frank was still hovering there, looking impatient.

Steele leaned close to her. "Has someone threatened you? Is there anything I can do to help?"

"No, it's only that . . ."

Frank was suddenly standing there next to them. "Let's go, Rita. We've got to finish making the arrangements."

She stood up, but Steele caught her hand. "Mrs. Culp. It's my job to find out what happened to your husband. Anything you can tell me might help."

Frank took a step closer. "Let go of her hand, Steele."

"It's all right, Frank." She pulled away. "I'm coming."

Steele called after them. "You know my phone number, Mrs. Culp. If you think of anything you want to tell me, anything at all, call me. Day or night."

She didn't look back.

After they were gone, Steele stayed in the chapel to try to sort it all out. What was she hiding? She didn't seem to be afraid, but she was being cautious, choosing her words. It was obviously hard for her to accept that her husband had stolen money from the casino, but Steele was sure she had a suspicion about why he might have done it. How much did she know about her husband's life? Sometimes wives knew very little about what their husbands did at work. If Culp hadn't told his wife about stealing the money, were there also other secrets he was keeping from her? The one thing she definitely didn't want to talk about was his plan to bring the two sons back into the casino. Why was that such a secret? She said she thought Craig might know more about that plan. James had also said Craig might know about it. Did that indicate Craig was in on it, whatever it was?

Steele turned to look at the door where Frank had been waiting. Frank never seemed to stray far from Mrs. Culp's side. Who was this Frank, this so-called friend of the family? From the way he dressed, and that Rolls-Royce parked out front, he must be a very rich family friend. How would she know somebody like that? Steele suspected Frank might be the one paying for the funeral. But why would a family friend pay for a funeral? And why such an extravagant one?

Steele looked at the empty dais on the stage, thinking about Culp could have been up to. James had said he thought his stepfather had gone to talk to the bankruptcy judge. Why would he do that? Was he thinking about trying to make a bid for the casino? Was that why he needed money? But stealing one-hundred dollar bills from the count wouldn't even come close to providing the kind of money he would need for that, even if the casino was in bankruptcy. So why was he stealing? Was he raising money for some kind of investment? Maybe it was a very risky investment, a way to raise money quickly. Were his killers involved? Maybe the investment was so risky it led to his death.

# Chapter 16

*R*udd came to the door. "Oh, there you are. Why are you sitting in here by yourself?"

Steele got up. "Just thinking."

"Did you talk to her?"

"I'll tell you about it when we're in the car." Steele led the way to the parking lot and on the way back to the casino he quickly summarized what he'd learned from Mrs. Culp.

Rudd thought about it for a minute and then said, "So you think that guy with the Rolls is paying for Culp's big funeral. Who is he?"

"She wouldn't say. Only that he was a friend of the family."

"Maybe I should take that job as an usher at the funeral. I bet I could find out who he is."

"Maybe you could, but I think it's more important to find out what led Culp to LA. I think the answer lies with Craig, her other son. We're going back to LA to talk to him."

"Back to LA? But I haven't had a chance to win my fortune at that slot machine."

"We've learned as much as we can in Las Vegas. From here, the trail leads to LA, and maybe Crueltown."

"Well, heck. I just hope nobody hits that big jackpot 'til I can get back here to claim it."

On the way out of town, Steele called Monroe's office. He wasn't in his office, but after Steele told the girl who was calling, she told him to wait while she paged him.

After less than a minute, Monroe came on the line. "Steele? Where are you?"

"We're on our way back to LA. I'm going to talk to Craig Vinelli. He works at a poker club in Gardena."

"Okay, did you talk to my two count people?"

"Yes. I don't think they knew what Culp was up to. They may have suspected something, but they were not in on it."

"You're sure?"

"I'm sure. They're not even convinced Culp really was stealing."

"Yeah, well, we know he was. They should have been more on their toes. Their job is not only to do the count, but to keep their eyes open. I should can them just to make that point to everybody else."

"Maybe you should let them keep their office jobs at least. To show you know they weren't in on it."

"I'll think about it."

"And it would demonstrate compassion."

"There's no compassion in the casino business, Steele. Our job is to ply people with drinks and entertainment in order to take their money away from them."

"Well, it's up to you, Mr. Monroe. My job is to find out who killed Culp, and why."

"Do you think you're getting any closer?"

"I have some leads. Could you email me some indication of when you noticed the shortages in the morning count?

"Sure, I'll do it right away. But you should know my superiors have been asking me about you. I'll tell you right out, they're a little edgy about your investigation."

"Why is that?"

"Not sure. All I know is they called me into today's big-shot meeting to ask about you. I got the feeling haircut was against retaining you, but suit said--"

"Are you referring to the two overseers from Omnivexx?"

"Yeah, didn't I say that? Anyhow, this whole thing about Culp has got 'em really nervous. If I was you, I'd wrap up your investigation as quick as you can. I'd hate to see them make us drop it before you find out what the hell is going on. I can still see those two words burned onto Culp's forehead. Nothing yet about that?"

"Not yet, but I may learn more when I get back to LA."

"Okay, I'll try to hold them off. Hurry it up, if that's possible."

"I'll do what I can."

After Monroe hung up, Rudd asked, "Was that Monroe?"

"Yes, he says his superiors are getting impatient."

"I bet they always do that," said Rudd with a grin, "as soon as they get their first look at your bill."

"I haven't submitted a bill yet. I think it's something else."

"What?"

"They may not have thought I would come to Las Vegas. In fact, I've been wondering why they hired me instead of a Vegas detective."

"Maybe they wanted the best."

"Maybe they didn't."

Rudd looked surprised. "What do you mean by that?"

"Never mind. Just thinking out loud."

As they drove out of town, Rudd continued to grumble about how close he'd come to hitting that Elvis slot machine. He was sure it was just about ready to hit.

As soon as they were out on the open road, Steele opened the small laptop computer that was attached to the console between the seats. He quickly checked his email and found one from Loren. It was a one-liner, typical of her. It was cheerful, even friendly, but it said this was not a good time for him to visit Paris. She had some important exams coming up. As usual, it ended with, "More later."

"Anything?" asked Rudd.

Steele scanned down the list. There was nothing from the information-search agency. "Nothing yet."

He took out his cell phone and called the casino to ask for Rachel Hill. When she answered, he told her they were on their way back to LA.

"So, this is goodbye? The morning-after brush off?"

"Very funny. I just talked to your boss. He says his superiors are getting impatient."

"Is that right? He didn't mention it to me."

"What has he mentioned?"

"About you? Not much. But he did say an odd thing this morning. He asked me what I thought about you."

"Why was that odd?"

"Only that he doesn't usually ask me things like that."

"What did you say?"

"I told him I was already missing you."

"What did you really say?"

"I told him I thought you were very competent."

"You said that with a straight face?"

"I'm pretty good at straight faces. Or maybe a famous detective like you would have already figured that out."

"Uh huh."

There was a silence on the line, then she said, "You didn't respond to my saying I missed you."

"Didn't I?"

"Uh oh, maybe I'm not supposed to say things like that."

"I don't mind."

"Well, it's true. You might have already ruined me. I'm starting to think there might be something to life besides this damn casino."

"There is. Do you ever get down to LA?'

"I could."

"If you do, call me before you leave. I'll meet you."

"You could have said you'd leave a key under the mat."

"Not in LA."

"I get it. So this really is goodbye. Well, if I ever get down your way, I'll give you a jingle. If I remember."

"Don't be sarcastic. Just call."

"Sorry. Okay, I'll drop the self-pitying routine and pull myself back together. Maybe I *have* been working too hard. Speaking of working too hard, what did you find out when you interviewed those two count people?"

"They didn't know what Culp was up to."

"You sure? My boss is ready to fire them, just to be on the safe side."

"I think they'll be even better at doing their jobs now."

"I'll tell him that, but he may have already made up his mind. Or somebody from Omnivexx may have made it up for him. Oops, here he comes now. Bye."

As soon as Steele clicked off the phone, Rudd said, "Sounds like she's ready to get serious. What're you going to do about that?"

"I've got other things to think about right now. A murder case, remember?"

"Don't want to build up her expectations, eh?"

"Shouldn't you be playing with the GPS or something?"

Rudd shrugged. "It's fine with me if you don't want to see her again. I understand. I don't like women who come on too strong either. Now take Jenny Dainty. There's a nice girl. You should get to know her better." He waited for a response, but when he didn't get one, he added, "Me, I like 'em sweet and cooperative. I bet a girl like Jenny would wake up and make you breakfast and not even--"

"When we get back to LA, I have another job for you."

"You do? What?"

"Do you know how to play poker?"

"Poker? Sure. When I was in the Army--"

Before he could finish, Steele's cell phone buzzed.

"I bet it's that Rachel again. I'm telling you, she's after you."

Steele looked at the number on the phone's screen. "No, it's Kelly." He pushed the talk button. "Hello Kelly, How was the Laker game?"

"Great. But I wasn't right behind Nicholson."

"So you're calling to complain?"

"Naw, it was a great seat. Second row. Just a little ways down the row from Jack. I waved to him at halftime and he almost waved back. But wait 'til you hear why I really called. We got another one."

"Another one?"

"Another forehead thing."

"Another body? With a message on the forehead?"

"That's right, and it's the same two words: 'Keep out.' This one was also found out by Crueltown. Dumped in the ditch. A kid this time."

"Is he skinny? A Led Zeppelin T-shirt?"

"How'd you know that?"

"I met him yesterday. He worked at the same casino as the first guy. We're on our way back from Vegas now."

"Uh oh, you'd better not tell Captain Pruett you know this guy too. He's already after you."

"After me?"

"Yeah. He wants to know how you happened to be out at Crueltown when they found the first body. He's a bit pissed off. Says you're interfering in his case."

"I'm not doing anything to interfere with his investigation."

"That's the trouble. He didn't do an investigation. He wrote off the first murder as a dug deal gone bad so when I called him about this second murder it made him look back. I kind of did a 'told you so.' Told him I didn't think you were convinced it was about drugs."

"You had to go and mention my name, didn't you?"

"Yeah. Maybe I shouldn't have. He seemed a little, uh, like I said, pissed off."

"I'll talk to him as soon as I get a chance. Have you done the autopsy on the kid yet?"

"Not yet. They just brought him in. I thought you'd want to know about it right away."

"Thanks. We'll be there later this afternoon."

"Okay, I'll put him first in line so I'll be done by the time you get here. The other stiffs won't mind. Hey, I'll give you odds that I'll find another one of those drug condoms in his stomach."

"I doubt it. They know the police aren't going to fall for the drug ruse twice."

Steele clicked off the cell phone and Rudd said, "They found another one? Words on his forehead?"

Steele nodded. "Same two words. Remember Gary? That young casino surveillance employee I mentioned? I think it's him."

"No kidding? So he ran off to LA and got himself killed too? What does it mean?"

"That's what we've got to find out."

"Okay, but it's an important clue, isn't it? It means Culp's murder did have something to do with the casino."

"Possibly."

"Well, it makes sense doesn't it? Culp steals from the casino and ends up dead. Then they find out the kid was in on it and he ends up dead too. Same two words on both their foreheads. It's obviously a warning to other employees not to steal."

"Casinos don't do business that way anymore. That went out with Bugsy Siegel."

"Sure they do," protested Rudd. "I saw it in . . . in the movies."

"Movies?"

"Well, maybe movies don't count, but why couldn't it be the casino? Otherwise, why do two employees from the same casino end up dead in the same way?"

"Casinos are now owned by corporations, big corporations that are often on the New York Stock Exchange. Murder, or any kind of scandal, is the last thing a corporation wants. The money Culp took would be insignificant to them. They hired me, at exceptionally high rates, to find out what happened to Cup before anybody else did. They want full information about it so they can have full deniability about it."

"You're sure."

"Actually, I'm not sure. I'm giving you my hypothesis. We have to--"

"Uh oh, I've heard this lecture before. We have to keep an open mind. Gather information. Wait for the data to tell us the truth."

"That's right."

"Okay, so why did you ask if I knew how to play poker? Are we going to gather data about poker?"

"Remember I told you Culp had two sons? The younger son, Craig, works in a poker club in Gardena."

"So that's where we're going?"

Steele nodded and reset the cruise control for eighty-five. The Ford's powerful motor responded.

"Eighty-five?" said Rudd. "Don't they patrol this road a lot?"

"That's what the radar detector is for."

They made it through Victorville and down the long hill into LA without seeing a single police car. As Steele transitioned off the 15 and onto the 10, Rudd spotted a MacDonald's and demanded they stop for hamburgers.

"They've got food at the poker club. I want to get to Craig Vinelli before anybody else does."

"You afraid Pruett will get there first?"

"I doubt if Captain Pruett is far enough along in his investigation to have learned about the Vinelli brothers."

"And you're not going to tell him."

"He told Kelly I was interfering in his case. So I won't interfere. By the way, Kelly said you were right about Pruett writing off the first murder as drug-related."

"Ah ha, I knew it. That condom in his stomach did the trick. The cops fell for it. So, who do you think might beat us to this Vinelli guy?"

"Whoever beat us to Gary."

"Uh oh, you think we'll find Vinelli dead with a brand on his forehead?"

"Let's hope not."

The traffic on the 10 freeway was exceptionally slow for midday, so Steele transitioned down to the 60. It was also slow, so he got into the middle lane and tried not to get impatient as they inched along. Rudd fiddled with the police scanner, trying to find out if there was a major wreck ahead. There was nothing but the usual chatter.

The slow pace of the congested freeway gave Steele time think about Rudd's hypothesis that the casino had been behind Culp's murder. Despite his comment about Bugsy Siegel, Steele had to admit the casino's connection to both murders bothered him. Although it was not likely that anyone at a modern casino would kill an employee just for stealing a few thousand dollars, there could be something else going on besides the theft. When things didn't add up, it was important to make sure you weren't adding up the wrong numbers. In this case, the unknown seemed to be the Omnivexx Corporation. They were the new owners of the Golden Palace, but no one seemed to know much about them. They had shown special interest in Culp even before he'd been found murdered. Why?

Steele was also bothered by the fact that his information-search agency could find so little about Omnivexx. That wasn't normal in the modern-day Nevada gambling business. The state, still trying to live down the old mobster-control days, now insisted on full-disclosure and accountability. Every prospective top-level gaming employee had to go through a rigorous screening by the state gaming-control board before they could be hired. But maybe the rules were different for a bankruptcy buyout. Monroe had said Omnivexx had left the Golden Palace's management team intact, but the two overseers that came in for weekly meetings seemed to exert a lot of control. What was their official position? Maybe because they were not directly involved in the day-to-day operation of the games, they didn't have to undergo the state's investigation.

When Steele came to the 110 freeway, he turned south and took the first Gardena exit. At the Four Aces poker club, he followed the signs to self parking. The lot was huge, with hundreds of cars already there even though it wasn't even completely dark yet. Steele drove between the rows of cars under the watchful eye of the armed guards in the parking lot towers.

"Hey, look at that," said Rudd, pointing. "Guard towers. What the hell?"

"Every LA poker club has them now. By tradition, poker players deal in cash. Sometimes they carry a lot of cash. When they started to have parking-lot armed robberies, local gang kids mostly, the clubs were forced to hire parking lot guards."

"Creepy," said Rudd. "Feels like we're driving into a . . . a prison or something."

"You get used to it." Steele continued to drive through the rows of cars.

"What are you looking for?" asked Rudd, "the perfect parking place?"

"I'm looking for Culp's car. It's an older model Honda. A silver hatchback."

"You think he might have come here?"

"I asked his wife if he might have come to LA to see his son. She wasn't sure but she . . ." Steele slowed to look at the license plate of a beat-up silver Honda Accord. "That's his car." He drove on.

"So he did come here," said Rudd. "But why is his car still in the parking lot? Does it mean they grabbed him here when he tried to drive away?"

"Not likely. It's parked very close to one of the guard towers. Apparently he left with somebody else."

"Who? His killers?"

"Possibly." Steele found a parking place, but when Rudd started to get out, he stopped him. "Wait a minute." Steele leaned forward and felt for the release latch under the dash. When the secret drawer fell open, he felt for the ring of keys and pulled them out.

"Car keys?" said Rudd. "What're you going to do?"

"These are master keys for Hondas and Toyotas. I'm going to go check out Culp's car."

Rudd leaned closer to look. "Wow, look at all those keys. Where'd you get 'em?"

"You remember that car-smuggling operation I investigated? The one that stole newer cars and took them down to Tijuana to wipe out the ID number and repaint them so they could be sold in Mexico City?"

"Oh, yeah, you pretended to steal a few cars yourself to penetrate the ring, and then you got the head honcho from Mexico City to meet you at that warehouse in Carson. Whatever happened to him?"

"He got away."

"And those are his keys?"

"That's right."

Rudd nodded thoughtfully. "So, he just happened to get away, and you just happened to end up with all of his master keys?"

"I thought they'd be useful. I testified against the rest of the gang I'd gotten to know, and without them he was out of business anyhow. He never stole any of the cars himself so I didn't think a jury would have been able to convict him."

"So you let him go?"

"I gave him a little rope. Based on my anonymous tip to the police, he got picked up a week later in San Diego driving a brand new Cadillac."

"Stolen?"

"Of course. You wait here while I go check out Culp's car. When I wave to you, lock my car and go to the club. I'll meet you at the front door and tell you what I want you to do."

"Got it," said Rudd.

Steele put the keys in his jacket pocket and headed for the poker club's front entrance. The nearest guard leaned against the railing of his tower and watched him go. Steele went inside the club and waited for a few minutes inside the glass doors, watching numerous cars come and go. Then he took off his jacket and folded it over his arm. He went back outside and headed for Culp's car. It took only a few seconds to find the right key to open the driver's door. He got in and looked over the inside. Culp was a neat person: no trash on the floor, nothing that might indicate where he'd been the day he disappeared.

He noted the car's mileage: eighty-six thousand miles. Not many miles for a car that old. Culp hadn't been much of a traveler.

Steele felt under the front seats. Nothing there. He opened the glove compartment and took everything out: registration and insurance papers, an out-of-date coupon for one-dollar off Kellogg's Corn Flakes, a blue comb, two ball-point pens, some loose change, a Safeway Rewards card, and a blank Golden Palace notepad. Steele clicked on his little penlight and looked carefully at the surface of the notepad paper. There were impressions, but no recognizable letters or numbers. He stuffed the things back into the glove compartment and closed it. He looked under both visors. Nothing.

On the back seat, he found a plastic K-Mart bag. Inside was an unopened package of underwear, and a torn-open package of black socks. It looked like one pair of socks was missing from the package. There was also an empty shirt package. The K-Mart receipt in the bottom of the bag was dated February 6, 11:31 PM. It was from a store in an outlying eastern suburb of LA. Culp must have pulled off at the first major freeway exit he saw when he hit the LA area and went shopping for a change of clothes. February seventh was the day he'd been reported missing. It meant he'd left Las Vegas in a hurry, right after he got off work on the sixth. The new clothes indicated he didn't want to go to his house before leaving town.

The car held no more clues so Steele got out and locked the door. He headed back to the club's front entrance, nodding to Rudd as he passed his car.

He waited for Rudd in the club's very comfortable front lobby. Its expensive-looking, but worn, fake-leather chairs made it look more like a hotel lobby than a poker club.

Now that it was starting to get dark outside, more and more poker players were arriving. Steele sat down to watch them while he waited for Rudd. The players were mostly of a type, serious-looking males of all ages, and a few hard-looking middle-aged women. They were all moving fast, all focused on getting to the poker tables as quickly as they could. They were very unlike the happy-go-lucky gamblers that lined up in front of the slot machines in Las Vegas; these were people who took their gambling seriously.

Rudd arrived and sat down in the chair next to him. "Well, did you find anything?" he asked.

Steele shook his head. "Not much. Culp came to LA on the night of the sixth. There's no way to know how long his car has been in the parking lot, but if he was coming to LA specifically to see his stepson, his car may have been here since that night. This club is a twenty-four hour operation so a car could be in that lot for a long time before anybody would notice it hadn't been moved."

Rudd glanced toward the poker room. "Did you say they had free food in there?"

"That's right. For the players. Here's what I want you to do. Go to the signup desk and sign up for a low limit Hold'em game. You got money?"

"A little."

"Buy in for a hundred. Keep track of your losses. I'll pay you back."

"Hey, what makes you think I'll lose?"

"Only play good starting hands and maybe you won't. Don't chase straights and flushes."

"Got it. What're you going to do?"

"Talk to Vinelli."

"So why am I playing poker?"

"While you play, you're going to ask if anybody's heard about the murder of a guy who used to play here. A big guy who got killed and dumped out at Crueltown. Describe Culp. See if anybody remembers him."

"You think there's a connection with this club?"

"That's what you're going to find out. If nobody has heard anything, wait a few hands and leave. Say you're going to get something to eat. Then go sign up for another table."

"I do need to eat. I'm starving. Where's the food?"

"It'll be on a cart near the tables."

"No kidding. And it's free? Is it any good?"

"It's terrible. Greasy crap like soggy pizza or cold fish sticks."

"Just my type of food," said Rudd, grinning.

"Sometimes they have sandwiches. They might not be quite as bad. Move from table to table. Play the good listener. Don't tell them you're a reporter."

"Hey, you don't have to tell me. Getting info is what I'm good at."

To give Rudd time to get to a table, Steele bought an LA Times and read a small article in the crime section about another body that had been found out near the harbor. It said that like the first body, there were strange markings on the forehead, but the police were not releasing any more information because it was an ongoing investigation. The article quoted "informed sources" as saying it was probably yet another drug-related murder.

Steele threw away the paper and went into the poker room. The huge room was busy with hundreds of tables in action. Steele spotted Rudd at a nearly-full Hold'em table. He seemed to be having a good time, chatting away as he played. The other players seemed cheerful also, probably happy to have a new fish from which to extract a little money.

Steele went to the sign-in desk and asked for Craig Vinelli.

The woman at the desk stood up to look for him. "There he is." She pointed at a short, heavy-set man who was sitting at one of the empty poker tables, going over some papers. He looked like a heavier version of his brother, but unlike James, there was something decidedly unfriendly about him.

As Steele approached, Vinelli didn't look up, but Steele was sure the man had spotted him.

Steele sat down in one of the empty chairs at the table. "Craig Vinelli?"

Vinelli finished making a few notes on the papers, then, without looking up, he said, "You Steele?"

"That's right. Did your mother tell you I was coming?"

"She said you might. Tall handsome guy with a limp, she said. That about sizes you up. What can I do for you?"

For the first time, Vinelli looked up and Steele was struck by the angry look in the man's eyes. "I expect your brother told you I've been hired by the Golden Palace casino to investigate the death of your father."

"He wasn't my real father."

"I know that. Had you seen him recently?"

"Recently? You mean here in LA?"

"His body was found down by the harbor. Not far from here."

"What are you implying?"

"I'm not implying anything, Mr. Vinelli. I'm simply trying to find out why he came to LA. And why he was killed."

"I don't know anything about it. If you want to know the truth, I hardly knew the man. We mostly grew up without him. All he cared about was that casino. He was supposed to be married to my mother, but he was actually married to his job."

"Didn't he get you and your brother jobs at the casino?"

"Sure, he got us jobs, but he wasn't doing it to help us. It was all part of his big plan."

"Big plan?"

Vinelli stared at him. "Is that how you detectives do it? Play dumb to keep a guy talkin'?"

Steele waited for Vinelli to continue. When he didn't, Steele decided it was time to show him how much he already knew. "Your mother told me about his plan to bring you all back together at the casino."

"Shit. I should have known she'd talk. She never could keep her mouth shut. But it doesn't matter. You'll never figure out who killed him. That type is invisible."

"What type is that?"

"The type who . . . Come on, Steele, I saw his body. You probably did too. That neat little hole in his head. Professionals. You don't have a chance against them. I can't imagine why the casino would even bother to hire you. Besides, it's too late now."

"Monroe hired me to find your stepfather, and after his body was found, he told me to continue my investigation."

"Monroe, eh? He's another one like my old man was. All he cares about is that casino."

"But he really does want to find out who killed your stepfather."

"Yeah? Ask yourself why."

"Meaning?"

"You figure it out. You're the big-shot investigator." He went back to writing on the paper.

Steele wondered if it was worth continuing. Clearly, the man was not much interested in talking about what happened to his stepfather. But the fact that Culp's car was in the club's parking lot had to mean he had been there and Craig must have talked to him. Did Craig know the killers? Could he be part of it? Steele decided to push harder. "Listen, Vinelli, I know your stepfather came here."

Vinelli looked up. "Who says."

"Did he come to you for money? Or was it something else?"

Vinelli stared at him. "Who've you been talking to?"

"I talk to a lot of people. Why did he come here?"

Vinelli stood up. "I think it's time for you to leave."

Steele stayed seated. "Sit down, Mr. Vinelli. Don't you get it? I'm trying to help you. You could be danger too."

"I can take care of myself."

"I'm sure you can, but I was hired to find out what happened to your stepfather and that's what I intend to do. If you were involved in something with your stepfather, that's between you and the casino. Or you and the police. My job is to track down Culp's killers, and believe me I will do it, with your help or without it."

But Vinelli did not sit down and he wouldn't look at Steele. "I have nothing to say to you. I told you to leave. If you don't, I'll have you thrown out."

"I would advise against that," said Steele, sitting back in his chair. "If I walk out of here without finding out what I need to know, I'll have to call the police and have them come here to get Culp's car."

Vinelli hesitated, then sat back down. "What the hell are you talking about?"

"So you didn't know his car is still in your parking lot."

Vinelli looked toward the front door. "You're crazy."

"It's good that you didn't know it was out there. Of course when the police come to question you, I don't know how you're going to convince them of that."

Vinelli leaned closer to whisper. "You're saying his car is in the parking lot?"

"It is. He came here to see you, didn't he?"

Vinelli leaned back in his chair. He seemed to have composed himself somewhat, but he nervously scratched under his chin as he stared at Steele. "Just because his car is in the parking lot . . . you can't prove I ever saw him."

"He came here late on the night of the sixth. I'm sure the police can find someone who saw him here with you."

Vinelli shrugged and looked away. "So what? What's wrong with a man visiting his stepson?"

"The night of the sixth, he got off work, left the casino, and drove straight here. He didn't even go home to get a change of clothes. Why would he do that, Mr. Vinelli?"

"Maybe he was tired of all the shit they gave him at that casino."

"You're still not being straight with me. Do I need to say it? Your stepfather left Las Vegas and came straight here. He was never seen alive again. The police will eventually make the connection and come here to find you."

Vinelli thought about that for a long minute. Then he seemed to make a decision. He stood up. "I have nothing more to say. Get out of here or I'll have you thrown out."

"I'm warning you, Vinelli, talk to me or talk to the police. And don't even think about having that car moved. The police will call that evidence tampering."

Vinelli stared at him for several seconds, as if undecided about what to do. Then he turned and walked away without looking back. Steele watched him walk to the nearest security guard. He pointed back toward Steele. Steele was not surprised when the guard came to say he would have to leave. The guard was an older man and he was very polite about it, so Steele left quietly, nodding toward the door as he passed Rudd's table.

Steele waited for Rudd in the car, thinking about Vinelli's attitude. The man was nervous and antagonistic, unwilling to reveal anything. The only new information he provided was that he resented his stepfather's spending more time at his job than he did with his family. But his brother claimed Craig and his stepfather had been close before Craig moved to LA. Had there been some kind of falling out? Was that why Craig left Las Vegas and moved to LA? Maybe the falling out came after Craig was fired from the casino and Culp didn't do anything about it. James seemed to resent that; maybe Craig was even more upset about it. But if that was true, why would Culp think he could turn to Craig for help? He'd driven straight from Las Vegas to the Four Aces poker club. He must have come to Craig for help. But maybe Craig refused and threw him out. That would explain why Craig didn't know the car was still in the parking lot.

Steele took out his smartphone and made a few notes. Staring at what he had written, he realized there was another possibility. Craig could have introduced his stepfather to somebody. Culp might have left his car in the parking lot and went away with that person. That thought stopped Steele. Could Culp have met his killer at the club?

# Chapter 17

**W**hile he waited for Rudd, Steele tried to decide if he should call Pruett to tell him where Culp's car was. Maybe he could convince Pruett to leave the car where it was and have it watched. But the more he thought about it, the more certain he was that Pruett would go by the book: he'd have the car towed and bring Craig in for questioning. Steele decided against making that call. Better to leave the car where it was and then wait and see what Craig would do. The only danger to that plan was that Craig might take off. But he probably wouldn't do that; a man was not likely to walk away from such a good job, at least not without a good reason. He wasn't a suspect yet. That led Steele to another thought: if Vinelli *did* disappear, it might mean it was not the police he was afraid of, but the killers. Did he know, or suspect, who had murdered his stepfather? If so, he was in great danger. They wouldn't want him alive as a potential witness. Craig's next step would tell the tale. If he ran, it meant he not only knew who had killed his stepfather, but also that they knew him. Steele made a mental note to call the poker club often to find out if Craig was still there.

Rudd seemed to be taking his time at the poker tables. He was probably starting to enjoy the games, or the socialization, and would continue to play until he ran out of money. To fill the time, Steele took out his smartphone and Googled the words "Vinelli" and "genealogy." The first listings that came up were for a few Vinellis that had settled in New York during the late eighteen hundreds. Another large group appeared shortly after the first world war. A few of the family history research sites said the Vinellis had come from Sicily. That made Steele wonder if they had connections with the early gangs of New York City, many of which had also come from Sicily. Searching more recent genealogy links, Steele saw that most of the more recent Vinelli births and deaths were in and around New Jersey and Chicago. He was still reading about the Vinelli family tree when he saw Rudd heading for the car.

Rudd got in frowning. "You owe me a hundred and twenty bucks."

"I told you not to chase straights and flushes. What did you find out?"

"Well, at the first table nobody seemed to know anything about it. At least they said they didn't. But when I moved to another table, one guy said he'd seen a story about it in the paper."

"Your story?"

"Yeah. When I filed my story that first day, all I knew was they'd found a body with some words burned into the forehead. The guy had read it and everybody at the poker table started to talk about what the words might have been. So you see, people really do read my rag."

"I hope you didn't tell them you'd written the story."

"Naw, all I said was I thought it was a pretty good story. They thought so too."

"So, had anybody seen Culp in the club?"

"Nope."

"Did anybody react when you talked about the murder? Had they heard anything about it, outside of your story?"

"Naw. These poker guys don't seem to know much about anything, except for poker and sports. And horse racing. There was a big TV up on the wall and we had to stop one hand while everybody turned around to watch the end of a horse race. I got their attention back by saying the body was found out by the harbor, by Crueltown. One guy said if the body was found out at Crueltown, then the killing must have been over drugs. I said I thought I'd seen a guy who fit the description playing cards here, an old guy with gray hair, a big guy. They said dozens of guys who played poker in Gardena fit that description, but nobody acted like they knew Culp so I guess this was a waste of time."

"It wasn't a waste of time. It tells us he wasn't a regular at this club. If any regular player fitting Culp's description had been murdered, they would all know about it. At first I thought Culp might have been using the poker games to launder the hundred dollar bills he was stealing from the casino, but it doesn't look like it. Even if he'd only been in there a few times, they'd remember a not-so-good player always cashing in hundreds."

"Those guys in there are real smart gamblers," said Rudd. "They always seemed to know what I had. I don't think Culp was that type."

"I agree. In fact, this might have been the first time he'd been to this club."

"So he came here to see his son. What did you find out from him?"

"Not much. He wouldn't even admit that his stepfather had been there, and when I told him Culp's car was still in the parking lot, he seemed surprised and then he had me thrown out."

"No kidding? What does that mean? Did he have something to do with the murder?"

"It means he thought his stepfather had left."

"With his killer?"

"It's possible."

"So, did his own stepson introduce him to his murderer?"

"It's possible."

"Was it a setup? Did he have his own father killed? Like Abraham, except in reverse. Sort of."

"It's possible."

Rudd frowned. You keep saying, 'it's possible.' What do you really think?"

"It's too early to tell."

"But you must have a hunch."

"I don't have hunches."

"Okay, call it a hypothesis then. What do you think happened?"

"Craig might have introduced his stepfather to someone and Culp could have left with that person. But if it was a setup, as you call it, wouldn't he know the killers took Culp away? He would know he had to get rid of his stepfather's car."

"So he didn't introduce his own stepfather to the murderer?"

"More likely Craig introduced him to someone and that someone eventually led him to whoever murdered him. Culp probably came here looking for money. Vinelli might have introduced him to someone with money. Craig may not know how his stepfather ended up dead, but he's clearly worried. He may be trying to find out what happened on his own."

"Not such a smart idea," said Rudd. "He could end up dead too."

"He may not think he has any other choice. He may think the police would try to implicate him, arrest him as an accessory."

"I get it," said Rudd, nodding. "Culp comes here looking for money and his son introduces him to somebody and that somebody kills him. But why? Wasn't he just a harmless old man?"

"Culp could have had the money he stole from the casino with him."

"Ah, so it was about money. They killed him for his money. But how much could he have had? Wouldn't they just take it away from him? Why kill him?"

"Remember he ended up dead out at Crueltown. There are people in Crueltown who would knife you for twenty bucks, let alone a couple of thousand."

"So that's it. You've got it figured out. He met somebody at the poker club and they took him out to Crueltown and killed him for his money."

"If it was only that simple."

Rudd looked confused. "They didn't kill him for his money?"

Steele started the car. "It's possible they did. But there's more to it than that. Don't forget that message on his forehead and the drug-carrying condom in his stomach."

"Oh, that's right. Maybe they just needed a body to send a message."

"It's possible." Steele pulled out of the parking place and headed for the exit.

"Where we going now?" asked Rudd.

"Back to the morgue. I want to be sure that second body they found at Crueltown really is Gary."

"Oh no, not the morgue again. Kelly'll probably try to make me look at more stomach contents. I already feel a little sick."

"I warned you about the greasy food they serve in poker rooms. I hope you didn't eat the fish sticks."

"Not very many." Rudd put his hands to his stomach. "I'm still hungry."

# Chapter 18

*R*ush hour had the traffic on the Harbor Freeway backed up all the way to the 405, but Steele was able to work his way across five lanes of traffic and into the car-pool lane so it only took an hour and a half to cover the dozen or so miles to the morgue.

Inside, Kelly was waiting for them. "I just finished him," he said, gesturing toward the body under a plastic sheet on the examining table. Same words on his forehead, but you won't believe what I found in *his* stomach."

"Not another condom?" said Rudd.

"Nope. Come over here. I'll show you."

He pulled back the sheet and Rudd leaned over for a closer look. "Damn, look at that. 'Keep Out.' Right there on his forehead. Same as the other guy. And this one was beat up too. Not as bad as the first guy, but pretty bad."

Steele looked closely at the face. It was Gary. At the casino, the young security employee had been cheerful and casual; now his bruised face looked very sad. Steele looked closer at the two words on his forehead. He turned back to Kelly. "Identical?"

"You bet. Absolutely identical. I looked at the close-up facial photos from the first body and compared 'em."

Rudd looked at Steele. "How can that be?"

Steele traced the letters with his finger. "It's a brand."

Rudd grimaced. "A brand? You mean like a branding iron?"

"By God," said Kelly, "I bet you're right."

"And was this guy alive when they did it?" asked Rudd. "Just like the first one?"

"Fraid so," said Kelly.

"Ouch," said Rudd, touching his own forehead. "Branded like a damn cow."

"This one struggled a lot more than the first guy. His wrists were all torn up. Tied with rawhide. It was still around his wrists when they brought him in. And he was beat up real bad. So, aren't you curious about what I found in his stomach? It's all right there in the bag." He pushed the sheet further down and pointed to the plastic bag that was wedged between the naked body's legs.

"Yuck," said Rudd, "stomach contents."

"Right," said Kelly, smiling. "Hey, Rudd, why don't you open it and see what's in there."

"Not me," said Rudd, backing away.

"Actually, I put the, uh, special thing in another bag," said Kelly. "I'll show you."

He went to his desk and came back with another clear plastic bag. He held it up. "Whatta ya make of this?

Inside was a tiny pair of pink panties, probably from a child's doll.

Suddenly, Steele knew who the message was for. He turned on Rudd. "Why were you listening to the police scanner that night you called me about Culp's body?"

"Why, uh, because . . . because you told me too."

"I told you?"

"Yeah, don't you remember? You sent me an email. You said to keep my police scanner turned on that night. You said I might hear something interesting."

"The message was sent from my regular email address?"

"No, it was from your Google Gmail account."

"I don't have a Gmail account."

"Oh."

Steele turned to Kelly. "Cover him up. I want you to call Pruett."

Kelly stared at him. "The doll's panties means something to you?"

"They do. Do you have a cell phone? Call him right now."

Rudd took the plastic bag out of Kelly's hands to look at it more closely. "What is it, Steele? You act like you just saw a ghost. What does it mean?"

"It means Furtado."

"Furtado?" said Rudd. "The kidnapping case? The guy who

kidnapped and killed that little Rutherford girl?"

"I'm sure of it."

Kelly took the bag back from Rudd. "You're saying this Furtado character made this guy swallow these doll's panties before he killed him? Just to send a message to you?"

"Yes, and it means the 'Keep Out' message was meant for me too. I should have realized it, but I was sure Furtado was still in prison. He must have escaped. The 'Keep Out' message actually means the opposite. It means come in and get me. He's waiting inside Crueltown."

# Chapter 19

*R*udd held up the bag. "You mean these doll's panties, and the "Keep Out" words are both a challenge to you?"

"I think so. Don't you remember how important the child's panties were in Furtado's trial? The prosecuting attorney kept on holding them up in front of the jury."

"So he's after you because you shot him and because you testified against him. But wait a minute, your testimony against him put him away for life, didn't it?"

"That's why we have to call Pruett. Somehow, he must have got out."

"Damn," whispered Rudd. "Furtado. On the loose again. I can't believe it" He held his cell phone out to Steele.

But Steele wouldn't take it. "No, Pruett already thinks I'm interfering in his case. I want Kelly to call him. We have to find out if Furtado really has escaped. It hardly seems possible, but it all adds up. The message on the Culp's forehead, the doll's panties, even the drug-carrying condom in Culp's stomach. It's exactly the kind of game he likes to play."

"I remember Furtado's trial," said Kelly. "They said he ran some kind of drug smuggling operation out of Mexico, but they couldn't pin anything on him."

"But Steele went into Crueltown and got him," said Rudd. "At the trial, Furtado swore he had nothing to do with killing the little girl, but Steele's testimony got him convicted of planning the kidnapping and being an accessory to her murder."

"I'll make the call," said Kelly. "Let's go to my office so I can put it on the speakerphone."

In Kelly's tiny, cluttered office, Steele and Rudd waited while Kelly punched in the number.

Pruett answered on the first ring. "Yeah? Whatta you want, Kelly?"

"I just talked to Steele. He thinks these 'Keep Out' murders could have something to do with Furtado."

"Furtado? The drug smuggler? Naw, he's in prison. Up in Soledad. Steele should know that, he put him there."

"Steele thinks he might have escaped."

"Is Steele there? I need to talk to him."

Kelly put his hand over the phone and looked at Steele questioningly.

Steele shook his head.

"He, uh, just left. Maybe you should check with the prison, just in case."

"Sounds like Steele's gone off the deep end this time, but hang on, I'll call Soledad on the other line."

He was back in less than a minute. "Damn, Furtado *is* out. But he didn't escape. He's out on a million-dollars bail. Somehow his lawyer got him a new trial. Hang on, they're sayin' somethin' else. Okay . . . okay . . . I got it. Listen, Kelly, if you see Steele, tell him to call me right away. They're saying Furtado is supposed to go before the judge day after tomorrow. Some kind of pre-trial hearing."

"I wouldn't count on it," whispered Steele.

"What?" said Pruett. "Did you say something?"

"I said I wouldn't count on it," said Kelly. "All right, Captain, if I see Steele I'll tell him to call you." He hung up. "You'd better call Kelly pretty soon or he'll have his men out looking for you."

"If Pruett wants me, he should know where I'm heading."

"Not Crueltown?" said Kelly.

"Crueltown. That's what I want you to tell him."

Kelly shook his head. "You know he can't go in there."

"Up to him," said Steele as he headed for the door.

Once they were in the car and on their way, Rudd touched Steele's shoulder. "You can't go out there, Steele. What if Furtado is expecting you?"

"He is expecting me. For some reason, he wants me there. It's why he lured Mrs. Culp there. He wasn't after her, he was after me"

"But why?"

"I don't know. Revenge, I guess. He always did like his games. Remember the series of notes he sent to your newspaper? All those tongue-in-cheek clues about how to find the girl?"

"Sure I remember. How could I forget? You were the one who figured out the clues all led to Crueltown. You almost got yourself killed out there."

"It seems like his game is not quite over."

"I'm telling you, Steele, you burned him once before. This time he'll be smarter."

"Let's hope he's not as smart as he thinks he is."

Rudd shook his head and again lightly touched Steele's shoulder. "Don't do it, Steele. Please. Let the police take care of it."

"He knows they won't go into Crueltown. It's what he's counting on."

"So you're really going in there again."

"I have to. He's killed two already, maybe just to send messages to me. If I don't respond to his challenge, I think he will keep on creating bodies to send me more clues."

"Then he's gone completely mad."

"Probably."

"But he's still smart. And remember, he didn't know you back then. This time he'll be ready for you ."

"Then let's not keep him waiting." Steele pulled onto the Harbor freeway and headed for Crueltown.

# Chapter 20

*B*y the time they got to Crueltown, it was dark. Steele drove slowly along next to the back fence.

"How you gonna get through the fence?" asked Rudd.

Steele slowed the car to a crawl. "The county keeps on patching the fence, but every time they do, a new hole pops up somewhere else. The people who go in there usually cut their holes behind some bushes. Watch for a likely place."

They drove along slowly and after awhile Rudd said, "How about there?" He pointed at some heavy underbrush behind an abandoned old truck chassis.

Steele stopped the car. "That could be it. Hang on, I'll go look." He turned off the car and got out. He hurried up the slight incline and pushed through the bushes. As he expected, there was a good-sized hole cut in the fence. The trodden-down dry grass showed it had been recently used.

He went back down to the car and opened the trunk. He unlocked the strongbox that was bolted to the floor and took out a short-range radio receiver. Then he closed the trunk and got back in the car. "There *is* a hole in the fence up there. Here's what I want you to do. I've got a tiny microphone and transmitter sewn into the shoulder of my jacket. With this radio receiver, you should be able to pick up anything I say." He handed it to Rudd. "Try It. Use the ear piece."

Rudd stuck the earpiece in his ear. "Like this?"

Steele nodded. "Can you hear me?"

"Yep, loud and clear."

"As I go in, I'll be telling you where I'm going. If I get in trouble, it'll be up to you to save me."

Rudd stared at him wide-eyed. "Save you? Inside Crueltown? You're joking, right? I don't even have a gun."

"There's a fully-loaded snub-nose 38 mounted under the dash. The barrel is shoved onto a big cleaning brush I had welded under there. The 38 is loaded. Just pull it off its mount and it's ready to go."

"Now wait a minute, Steele. There's drug dealers and dope addicts and killers in there, and you want *me* to come in guns blazing?"

"No. If you hear me say I've found Furtado, call Pruett. Tell him we may be able to flush Furtado out if he comes with sirens on and lights flashing. Ask him to get a helicopter up. Then take the gun, go to the fence, and fire three shots into the ground."

"Oh, I get it. You want me to try to scare them off, make them think you've got reinforcements coming in so they'll scurry off into the darkness like rats."

"It will probably be more of a distraction than anything, but it might make them think twice about holding me. After you've fired the shots, get back in the car and lock the doors. Then start the engine and be ready to take off. The windows have been bullet-proofed but they won't stop a large-caliber rifle bullet. Don't take any chances. If anybody but me comes out, get the hell out of here fast."

"If you don't come out? Now wait a minute, maybe you shouldn't be doing this alone."

"You want to come with me?"

"Maybe I should."

"Don't even think about it. Believe me, I'll do better in there by myself."

"Well, don't forget what happened the last time," said Rudd. "Nobody would go in to help you, even when I begged them. Pruett tried to get his bosses to let him take a SWAT team in, but they said their hands were tied. Afterwards, I lambasted them all in my story. For not helping you, for being such chicken-shits. But it didn't do any good. They still won't go in there."

"Their hands *were* tied. They don't have jurisdiction. Nobody does, not until they decide which city is responsible for this area."

"Yeah, I know. But think about it, Steele. I mean if Furtado is waiting for you, maybe he'll just shoot you the moment he sees you."

"He didn't go to all this trouble, leaving those clues, just to shoot me. I know Furtado. He sees himself as a cat, playing with a mouse."

"But what if you get caught . . . like . . . like in his trap? Maybe we should just wait him out. He's got to come out of there sooner or later."

"I was hired to find Culp's killer. I think I've found him. Now I have to go get him. Pay close attention to what I say on that radio receiver." Steele got out of the car.

"All right, but be careful, damn it."

"I plan to." Steele closed the car door and headed back up the hill. When he got to the hole in the fence, he crawled through and went to the edge of the hill. He looked down at Crueltown. A dirty shroud of fog hung over the whole place and it smelled like the nearby oil refineries. Through the smoke and mist, Steele could see several campfires burning down there in the spaces between the dark shapes of the abandoned trailers. Nothing seemed to have changed in Crueltown: it was the same old dark and dirty place. Steele knew the same kinds of people would be there as the last time: the dope-dealers and the drifters, the illegal immigrants and the bail jumpers, the worn-out prostitutes and the kid car-strippers, along with assorted small-time hoods hiding out from the law. Mixed in with them would be the runaways, the mentally ill, and the hopelessly addicted, all hiding from whatever had driven them in there. He took the Beretta out of his ankle holster and put it into his jacket pocket, keeping his hand on it as he worked his way down the hill. He whispered into the hidden microphone: "I'm through the fence. Heading down toward the trailers."

At the bottom of the hill, the ground was mushy underfoot and smelled like a mixture of old oil and new sewer. He considered taking out his penlight to look for a dry path, but decided against it. Even a small light would stand out in the blackness of Crueltown. If there ever had been any electricity in the place, the county had cut it off long ago. The distant city lights reflected off of the harbor-area smog, but it was still too dark to see much detail. Old trailers that were deteriorating into the muck littered the horizon like the carcasses of strange ancient animals. Patches of standing putrid water lay in all directions.

He continued on, moving slowly, trying to avoid the wettest places. His damaged knees were hurting because of the uneven ground, but he kept going.

In the darkness ahead, he heard a variety of dogs barking, but no human sounds. A little further on he saw the reflection of what must be water. Probably a swampy area, but it looked as if there might be a somewhat dry path around the edge. He started toward it, but then he saw movement, a shadow.

He pulled back and whispered into the microphone: "Somebody ahead. I'm stopping."

"Lookin' for something?" The voice in the darkness sounded young; maybe a teenager.

"Yeah," said Steele. "What've you got?"

A young man in a black leather jacket stepped out. He had very long hair and was wearing low-riding torn-up jeans. A glint in the dim light indicated at least one nose ring. "Pot, smack, speed," he said in a flat voice. "Anything you want."

"What I want is to see Furtado."

"Never heard of him."

"Of course you have." Steele took out his pistol. "Take me to him"

"Hey Bro, no need to get unfriendly," said the young man, holding up both hands. "Follow me."

Steele let the boy get a little ahead and whispered into the microphone, "Not sure where he's taking me. Heading south."

The boy stopped and turned back. "You say something?"

"Just mumbling to myself."

"Takes all kinds, I guess. You got serious money on you? Furtado won't like me bringing in somebody without serious money."

"I have enough."

The young man continued on, leading Steele on a meandering path between many different kinds of old trailers that had tipped this way and that as they sank into the mud. Heaps of garbage were spilling out from between the trailers and Steele recognized a variety of odors as he passed by: mold, sour milk, rotten eggs, human and animal shit, plus the occasional food odors of decomposing chili, tortillas, beans, meat, and oddly, bananas.

Steele saw more campfires ahead and as they approached the firelight, he put his pistol back into his pocket. But he kept his hand wrapped around the grip and his finger on the trigger.

Before they got to the first of the campfires, a man whose face was hidden by a slouch hat, suddenly stepped out of the shadows. "Hey, bub, you lookin' for a girl?"

Steele ignored him and kept going.

"I got all kinds," the man called after him. "You want a big fat juicy one? Or how about a little kid? You can do whatever you want to her."

The man disappeared back into the shadows and as the boy led him past the campfire, Steele saw a stooped-over old Hispanic woman cooking something in a blackened pot that was nestled down into the coals. She didn't look up as they passed, but Steele could feel her eyes on his back as they continued on. They passed more dark, musty-smelling trailers and Steele was sure he heard cries and moans from behind the buckling walls that seemed to press in toward them from every side.

They passed more campfires. Their low-lying smoke, mixed with the smog from the nearby oil refineries, hung over the area like dirty yellow fog.

Two tired-looking old men squatted close to one of the fires. One of them was missing an arm. They were eating something off of tin plates. Their eyes, reflecting the yellow-orange firelight, followed Steele as he passed.

They went on until the random clutter of trailers suddenly ended and there was only darkness ahead. It was some sort of no-mans land, muddy and stinking, with pools of stagnant water. It looked like it had been bulldozed to clear the way for . . . what?

"Coming to open ground," he whispered. "No trailers. Still heading south." He imagined Rudd back in the car listening, probably wanting to say something back to him like, "No, don't go."

The kid stopped. "This is as far as I go. That'll be twenty bucks."

"Twenty bucks? For what?"

"For getting you this far without getting your throat cut."

Steele took out the money, but held it back. "Where do I go?"

"Just follow the path. Somebody'll meet you."

"Furtado?"

"Somebody."

Steele handed over the money and the kid disappeared into the darkness.

Steele went forward and soon saw the path the boy was referring to. Railroad ties had been laid out in a generally straight line across the swampy ground. Steele started across, tightrope walking past standing pools of foul-smelling water. Occasionally, the cold damp fog was interrupted by warmer areas that smelled like sulfur.

It was not easy to negotiate the railroad-tie path. The need to put one foot in front of the other put stress on the sides of his lower leg where the prosthetic foot was attached. Worried that the straps would loosen, he found it easier and safer to slide along sideways. Eventually, the railroad-tie path led to an old rusted-out trailer. Its windows had been knocked out and it was sunk halfway down into the mud. Steele took a chance and shined his little penlight inside. There was a bed with a dirty blanket on it, dishes in the sink, a half-full coffee cup on the table. Somebody had been in there recently. "An old metal trailer," he whispered. "Windows knocked out, but somebody's been living in it. Maybe it's a guard station, but nobody around now."

He snapped off the penlight and looked ahead. More open ground, but beyond it was something dark against the horizon. A house? Whatever it was, it was bigger than a trailer.

When Steele got closer, he saw that the dark shape was a cluster of newer-looking manufactured homes. Somebody had gone to the trouble to haul in several fairly-large homes. "Some sort of compound," he whispered into the microphone. "Manufactured homes, all pushed together into a circle."

The houses were sitting flat on the ground, and they were so close together there was not even enough space between them for a person to squeeze through. If the police ever did come into Crueltown, they would have a hard time penetrating that kind of strong defensive compound. He took out his gun and stayed where he was, watching for any movement. Except for the hum of harbor truck traffic in the distance, there was no sound.

Then he saw a light move across one of the windows of the nearest house. Somebody inside was moving, carrying a flashlight. The light went out. He waited, but it didn't reappear. "There's somebody inside one of the houses," he whispered. "I'm going closer."

He moved slowly forward, watching the window where he'd seen the light. If Furtado was inside, there would be guards outside. He stopped again to listen. Nothing. He started forward again and was almost to the house when the beam from a very-bright flashlight blinded him. "Stop right there, bud. Drop that gun or you're dead."

Steele stopped. He saw someone move to the side. It meant there were at least two of them. He couldn't see the man behind the flashlight, but the other guy was huge. He was holding what looked like a sawed-off shotgun.

Steele threw his gun over his shoulder, back toward the swampy path. When he heard the splash, he memorized how far he'd thrown it.

"Why'd you do that?" said the man with the flashlight. "Now it's in that crappy water."

"I figured I wouldn't need it."

"You were right about that."

"I bet it's him," said the big guy. "You Steele?"

"Who's asking?"

A laugh. The flashlight's beam moved to the big guy who was grinning as he pointed the shotgun at Steele. "It's him. I bet it's him. Tall, blonde hair. Just like the boss said."

"Shut up, Carl," said the voice behind the flashlight.

Carl shrugged and looked hurt. "What'd I say?"

"Just shut up and search him."

The blinding light came back to Steele. Carl came forward to pat him down and search his pockets. "He's clean. Nothing but this cell phone and a little flashlight."

"Check his ankles. The boss said to check his ankles."

"Okay," The big man stooped down and pulled up Steele's pants legs.

"Damn, look at this. He's got some kind of fake foot. And there's an empty holster hooked to it."

"No shit? Let me see." The man with the flashlight leaned closer. "How about that? He's a damn cripple. Okay, take him inside." He flashed the light on a door at the far end of the mobile home.

"Get moving," Carl growled, jabbing at Steele's back with the shotgun.

Steele walked to the door.

"Open it."

Steele reached for the doorknob.

"But don't move too fast or I might have to blow the back of your stupid head off."

Steele opened the door. It was pitch black inside.

"Now get in there, slow and easy or this shotgun could go boom."

Steele looked back over his shoulder. "Your boss wouldn't like that, Carl. He went to a lot of trouble to get me here." Steele jumped inside and slammed the door shut.

The blast of the shotgun splintered the door, leaving a ragged hole. Carl pushed his head through to look around and Steele punched the side of the big man's head as hard as he could. Carl let out a yowl and fell back. Steele ducked back just as the shotgun went off again, leaving an even larger hole.

A calm voice came out of the darkness: "Stop that shooting, you fool."

"But he hit me, boss. Son of a bitch sucker-punched me."

Steele heard the shotgun being reloaded.

The voice in the darkness said, "Back off, Carl. I'll take care of him."

"But, boss."

"Just stay where you are, Carl."

Steele knew that voice. It was a voice from the past. It was Furtado, talking as calm and measured as always, with little trace of a Mexican accent, even though he was supposed to have grown up south of the border.

"Welcome, Steele."

Steele estimated Furtado's voice was coming from about fifteen feet away.

"Just come toward me, Steele. Nice and easy."

Steele crouched down and moved toward the voice, feeling along the carpeted floor for anything that could be used as a weapon.

"You certainly are being quiet, Steele. What are you up to?"

Steele kept moving toward Furtado's voice. If he could get close enough, he might be able to surprise him.

"Did you search him?" came Furtado's voice.

"Yeah, boss, he's clean." Carl sounded like he was pouting. "And he's got some kind of fake foot. No kiddin'."

"Was he alone?"

"Yeah, boss."

"Look around for Rudd, that reporter I told you about. He might be hiding out there somewhere."

"Okay, boss."

"You needn't worry about Carl," said Furtado. "He won't fire again unless I tell him to."

Steele didn't reply. He continued to move slowly forward, crouched down, feeling his way along the wall.

"I assume in this situation you would take the offensive, wouldn't you, Steele? In fact, I expect you are now quietly sneaking toward me, trying to catch me off guard. But I must tell you I have a gun pointed at you."

Steele stood up. "So why don't you turn on a light? Why the games?"

Furtado chuckled. "But I like games. Don't you like games, Steele? Didn't you enjoy our little game of clues? You're supposed to be the famous detective. I thought you'd like some physical clues to follow."

Steele felt the wall behind him end. A corner. He followed the turn to the left, moving with his hands out, hoping to feel a door, a counter, anything to get behind. "It wasn't hard to figure out it was you, Furtado. Who else would get so much pleasure out of torturing people by branding them?"

"Oh, but I didn't torture anyone." Furtado's voice sounded almost cheerful. "You should know that about me by now. You've seen the fine clothes I wear. I like to keep myself presentable, and torture makes such a mess."

"So what are you saying? That you have your stooges do the killing and branding for you? That you didn't have the nerve to do it yourself?"

Furtado chuckled. "Good old Steele, challenging and direct, same as always. I have to admit the branding *was* my idea. Those troublesome young fellows down at my ranch were branding 'Keep Out' signs on every fence post in sight. I told the fools it would just make the border patrol suspicious, make them want to come in to see why we were trying to keep them out. But it gave me an idea. A 'Keep Out' message would be sure to make *you* want to come in. Those crazy cowboys down there didn't mind doing it for me. They said they'd always wanted to try it on a human."

"So you still get someone else to do your dirty work, just like when you had your men kill that little girl. I bet you watched though, didn't you? I bet you enjoyed it."

There was a long silence. "So you really don't understand me at all, do you, Steele?" Furtado no longer sounded so cheerful. "Or are you just trying to anger me? Ask yourself this, of what use would the girl be to me if she was dead?"

"So why was she killed?"

"Call it . . . human weakness. Men can be such animals. But, that's all in the past now, isn't it? Odd that it was that same human weakness that led to my current freedom."

Steele's searching hands felt a door, then a doorknob. "Is that right? So tell me, how did you get out of prison?'

"A long story. I'm afraid you won't have time to hear it."

"Oh, I suspect we have a little time. I don't think you're quite ready to kill me just yet. You're enjoying this too much." Steele opened the door a crack, but he felt no cool outside air. It must lead into another room, or maybe it was only a closet.

"I must admit I *am* enjoying this, Steele. I've been waiting a long time for this moment."

Steele opened the door a little more, but the hinges creaked. A light suddenly came on, swinging on its wire from the ceiling. Furtado was standing under it, pointing a long-barreled revolver at Steele's midsection. "You'll find nothing in that closet, Steele, unless you're looking for a broom. Come over here and sit down." He used the gun to gesture toward a wooden chair as he backed into the shadows and sat on a fairly new-looking sofa.

Steele didn't have any trouble recognizing Furtado, even in the dim light. He was perched on the forward edge of the sofa, sitting up steel-rod straight. He'd sat exactly that way all through his trial. Steele wondered if someone had once punished him for slumping.

Steele closed the closet door and went slowly toward the chair. The path would take him within six feet of Furtado. Was it worth a try to dive at him? If he could move slightly to the side as he made his move, the bullet might miss, or only hit him in the shoulder. Furtado was not a big man; maybe he could get the gun away from him even after he'd been hit.

"Easy now, Steele. I remember how tricky you are. This 38 is loaded with hollow-points. I've seen what they do to a man, and I'd hate to blow that kind of hole in you before we've had our little talk."

Steele sat in the chair and looked Furtado over. The man had lost a lot of weight, and he'd shaved his head. He had a new scar on his face. "You're uglier than ever, Furtado."

Furtado smiled and touched his cheek. "You mean this? Just a little souvenir of prison life. You have to show the gangs you're not scared of them. Did you know they make a special kind of knife in prison? Wide, so it leaves a noticeable scar."

"How resourceful of them."

Furtado smiled. "Still the same dry humor. And speaking of scars, it looks like you've got a new one on your jaw. Turn a little sideways so I can see it better."

Steele didn't move. He was watching that gun, looking for any chance to make a dive at it.

Furtado leaned closer to try to get a better look. "You do have a new scar. I heard those poppy growers almost nailed you over there in Baghdad. Blew your legs all to hell, did they? What's the matter, Steele, a bit too dangerous for you over there?"

Steele sat back in his chair and tried to look casual. "So, Furtado, you want to chat about danger. Then tell me, why are you hiding here in Crueltown with the other vermin? The real world out there too scary for you? Only two guards, and both of them a bit dim-witted at that. What happened to your gang, Furtado, if that's the right word for those losers you used to attract to yourself? Did you lose all your nice friends while you were living off the state up there in Soledad?"

"Interesting. You combine insults with probing questions. Does that usually work in your, uh, profession, if you can call it that?"

"Usually, but a few are not intelligent enough to know when they're being insulted. In case you didn't get it, Furtado, that was also an insult."

Furtado laughed, a quiet sort of amused chuckle. "You're a funny fellow, Steele. You know what? If I didn't hate you so much I might like you."

"Hate me? Why should you hate me? I was just doing my job."

"Your job? Was it your job to shoot my leg? To completely shatter the bone?"

"I could have shot you in the head."

"Maybe it would have been better if you had. Part of your bullet is still in my leg. The pain reminds me of you every time the weather changes."

"Nonsense, Furtado, there's no bullet in your leg. They rushed you to the hospital as soon as I brought you out."

"Oh yes, they said they'd cut the bullet out, but they didn't get it all. I told the prison doctor that, told him how it pained me, how it kept me lying awake nights, remembering. He took some X-rays. Said he couldn't see anything. He was lying. I know part of your bullet is still in there. I can feel it even now."

Steele knew there was no point in arguing. He looked around the room. A long table against the wall held a variety of computers and communication equipment. The screens were all dark, but tiny green lights under the table showed all of the equipment was turned on. A bank of very large batteries lined the wall next to them. Why did Furtado need so much computer equipment?

"You like my little setup, Steele?"

"What's it for?"

"Another long story. No time."

"We've got nothing but time."

"Nothing but time? Are you stalling, Steele?"

"It's just you and me, Furtado. You said you wanted to talk, so talk."

"You're trying to get me to talk? Why, are you wearing a wire?"

Steele shook his head. "No wire."

"Open your shirt."

Steele unbuttoned his shirt. "You won't find anything."

"I won't waste my time trying to find it, but I suspect it's there somewhere. But why did you bother? You know the police won't come inside Crueltown."

"What if you're wrong?"

"Does that mean you think they will? What are you up to, Steele? I wish I could just shoot you. I'd enjoy seeing you whimper as you die, but they say they want Mister Drew Steele alive."

"They? Who is they?"

"Never mind. You'll find out."

"I'm afraid we won't have time." Steele put his hand to his ear. "Listen."

Furtado looked toward the door. "I hear it. Sirens. But they're a long ways away. They're not coming here."

"Yes they are. Listen. A helicopter." The sound of the helicopter *was* coming closer. Rudd must have made the call to Pruett.

Furtado stood up. "What the hell?"

The helicopter was coming closer and closer, beating the air, sounding almost angry as it approached.

Furtado turned back to Steele, pointing the gun at him. "I should have known you wouldn't come in here alone? Who is it?"

"Who do you think? said Steele. "It's the warden from Soledad. Those gangs up there said they weren't through with you."

The sirens were very close now, but no longer moving. Steele realized they must have stopped just outside the Crueltown fence.

Furtado went to the window. "The cops won't come in here. You're running a bluff, aren't you, Steele?"

The helicopter arrived, hovering low overhead, unbelievably loud, shaking the flimsy building. "You think that helicopter is a bluff?" yelled Steele. "Why don't you go outside and wave at them?"

Furtado leaned close to the window to look up, and as if in response, the police helicopter's powerful spotlight light passed over the trailer, momentarily filling the entire outside area with the brightness of daylight. At almost the same instant, there was a shot and the window's glass blew apart. Furtado went down and Steele reacted by jumping up out of his chair to smash the hanging light bulb with his fist. The room went dark and Steele got down on his hands and knees to quickly crawl away into a corner. As the helicopter moved away to search deeper into Crueltown, Steele heard several more shots from outside, including two loud bursts from a shotgun and what sounded like return fire from a pistol.

Steele found a table and crawled under it. Everything was quiet. Had Furtado been hit?

As if in response to Steele's thought, Furtado's gruff voice came out of the darkness. "They wanted you alive, Steele, but too bad. See ya." Several shots filled the dark space with sound. The flashes from the gun's muzzle showed Furtado standing near the window.

Steele didn't move.

"Did I get ya?" whispered Furtado. "Or are you playing hide and seek? Come out, come out, wherever you are."

Steele waited, not even breathing.

"So you got somebody to come in with you. Who's out there? Rudd? Did he bring the cops in? Shame on you, needing help just to come in and get me."

Steele waited, not moving, making sure he didn't make a sound. Would Furtado fire again? There was no more shooting from outside and the sound of the helicopter was moving away leaving only silence behind. The flashing red lights were still out there, but they were still the same distance away, probably still out on the road. What was Furtado thinking? Did he think the police were coming in?

Steele heard a sound. Was Furtado moving? Then he heard the squeak of that closet door. Was Furtado getting inside that closet? Maybe it wasn't a closet after all.

Steele knew there were computers on the table he was under. He reached up and felt for a switch on the front of a monitor. He pressed it and ducked back into the darkness as the monitor lit up. It gave off enough light for Steele to see that the room was empty.

A flashlight came on outside the broken window. A face peered in. "Steele, are you in there?" It was Rudd.

Steele stood up. "Turn off that light, Rudd. There are two guards out there somewhere."

"They ran off. I think I might have hit one of 'em."

Steele hurried to the shattered window. "Give me the flashlight."

Rudd handed it through.

"Find a place to hide. They could still be out there somewhere."

Steele hurried to the squeaky closet door. He cautiously opened it and shined the flashlight in. The closet was empty, but there was an open trap door in the floor. An escape tunnel. Furtado was gone.

# Chapter 21

*O*utside, Steele found Rudd still standing by the window, looking in. "Why didn't you hide?"

Rudd turned around and shrugged. "There's no place to hide around here. Besides, everybody ran off when the chopper came. You shoulda seen 'em run, Steele. Like you said, rats scurrying off into the darkness."

"Why didn't you stay in the car?"

"I heard on your little radio when they took you in to Furtado. I thought he'd kill you."

"He wanted to, but he said somebody wanted me alive."

"Who?"

"He didn't say. Let's get out of here."

"I don't think they'll be back. That helicopter scared the bejesus out of 'em. I bet they're still running."

"I wouldn't count on it. Help me find my gun and let's go."

Rudd waited on the railroad-tie path while Steele waded into the putrid water to retrieve his gun. After several minutes of searching, he found it and tried to wipe off some of the muck. It felt slimy and smelled like oil, but he knew it would still work. He kept it in his hand as they hurried back across the open area and through the rows of trailers. The campfires still burned, but there was no one in sight.

"There were people all over the place when I came through," said Rudd. "But they all slipped away into the dark when they saw my gun."

"Well, keep it in your hand. We aren't out of here yet. What did Pruett say when you called him?"

"I told him to send in the cavalry, and don't forget the helicopter. At first, he said no way, that you were on your own. But then I told him you'd found Furtado. He said he'd see what he could do and he hung up on me. I guess he sent that helicopter, but it looks like they still won't come in."

"I didn't expect them too."

As they made their way back through the mobile homes, they didn't see a soul. The still-smoking campfires and the absence of people made the place feel like the aftermath of some sudden disaster. Although the people all ran for cover when the helicopter came and hovered overhead with its bright spotlight, Steele knew they were still there somewhere, hiding in the darkness. He kept his gun in his hand all the way back to the fence.

They found Pruett and two uniformed deputies waiting next to Steele's car.

"So, Steele, you're not dead after all," said Pruett.

"No thanks to you," said Rudd.

Pruett ignored him and stopped Steele with a hand to his chest. "Rudd said you'd found Furtado. Where is he?"

"Escaped."

"So it really was him? He's been in there all this time?"

Steele nodded. "He was waiting for me."

"After what he said about you at his trial, I'm surprised he didn't put a bullet in you."

"He was ready to when Rudd starting shooting. He saved my life."

Pruett glanced at Rudd. "Rudd? Shooting?"

Rudd stepped forward to jab a finger into Pruett's chest. "I knew you weren't going to help him, so I had to."

"You know I can't go in there," protested Pruett. "It could cost me my job. But when you called, I helped, didn't I? I didn't have to call in that chopper you know."

"You weren't any help at all," said Rudd. "Steele could have been--"

Steele stepped between them. "It doesn't matter now. What matters is Furtado is on the loose again. How did he get out of prison?"

Pruett shrugged. "Lawyers, of course. Seems his lawyer found out the prosecutor was all ready to add a rape charge to the kidnapping charge, but the DNA they got from inside the little girl didn't match up with Furtado. So they quietly dropped the rape part of it. When Furtado's lawyer found out about it last week, he went to the judge and said that was important evidence that had been withheld from their defense. The judge agreed and scheduled a new trial. They had Furtado moved back down to the LA jail and in the middle of the night, Furtado's lawyer got another judge to set bail. A million bucks. Furtado posted the bond and was out before anybody got wind of it. Most everybody assumed he'd run right back to Mexico."

"He did mention a ranch," said Steele. "It may be down close to the border, a place to smuggle drugs across from Mexico. If I was you, I'd have the border patrol look for him down there. They may already know the place. Tell them to look for 'Keep Out' signs on fence posts."

Pruett looked puzzled. "Keep out? The same as on the stiff's forehead?"

"That's right. It was done with a branding iron they were using to brand fence posts."

"Ouch," said Pruett. "Kelly told me the second guy had those same words on his forehead. What's it all about?"

"Somehow Furtado must have found out I was looking for Culp. He put those words on Culp's body to draw me in. He likes to play games."

"And the doll's panties in the second stiff's stomach. Another message?"

"Furtado's final clue. Also meant for me."

"So why didn't you tell me?" said Pruett. "You could have got yourself killed in there."

"Would you have gone inside Crueltown with me?"

"Don't be a smart-ass, Steele. I do what I can. But why did Furtado kill those two guys? And what does it have to do with Las Vegas?"

"I have no idea."

Pruett closed one eye. "No idea? Come on, what aren't you telling me?"

"I'm still trying to figure it out. For some reason, Furtado's got a lot of computer equipment set up in there. If I was you, I'd get a court order to go in and see what's on those computers."

"Fat chance of that. Don't forget I went down that court-order road the last time, after you found the kidnapped girl in there. They said I had to get approval from whoever had jurisdiction over the property and you remember how that ended up."

"Nobody would sign on the dotted line."

"Right. Nobody has jurisdiction. They all said just stay out until the federal courts decide the matter."

"Maybe they'll listen this time."

"I doubt it, but I'll try. What's your next move?"

"As you suggested, I'll try to find the connection between Furtado and the two casino employees."

"All right, but this time you'd better keep me in the loop. This is my investigation."

"I will."

"You'd better or I'll . . . I'll go after Rudd here for discharging a firearm inside the county limits."

Rudd put up both hands. "Who said I discharged a firearm? Besides, is Crueltown really inside the county limits? I'd like to see you prove it."

Pruett shook his head in disgust. "Just remember what I said. You have to keep me in the loop. I've got two unsolved murders on my hands."

# Chapter 22

After Pruett and the deputy drove away, Steele remounted the .38 under the car's dash and took out an oiled rag to clean his automatic.

"That Pruett," said Rudd. "He wants you to solve the case for him. I'm in there risking my life and he's sitting out here waiting to see if we end up dead. I can't believe it."

Steele glanced over at him. "Why didn't you do what I told you? I said to fire off a few shots and get back in the car."

"I don't know what came over me. When I heard that voice on your radio sayin' he was going to blow a big fat hole in you, I called Pruett. Then, when I heard a gun go off and you didn't talk anymore, I just figured . . . I don't know what I figured. That maybe you were dead or something. I just had to . . . you know, get in there to see what was happening. By the time you started talking to Furtado, I was already in. I followed your directions and found you about the same the time the police chopper got here. When I saw Furtado at the window holding that gun, I just . . . pulled the trigger."

"Too bad you missed."

"Well, I didn't exactly miss."

"You weren't trying to hit him?"

"Sort of trying. I thought maybe I could just hit him in the leg. I'm just the reporter here, remember? I never shot anybody before."

"But you shot at Furtado's guards. You said you might have hit one of them."

"That was different. A big guy came out of the dark firing a shotgun at me and I just . . . I guess I shot back without thinking. I'm glad I didn't have time to think. Otherwise I might have peed my pants."

Steele looked at his old friend. His face was sweaty and he was staring straight ahead, pinching the bridge of his nose.

"You did fine," said Steele, "more than anyone else would have done in your situation. It was remarkably brave of you."

Rudd stared down at his hands in his lap. "If you'd have seen how bad my hands were shaking, you wouldn't have thought I was so brave. I couldn't have hit anything except maybe by accident."

"It takes more than bravery to kill a man. It takes . . ." Steele hesitated, not sure he wanted to talk about what it felt like to kill a man. Hopefully, Rudd would never find himself in that kind of situation again. "You say you were scared, but it takes a brave man to do something like that, even more so when you're afraid. I won't ever forget it."

"Aw, hell," said Rudd, looking away. It seemed as if he was going to say something else, but he just looked out his window.

Steele put the car in gear and pulled out onto the deserted road. What *did* it take to kill a man? Maybe it always did come down to knowing the other man was going to kill you, like Rudd said. It was a lot easier when you didn't have much time to think about it. In Iraq, they always came at you in numbers, shooting as they came. You fired back to save your own life and they went down like practice dummies, almost as if they were not real humans. Only later, when you had time to think about it, did you start to wonder if those men had families, wives and children who would be waiting for them back home. The soldiers in Iraq didn't like to talk about it. In fact, they all agreed it was better not even to think about it. But Steele *did* think about it. He thought about it often, especially at night when he should be sleeping and not remembering.

Rudd brought him back from his thoughts by turning up the police scanner. Steele glanced at him. "You expecting them to say something about what happened?"

Rudd shrugged. "You'd think they'd at least mention the helicopter."

"Everybody probably thought it was just another car chase."

"Yeah, guess you're right. Where we heading?"

"Back to my place. I have to make some calls."

"Good," said Rudd, "I'm hungry as hell. Got anything to eat

there?"

"I expect we can find you something." Steele smiled to himself. Rudd was ready to forget about his brush with death and move onto more important things, like eating.

"Great," said Rudd, cheering up, "you know, it's not all that late. Maybe some of the gals at your place will still be out at the pool."

Steele just laughed.

The drive through the harbor district was slow because of the many flatbed trucks lining up for the ship offloading. The night was always the busiest time at the harbor. Inching along behind the slow line of trucks, Steele thought about what Furtado had said about somebody "wanting Mister Drew Steele alive." The way he'd said it made Steele wonder if he was mimicking someone with a foreign accent. And then there was the mention of Iraq. Furtado had said "those poppy growers almost nailed you." Poppy growers. Did Furtado know he had been in Afghanistan as well as Iraq? Steele never knew who had set him up for that roadside bombing in Baghdad, but he had always assumed it was the drug traffickers. Whoever it was, it was obvious they were there waiting for them; the bomb had been set off by remote control. Afterward, Steele was sure he was the target because the convey had been in support of his mission to break the al-Qaeda drug smuggling business. Could Furtado have some kind of connection with al-Qaeda? It hardly seemed possible. How could a Mexican drug smuggler like Furtado even meet them? Maybe al-Qaeda was expanding its drug operations from Europe to the United States as part of a plan to destroy the country from the inside out.

As Steele drove past the harbor, he began to wonder if Furtado's elaborate game of spider and fly was more than just revenge. Furtado was obviously planning to turn him over to someone. Maybe al-Qaeda had posted a reward for him. Furtado wouldn't like losing his chance for revenge so he must have made a deal to let somebody else do the killing. Maybe they promised him Mister Drew Steele would be questioned and tortured. Furtado would only give him up for a deal like that.

Before they reached Steele's condo, Rudd was again complaining about being hungry. "I bet you won't have anything good at your place. Everything you eat is too healthy for a guy like me."

"You can call for takeout," suggested Steele.

"Hey, that's an idea," said Rudd. "How about we get some pizza? We could get a couple of large ones and some beers and relax for a change. We've been on the go since this whole thing started."

"Unfortunately, we may not have much choice but to sit tight and wait. Furtado will have gone underground. We'll have to wait for him to make his next move."

"You think he's still around? Why wouldn't he just run back to Mexico?"

"If he was going back to Mexico, he would have gone as soon as he got out of prison. Something kept him here, something so big he can't leave"

"Maybe he just stuck around to get back at you."

Steele shook his head. "It's true he put the 'Keep Out' brands on the murdered men's foreheads to play a game with me, but there's something else going on. He wouldn't turn me over to someone else unless there was something important in it for him."

"Maybe lot's of money."

"I expect so, but I still think there's more to it than that. He wouldn't give up his chance at revenge for mere money."

"So what is it? A big drug deal?"

"Probably. Now that he's out of prison, he'll want to pull his gang back together and get back in the game. If I know Furtado, it'll be something dramatic. That's his style."

"But what about Culp and that Gary kid? Do you think his big deal has something to do with their murders?"

"It's possible. Maybe they got in the way of whatever he was planning."

Rudd frowned. "I still think the casino might have knocked them off. They could have hired Furtado to do it."

"Furtado is a drug importer, not a hired killer."

"Okay, then we're back to drugs, back to that condom in Culp's stomach. That's where this all started. Maybe that's the answer. Maybe Culp was so desperate for money he was willing to act as a drug-carrying mule for Furtado."

"I don't think so," said Steele. "We know Culp needed money, even though we don't know why. Then, when he thought Monroe was on to him, he knew he had get out fast. But he still needed the money. He went to his stepson for help. Maybe Craig introduced him to people with money."

"You think Craig knew people with money?"

"I'm sure he knew a lot of them. Some of the poker players who come into the Four Aces club throw around a lot of cash. It's Craig's job to know who they are. But he probably didn't know them as well as he should have."

"Uh oh. I can see where you're going with this. You think Craig introduced his stepfather to Furtado."

"No, Furtado would have been in hiding. Remember, he just got out of prison. But Craig could have introduced his stepfather to someone who took him to Furtado."

Rudd shook his head in disgust. "Man alive, putting your own stepfather into the hands of killers."

"I doubt if Craig knew he was putting him in real jeopardy. He could have simply introduced him to a few big-money players "

"Oh yeah, what if the kid hated his stepfather? Maybe he set him up to get back at him."

"Craig did resent his stepfather, but I doubt he wanted to see him hurt. Remember, it would be hurting his mother too.""

"So they took him to Furtado and he killed the old guy for his money. Sad. But wait a minute." Rudd pointed to his own forehead. "How about those two words, 'Keep Out.' How would Furtado know you'd get the message?"

"He sent you that email telling you to listen to the police scanner the night they dumped Culp out next to the Crueltown fence."

"Oh, that's right. But how did he know you'd been hired to find Culp?"

"He talked to somebody at the casino."

"He did? Who?"

"You know who. The other body that showed up with the same two words on the forehead."

Rudd snapped his fingers. "Oh, that's right. Gary. And he ended up dead too. But how did Furtado get to him?"

"Culp must have told him about Gary. Furtado probably wanted to know where Culp got all those one hundred-dollar bills so they beat it out of him. In the end, Culp would have told them about his scheme and how he worked with Gary to cover up his stealing. Maybe he thought they'd let him go if he let them in on it. Then Furtado could have called Gary with some kind of story, maybe he said he was a friend of Culp's. That's when he found out I'd been hired to find Culp and it presented Furtado with the perfect way to draw me in. He killed Culp and used his body to send me those messages. He had his men dump the body where he knew the police would find it and he sent you that fake email message to be sure you'd find out about it and tell me."

"So Culp was still alive when you got hired to find him."

"I expect he was."

Rudd shivered. "Jesus. That means they killed him just to send you that message. But how did Gary end up in their hands?"

"Maybe Culp told them something they could use against Gary. After Culp's body was found, Gary would have been scared. Really scared. Maybe Furtado told him he was a friend of Culp's. He may have offered Gary a place to hide, or a way to get out of the country. Whatever he told him, it was enough to lure Gary to LA."

"Where they killed him."

"Yes, but not before they tried to get something out of him. Kelly said he'd been badly beaten also."

"I bet they were trying to find out what he'd done with his share of the stolen money," said Rudd.

"I suspect you're right. Whatever it was, when they were done with him, they forced him to swallow those doll's panties and then they branded him. They killed him and dumped him outside the Crueltown fence, right where they'd left Culp."

Rudd looked like he was going to be sick. "Damn, Steele, what kind of people are these? How can humans do such things?"

Steele didn't answer, but he did think about Rudd's question. In fact, he often thought about the kind of people who murdered without compunction. For years he had been trying to learn more about how people like Furtado could live with themselves after committing such crimes. He had interviewed a number of murderers and every one of them had somehow come to believe their acts were justified. They all found a way to convince themselves that either the victim deserved it, or it was "necessary" in order to accomplish some goal. They had depersonalized the victim, often feeling that they were just in the way. The logic of it might seem mad or mindlessly out of control, but Steele had learned that even serial killers found some way to convince themselves that it was "the right thing to do" under the circumstances. Something had happened to them, something that made them different from others, made them unconcerned about the lives of others. Often it was something that had happened when they were kids. Had something like that happened to Furtado?

"That got you to thinking, didn't it?" said Rudd. "I bet you're thinking about your past cases, all those other murders."

"I was. And I was also thinking about Furtado. He is not a madman. This is all part of some larger plan, something big. He wanted revenge so he drew me in, but he took some big chances to do it. And yet, he agreed to turn me over to someone else."

"Who?"

"I have an idea who. It might have something to do with what I was doing in Iraq."

Rudd looked surprised. "What? How did you make that connection? I thought you were over there doing something for the U.S. embassy."

Steele nodded. "That's right. You know I can't talk about it. I'm only telling you now in case something happens to me."

"You mean if you get killed? What am I supposed to do, tell somebody?"

"Just remember what I said. Furtado must have agreed to turn me over to someone and it has something to do with why I was in Iraq."

"Hey, knock off that kind of talk, Steele. Nothing's going to happen to you. You've been through lots of things like this. You've been up against even tougher guys than Furtado. Besides, I bet he's already run back to Mexico. I bet we never hear from him again."

Steele didn't reply and they drove the rest of the way to the condo village in silence. Steele turned into the driveway. The guard recognized him and hit the button to lift the gate.

"Hey, I just thought of something else," said Rudd. "When his stepfather ended up dead, why didn't Craig go to the police?"

"Somebody got to him."

"Furtado?"

"Probably one of Furtado's gang. When I talked to Craig at the poker club, I could see he was scared. He was agitated, very nervous, and he wanted me out of there fast."

"You think somebody was watching him there at the club?"

"The person Craig introduced his stepfather to could still be hanging around. Maybe he's a regular player there."

Rudd let out his usual low whistle. "That's right, you said you hoped Craig didn't end up dead too."

"He still might. If he is being watched, by now Furtado will know I was at the club today. I tried to warn Craig, but he wouldn't listen. He said he knew how to take care of himself. For his sake, I hope he does."

"Maybe you should warn him again."

"I plan to. I'll call him as soon as we get inside."

As soon as they were inside the condo, Rudd said he was going to change into his swimming suit and go check out the pool.

Steele immediately called the poker club. He asked for Craig Vinelli, but the receptionist said he'd gone home with a sudden illness. She said she didn't know when he'd be back.

Rudd came out of the bathroom frowning. "Did you wash this swimming suit?"

"No, why?"

"I shouldn't have left it hanging in the bathroom wet. It must have shrunk."

"Or else you got bigger. It's been a while since you wore it."

"Very funny. Did you call the poker club? Was Craig there?"

"They said he had a sudden illness."

"So he's run off."

Steele nodded. "If he's smart, he'll run far and fast. Furtado will have his men out looking for him. He's the only one still alive who can link Furtado to Culp's death."

"Besides you."

"Besides me," agreed Steele, "but my information came from Furtado himself. In court, that's called hearsay and not admissible evidence. Craig is the direct link a prosecutor would be looking for." He handed the phone to Rudd. "You were going to order a pizza?"

"Only one? Don't you want any?"

"I'm not hungry. You go ahead. I'll be upstairs in my office. I've got some calls to make."

"Okay. While I wait for the pizza, maybe I'll just go down to the pool for a bit. See if any of your neighbor gals are having a pool party tonight."

Upstairs in this office, Steele punched in the director's number. It had been some time since he'd dialed it, but he still had the number memorized. He waited through the flat-voiced answering-service monologue: "There is no one available to take your call right now. Please leave a number and we'll get back to you." He waited through the long dead-air silence and then there was the usual full minute of dial tone. Then silence. Finally, it beeped once. Steele said, "I'd like to speak to the director. This is DS47355." Then he hung up to wait for the return call.

When the phone rang, he picked it up and waited. Dead air. It was as if no one was on the other end of the line. Steele waited patiently. Finally, someone said, "Yes?"

"I need to speak to the director."

"The director? I'm afraid you have the wrong number, sir." Steele recognized that voice. It was Ruth, her pleasant voice as calm and patient as always.

"Hello Ruth. It's Drew Steele. I need to talk to him. Priority."

"Well, hello, Mr. Steele. We haven't heard from you for a while. Are you fully recovered?"

"Yes. How are you, Ruth? How are things back there on your side of the country?"

"I'm fine, but as for the weather, well, you know what it's like this time of year in D.C. We don't all get to live in sunny California. You sure this is a priority call?"

"Yes, it's regarding operation Hopeful Horizons."

"Just a moment, I'll see if the director is free."

After a short wait filled with soft elevator music, Ruth came back to say she would connect him now.

"Hello, Steele, how's the legs?" The Director's voice was friendly, but reserved, as usual.

"Much better, sir, but I have some disturbing news. Recently, two different sources knew I had been in Iraq."

"Well, that may not be all that surprising. There's been a hoard of reporters asking about private contractors lately. And there was that documentary on PBS about who's really fighting the war over there."

"This sounded like they had specific information. They knew I'd been stationed in Baghdad."

"You want us to check it out?"

"I think you'd better. I didn't want to bother you with this until I had something more definite, but now it looks like there may have been a leak about the Hopeful Horizons operation. The Golden Palace Casino in Las Vegas has recently been taken over by a group known as the Omnivexx Corporation. They knew I had been in Iraq and that I'd been injured."

"Are you getting all this, Ruth?"

"Yes, sir."

"But there's a bigger problem," continued Steele. "Before I went to Afghanistan, I was involved in a case that put a man named Furtado in prison. A Mexican drug importer. He's out of prison now. He also knew I had been in Baghdad. He thinks I was assigned to the U.S. embassy in Baghdad, but he referred to what we were doing there as 'chasing after poppy growers.'"

"Well, at least the cover story about you being attached to the embassy is still working. But I see what you mean. No one outside of the operation should know about your undercover work inside the al-Qaeda drug supply network. That operation was on a need-to-know basis."

"It was, but don't forget the Iraqi military insisted on knowing the details before they would approve the operation."

"So you think that's where the leak was? Baghdad? What about Afghanistan?"

"No one in Afghanistan knew I was working undercover there. As far as the Afghani government knew, I was just another foolhardy journalist digging for stories. And Furtado only seemed to know about Iraq."

"You think the leak came from somebody in the Iraq government."

"Most likely. And they'd have to be fairly high up. Not many knew about the Hopeful Horizons operation."

"Hopeful Horizons. Where do they come up with these names? Sounds like a senior rest home or something. All right, we'll check it out. If there was a leak, by now al-Qaeda will know who you are. We'll have to bring you in."

"I'm not willing to live like that, sir."

"But, Steele, if al-Qaeda knows it was you that penetrated their drug-supply operation, they'll go after you hard. Sooner or later, they'll find you. We can't protect you if you stay out in the open."

"I know that, sir, but this man Furtado may have the answer. If he has some kind of connection with al-Qaeda, I may be able to find out who his contacts are."

"Why would al-Qaeda get involved with a Mexican? He's probably a Catholic, isn't he?"

"I don't know anything about his religion, but that may not matter to whoever is running al-Qaeda's heroin operation. The ones I met in Afghanistan were less concerned about ideology than with profits. They were not really part of al-Qaeda, but they were willing to work with anybody who had worldwide distribution resources. Let me tell you about Furtado. He's been importing heroin into the United States for years and he's become one of the biggest distributors in the West. Business is business, and in the heroin business, the U.S. is the market. Al-Qaeda may have begun working with the Afghan poppy farmers specifically because they wanted to import heroin into the United States. To prove how corrupt American morals are. But now it's starting to provide them with much-needed funds for their terrorist operations. If they were trying to find existing U.S. importers to work with, Furtado would show up on their list."

"Do you want this Furtado eliminated?"

"He's involved in a couple of murders here. If I can prove it, he'll be in prison for life. But first, I'll try to find out what his connection to Afghanistan or Iraq is."

"You know where to find him?"

"He'll find me."

"That sounds ominous. But it's up to you. We'll check out potential leaks in Baghdad and let you use your own discretion with regard to this Furtado character. In truth, we'd prefer that you take care of him. Such things are best dealt with . . . shall we say, on the local level. We are, after all, merely an information resource."

Steele had heard that joke many times, but this time he was in no mood to leave it at that. "Yes, sir, but speaking of information, there may be some very useful information here in California. Tell your Southern California operatives that Furtado has a bank of powerful computers running inside Crueltown. I suspect they're used to run his drug operation, now that they've gone international."

"Crueltown? What's that?"

"It's a sort of no-mans land between police enforcement districts.

Your people here know what it is, and where it is. If Furtado has a connection to al-Qaeda, those computers in his Crueltown hideout may hold the answer. I have a feeling your specialists would find a great deal of useful information there."

"Are those computers well guarded? In this . . . Crueltown place."

"Not really. I don't think Furtado has more than a handful of local thugs with him. There are a lot of other people inside Crueltown, homeless mostly, and undocumented farm workers, and a few small-time hustlers, but I expect they would all scatter as soon as your men went in."

"Now, Steele, you know it's not that easy to assemble a strike force on such . . . speculation."

"It's up to you, sir. But cleaning out Crueltown would also be a great help to our local law enforcement here. Crueltown is a real thorn in their sides, and . . . well, as I said, your local people will know about it."

There was a silence on the line. Finally, the director said, "All right, I'll see what I can do. Do we have a secure phone number to get back to you?"

"Yes, the number I'm calling from now is secure. Ruth has it. She also has my cell number, but don't use that one, even for non-secure calls. Furtado's men took my cell phone away from me earlier tonight."

"I'll bet there's an interesting story behind that. The next time I'm out in California, we should have lunch. You can tell me all about your latest near-death experiences."

"I'll look forward to that lunch, sir."

After he hung up, Steele sat there mulling over the director's response. He didn't seem too surprised that the Hopeful Horizons operation had been compromised. He must already have suspected there was a leak. He'd blamed it on the press, but Steele was sure that wasn't the source. Either al-Qaeda had penetrated the Hopeful Horizons team in Afghanistan, which wasn't likely, or someone in the Iraqi military had gone over to the other side, which was quite likely. The real question was how such information could have trickled down to a local drug dealer like Furtado? Furtado had said somebody wanted to get their hands on "Mister Drew Steele." Had al-Qaeda put a large reward on his head? Normally, in such situations, al-Qaeda wouldn't care whether the head was attached to a body or not, but in this case it was clear Furtado was supposed to turn Mister Drew Steele over alive. It could only mean they wanted to question him before they killed him. Then they would remove his head and put it on display as a further warning to anyone who might try to disrupt their drug-supply chain. The possibility of being beheaded was a given among the members of the Hopeful Horizons team. Steele remembered the day two members of the team, two of the younger, crazier men, had gone to a local Baghdad tattoo parlor to have dotted lines tattooed around their necks along with the words "Cut Here." Over beers that night, they showed off their new tattoos. They laughingly suggested that Steele, as the team leader, should also have it done. Steele had replied that he was sure al-Qaeda wouldn't need an instruction manual. That got a good laugh out of the men. Sadly, those two were in the Humvee along with Steele. They hadn't survived the blast. Their bodies were shipped home, heads still attached, victims of roadside bombs, not an al-Qaeda executioner's sword. As usual, their deaths were recorded as "industrial accidents," but Steele couldn't help but wonder what the employees of the mortuaries back home thought of those strange dotted neck tattoos that kept turning up on the necks of deceased industrial accident victims.

# Chapter 23

$S$teele's thoughts were interrupted by the doorbell.

He went down and looked through the peephole. It was the pizza guy. He opened the door and paid the young fellow. He asked him to stop by the pool on his way out to tell Rudd his supper was here.

A few minutes later, Rudd arrived, complaining about how unfriendly the girls at the pool were. He tucked a napkin under his chin and parked himself in front of the TV with his pizza, grumbling about how small so-called extra-large pizzas were these days.

Steele went back up to his office to check his email. The first email on the list was from the information search agency. They said they had tracked down an old newspaper story about the murder of a man named Vinelli in Chicago. The crime had never been solved and the police report had been filed as inactive, under the label "Probable Organized Crime Reprisal."

Steele forwarded the report to Monroe.

As he scanned through the rest of his email, his business cell phone rang. He didn't recognize the number, but picked it up anyway. "Yes?"

"Mr. Steele? This is Rita Culp."

She sounded worried, maybe even scared. "What can I do for you, Mrs. Culp?"

"I think I may need . . . I mean, you said I should call you if anything happened."

"Is it about your son, Craig?"

It took several seconds before she answered. "Yes. Have you seen him?"

"I talked to him earlier today. Has he been in touch with you?"

Another pause. "Not since . . . what I mean is, if I wanted to hire you, would you help me with something?"

"Mrs. Culp, if Craig has been in touch with you, you'd better tell me about it. I think he may be in danger."

"Really? Why do you say that?"

"What did he tell you, Mrs. Culp?"

"Well, he didn't say there was anything wrong . . . exactly, but he sounded worried."

"Did he say anything about your husband's car?"

"Yes, how did you know?"

"Just tell me what he said."

"He said the strangest thing. He said Ken's car was in the parking lot, right there at the poker club where he works. I tried to get him to tell me why it was there, but he said he'd explain later. He wanted to know if Ken had a spare key hidden anywhere in his car. I told him Ken used to keep one under the car somewhere, but I wasn't sure where."

"He said he'd find it, and he'd bring it back to me when he could. Then he asked me for money. He said he needed a lot of money, and fast."

"Did he say why he needed the money?"

"No. I said I would try to borrow some, and then I said I'd fly down there and bring it to him. But he said no, that I was not to come back to LA no matter what happened. I did manage to borrow some money, from a . . . friend, but when I called the casino they said he'd gone home sick. I've been calling his apartment, but he doesn't answer. I'm worried, Mr. Steele. I'd hire you to find him if you think you can."

"I doubt I could find him, but I'll see what I can do. What's his address?"

"Well, actually, I don't know where he lives. He never did tell me. He says he moves a lot, but I know he just doesn't want me to tell me. I guess he doesn't want me dropping in to see him unexpectedly. He's always been like that, secretive. But I understand, he wants to do things his own way now with no help from . . . the family."

"Mrs. Culp, I think he's has gone into hiding. Hopefully, somewhere where nobody will be able to find him, not even me."

"Hiding? But why would he need to hide?"

"Remember those men who chased us that night?"

There was a long silence. Then, "Do you think they're after him now?"

"It seems likely. But Craig seems to me to be a pretty smart guy. I suspect he has a good place to hide."

There was another long silence before she responded. "You're scaring me, Mr. Steele. Why would they want to hurt him? Has he done something wrong?"

"You tell me,. Mrs. Culp.

There was a pause before she said, "I don't know. I don't understand anything. I just wanted to help my son. I wanted him to come home, to come to Ken's funeral. Now I don't even know where he is."

"Mrs. Culp, I'll try to help him if I can. But you must tell me the truth. You must tell me why your husband stole money from the casino. Why did he need money so badly?"

"I already told you, I have no idea."

"But you do, Mrs. Culp. He wanted to bring your two sons back to the Golden Palace, didn't he? Was that your idea?"

Another silence, then, "No."

"No, it wasn't your idea, or no, you won't tell me?"

"It doesn't matter anymore. He's going to be buried tomorrow afternoon."

"It might matter to your son. It might matter very much to Craig."

"Why do you say that?"

"You know why, Mrs. Culp. Your husband came to Craig to get money, didn't he? Craig said he'd help him, but in the end it caused your husband's death."

"You don't know that."

"I think I do. And I think you do too. Your husband needed money badly. He came to Craig to help him get it. Maybe Craig had gotten himself involved with the wrong kind of people. Maybe it was something that had to do with drugs."

"Craig wouldn't do that. He wouldn't have had anything to do with illegal drugs."

"You said yourself he was secretive, and that he wouldn't even tell you where he lived. Why do you think that was? I suspect Craig introduced your husband to the people he was involved with, and they killed him."

"Craig wouldn't have done anything like that."

"The evidence says he did. You saw yourself what lengths those people were willing to go to, that night when they chased us, shot at us. You must see that your son is in grave danger. If I'm going to be able to help him, you have to tell me what this is all about."

For a long moment, there was no response. Then she began: "It started a long time ago. In Chicago." Her voice was quiet and shaky, but then it got stronger. "I married one of the Vinelli boys. His family had a bit of a bad reputation, but what did I know? I was right out of high school and he had the coolest car around. He had money. We did fun things. He bought me expensive things. We were only married for a few years before he was killed, shot dead, right on one of Chicago's busiest streets. After he died, his family was very nice to me, offered to take care of me. But they wanted to run my life, wouldn't let me see anybody. They paid for my house, but they wouldn't let me go out of it. They said my life was in danger. One day I'd had enough of them, so I packed up my two boys in the middle of the night and moved us to Las Vegas. I got a job at the Golden Palace. I met Ken soon after I got there."

"I notice your two sons kept the Vinelli name. Wasn't Ken willing to adopt them?"

"Oh, yes, he wanted to, but I . . . wouldn't let him. You see, the Vinelli family kept tabs on me. Frank kept on showing up at the casino and--"

"Is that the Frank I met at the mortuary?"

"Yes, he's my first husband's brother. He's the senior Vinelli now and he says he's keeping a promise the family made to me after my first husband was killed. He says my two boys are Vinellis and a Vinelli will always be taken care of. Over the years, he's done some wonderful things for the boys."

I'm surprised Ken would allow that."

"Ken didn't like it very much, but the Vinellis can be very persuasive. When Craig broke his arm badly and needed an expensive operation to get it fixed right, they had him flown to a wonderful clinic back in Chicago. They had to redo the orthopedic surgery on his arm twice, and the Vinellis paid for it all. Ken wasn't happy about their interference, but we kept on having problems we couldn't pay for. Like the time James needed a very expensive tooth implant. They paid for that too. And there was that wonderful summer camp back in Minnesota. The boys loved going there every summer. Ken wanted what was best for the boys, so he kept quiet. But I could tell he wasn't happy about it. He thought the Vinellis were trying to keep the boys from caring about him, trying stop them from . . . loving him. Maybe he was right."

"So was that why your husband needed money? Something for the boys? Was he trying to outdo the Vinellis?"

"In a way. As it turned out, Frank was up to something. He wasn't just coming out to Las Vegas to visit the boys, he was interested in the casino. You see, the Vinellis were involved with a casino back in Atlantic City so when the Golden Palace went into bankruptcy, they decided to make a bid for it."

Suddenly, an important piece of the puzzle fell into place for Steele. "Are the Vinellis involved with the Omnivexx Corporation."

"Involved? I'm pretty sure they *are* the Omnivexx Corporation. They don't run any of the day-to-day operations, but I know they make all the important decisions behind the scenes. I really don't know much more than that. Frank says it's family business and he can't talk about it. My first husband didn't like to talk about what he called 'family business' either. That's the way it is with the Vinellis. The men take care of the business, and the women are supposed to stay home and have kids."

"I think I'm beginning to understand," said Steele. "Your husband resented very much the Vinellis taking over the casino. Becoming his boss, as it were."

"He surely did. At first it seemed like he was going to just keep quiet, like he always did, for the sake of the boys. But they made a lot of changes at the casino, fired a lot of people, and Craig started making trouble about it. Frank came to me and told me to put a muzzle on Craig. That's exactly how he said it. He said a Vinelli is supposed to keep quiet and leave the business decisions to the elders of the family. Well, Craig wasn't about to go along with that. He even started talking to the other employees about starting a union. Frank went to Ken and told him he'd better keep Craig quiet or else. Ken tried to calm Craig down, he really did, but Craig was drinking a lot at that time and wasn't about to keep his mouth shut. When they finally fired Craig, and then later, James too, Ken got really upset about it. Frank told him it was his own fault, that he should have kept the boys quiet, that the boys should have been grateful after everything the family had done for them."

"So your husband decided to get back at them."

"I guess so. At first he just went quiet. He went to work every day and kept his mouth shut. He'd come home at night and lock himself in his study. I knew he was up to something, but he wouldn't talk to me about it. Finally, I demanded to know what was going on. He broke down and cried. He admitted he'd been doing things on his own to get the boys back their jobs. He said he knew the Vinellis had been kind to me and to my boys, but he couldn't take it any more. He said he'd been to see the bankruptcy judge about leading a management takeover of the casino. He said the Omnivexx takeover proposal would only be approved if they could get through all the Nevada state gaming requirements. He said he was going to prove to the judge that the Vinellis were into illegal activity, and had been for many years. The judge said to bring him proof and he would look into it. But the judge said even if the Omnivexx bid was disqualified, Ken's bid for the casino would not be taken seriously unless he could show he had significant money behind him. Ken said he'd get it, somehow."

"So that's why your husband needed money so badly. Not only to lead a buyout of the casino, but to get rid of the Vinelli's influence. To show he could take care of the boys himself."

"Yes. After he admitted to me what he was planning, he talked about nothing else. I'm afraid I didn't handle it very well. I told him he was acting crazy, that he should just keep quiet and hang on to his job until he hit retirement age. He would have had a good pension. I told him the boys had found other jobs and were probably better off away from the situation."

"But he wouldn't let it go."

"No, he wouldn't. He stopped talking to me about it, but I knew he was still up to something. He got very sullen. I'm surprised nobody at the casino noticed how he was acting."

"That must have been when he started stealing money from the casino."

"I . . . guess so. At first I couldn't believe it when you told me he's done that. It was so unlike him. But now I realize he must have hated the Vinellis so much he would have done anything to get back at them."

"Not only was he willing to steal from them, but in order to carry out his plan, he must have also been willing to take terrible chances to raise the money it required."

"That's the part that *was* like him. When he got an idea in his head, he wasn't likely to let it go."

"He must have told Craig about his plan."

"I suppose he did. Maybe he thought Craig would want to get back at them too."

"Mrs. Culp, I have to ask you this. Do you think the Vinellis would try to hurt your husband? Could he have run away to LA because they threatened him?"

"I asked Frank that as soon as I found out Ken was dead. He swore they had nothing to do with it."

"Do you believe him?"

"He swore on the family name. The Vinellis take that sort of thing very seriously. He swore that he didn't even know where Ken had gone. They wanted very much to know. He said that's why they hired you to find him."

"But they may have threatened him. It would have put even more pressure on him."

"It's possible. I know that's how they used to do things back in Chicago. But Frank says the family is different now, that they are only involved in legitimate businesses."

Steele doubted that was true. What if the Vinellis knew Culp had gone to see the bankruptcy judge? The judge might have notified them that their petition to conduct gaming in the state of Nevada was in question. If so, Culp's actions had the potential to cost them dearly. But if the state was investigating them, they would be crazy to eliminate the person who'd told the judge about their past, especially in such a flagrant way. They never would have put that "Keep Out" message on Culp's forehead. That had to be Furtado's special little touch. Knowing how things were done in Chicago, Steele was sure that if the Vinellis had wanted to eliminate Culp, he would have just disappeared. No body would have ever been found.

"Are you still there, Mr. Steele?"

"Yes, I was just thinking. I understand why you had to keep silent until now. Thank you for telling me."

"If the Vinellis find out I told you all this, they will see me as disloyal. It could go hard on my sons. The family gets very upset about disloyalty."

"I understand. They won't find it out from me. You can be sure of that."

"And you'll try to help Craig?"

"I will. I'll call you if I find out anything about where he is."

After she hung up, Steele sat there thinking about what motivated people. As it turned out, Culp died because he wanted his stepsons to love him. He was willing to do just about anything to get their love. Steele thought about the autopsy report, about the terrible beating Culp had taken. Was it to protect Craig? If so, he had shown the depth of his love for the boys, right to the end.

"Hey, Steele, come here and have some of this pizza before it's all gone."

"No thanks."

Rudd got up and came to sit in the chair next to Steele's desk. "You never eat. No wonder you're so skinny."

"I guess so."

"Hmm, that was a distracted response. What are you thinking about?"

"Mrs. Culp called. Craig has disappeared."

"So he's made a run for it. Probably for the best if he doesn't want to end up with that 'Keep Out' message branded on his forehead."

"She told me some things that make me think Culp met Furtado through her son Craig."

"Is that right? So did Culp get involved in a drug deal?"

"I doubt it. Maybe one or more of Furtado's gang had been playing cards at the poker club. Craig may have done some business with them in the past, drugs, money laundering, something like that. He could have introduced Culp to Furtodo's men. When Culp said he was trying to raise money to buy a casino, they would have taken him to Furtado. It wouldn't have taken Furtado long to discovered Culp had accumulated a lot of cash."

"The money he stole from the casino."

"That's right. I suspect they killed him, trying to get him to tell them where it was."

"Do you think Craig has it?"

"Could be."

"Okay, that all makes sense, but why use his body to send a message to you?"

"Furtado's little game. When he found out I'd been hired to track Culp down, he saw it as a way to draw me in."

"So, Furtado didn't leave town after we flushed him out of Crueltown?"

"Do you think he was in that BMW that chased us?"

"It wouldn't be like Furtado to act out of control like that. But it was probably his plan to use Mrs. Culp to get to me."

"So he was calling the shots. Literally." Rudd grinned. "The shots. Get it?"

Steele ignored the joke. "He must really want to get to me. You'd have thought he would run right straight back to Mexico as soon as his lawyer got him out of prison, but he didn't. Something is keeping him here."

"Right, he's after you."

"Yes, but he could wait to do that. There must be something important happening right now."

"What?"

"I'm not sure. Something to do with drugs. A big deal of some kind."

Rudd squinted. "All right, Steele, what aren't you telling me?"

"I told you everything I know. It's just a feeling I got while I was talking to him. I think he's into something big, and that's what's keeping him here in LA. Furtado was a drug importer before he was in prison, one of the biggest. Now that he's out, I think he's trying to reestablish his business and his reputation. There's some kind of big drug deal coming down that will put him back in the center of the Western U.S. drug business."

"So where is he now? Inside Crueltown?"

"He may still be in there, but he'll have his guard up now. It would take a SWAT team to get him this time."

Pruet held up both hands. "No way. You saw what Pruett did. He was willing to stand by and let us get killed in there. In fact, I wouldn't be surprised if he got called on the carpet just for sending that helicopter out there. It could have indicated they had jurisdiction over the place."

Steele shrugged. "You're right. We'll just have to wait for his next move."

"And what will that be?"

"He went to a lot of trouble to get me. He'll try again."

# Chapter 24

*R*udd went back to the TV to finish the rest of his pizza.

Steele was just starting to read his latest email messages when the desk phone rang. He glanced at the calling number and saw that it was coming from his own cell phone, the one Furtado's men had taken away from him at Crueltown. Was Furtado calling to bait him again?

Steele picked up the receiver. "Hello, Furtado. Forget something?"

He heard Furtado's low chuckle. "Good evening, Steele. I didn't expect to find you at home yet. I thought you'd be out looking for bad guys."

"No, Furtado, I was just sitting here waiting for your call. What kept you?"

"Ah, glad to see you're still in good spirits, Steele. And I'm glad to hear that you're still safe and sound. I want you for myself."

"Anytime, Furtado. Just you and me. How about it? I'll meet you anywhere you say."

"All right, how about if you come here now. I'll be waiting for you."

"Fine. Just tell me where you are."

"I will, but first, I've got somebody here that wants to talk to you."

There was a brief moment of dead silence as if Furtado had put his hand over the phone. Then, "Hello, Mr. Steele. This is Jenny. I think I've made a big mistake. I--"

Furtado came back. "She's a real cute little number, isn't she, Steele? You ought to see what I'm looking at right now. She's not bad looking once you get her clothes off." His harsh laughter gradually turned into a coughing fit. When he recovered, he said, "I think she's too good for you, Steele. I may have to do something about that."

"Let her go, Furtado. She doesn't know anything."

"But she knows you, doesn't she? And now I know her. I've got her sitting right here on my lap. I can feel her tight little ass right through my pants. Nothing much to her tits though. I'm feeling them right now."

Steele heard a little shriek in the background, then men laughing.

"But you know, Steele, I think I'd like her better if she had more to her. Without her clothes on she's kind of skinny, like a little girl and I'm not into that kind of thing. But a couple of the older guys here are. You want me to turn her over to them?"

"Get to your point, Furtado."

"The point is, if you don't get your butt over here pretty quick there won't be much left of her for you."

"Tell me where you are."

"I'm at the harbor."

"The harbor's a big place."

"Truck-loading gate six. I'll have somebody meet you there. Come alone or I'm afraid these big boys might split your little Jenny wide open. From the way they're looking at her I can tell they're . . . shall we say, impatient to get started."

"Tell them if they touch her I'll find them. They will be very, very sorry."

"Oh, they're really scared. That's why they're laughing."

"Does that mean you have me on speaker phone? Listen up, all of you. I only want Furtado. If you have any semblance of intelligence left, you should get out of there fast while you still can. Do not touch her. I'm warning you. I have resources you can't imagine. Hurt her and we will hunt you down."

"Nice try, Steele. But they're still laughing. I think their baser instincts are driving them. More powerful even than fear, I expect. As I said to you earlier when we had our talk out at Crueltown, men can be such animals."

"Are you really at the harbor, Furtado?"

"Would I lie to you?"

"I could have the harbor surrounded right now."

"But you won't, will you? Your little girl friend's life depends on it."

"She's not my girl friend. I hardly know her."

"Come now, Steele, you can't expect me to fall for that one. She called your cell phone to invite you over for a cozy supper, just the two of you. Said you'd promised to come over tonight to look at her car. Tell you what, Steele, get here within a half hour and I may be able to hold them off. I might even let her put her clothes back on."

"I'll be right there."

"Good, good. Looking forward to seeing you again."

The line went dead. Steele looked up Pruett's number and punched it in.

"Yeah?"

"Captain, this is Steele. I just got a call from Furtado. I'm going to meet him now."

"You're going to meet him? Are you crazy?"

"He has a hostage. A young woman."

"Damn! Okay, I'll call the hostage negotiator. Where shall I meet you?"

"I don't think Furtado would be willing to negotiate with anybody but me. It's me he wants. I don't know why."

"Is he alone?"

"He's never alone. He always has his guards with him."

"Then we're talking SWAT."

"That's up to you. But let me go in first and talk to him."

"Go in where?"

"I can't tell you yet. The hostage's life depends on my cooperation. If I refuse to go, he'll have no more use for her. And I'm sure he has an escape plan."

"Don't do it, Steele, he'll just kill you."

"For some reason, he needs me alive. I'll tell him I will cooperate, but only after he lets the hostage go. After I go in, I'll keep an open line to Rudd. Once the hostage is free, he'll tell you where I am so you can send in the troops to rescue me."

"Now just a damn minute, Steele. You're interfering in a police operation. This is a double-murder case. I've warned you before about--"

"Keep this line free, Captain. If you want to move some men into place, have them assemble at Crueltown."

"Crueltown? Is that where he's holding her? You know I can't go in there."

"He's not in there. I just don't want him running back there."

"So he's near there? Come on, Steele, you can't do this alone. Just tell me where he--"

Steele hung up the phone and went to his file cabinet. He unlocked it and took out another radio receiver and tested it by speaking into the transmitter hidden in his collar. He also took out a sub-compact .22LR Beretta automatic and a .25 silver pen gun. He put the pen gun in his shirt pocket. Then he hurried downstairs. "Let's go, Rudd."

Rudd looked up from his chair in front of the TV. "Where are we going this time. I'm not done eating yet." He had an assortment of food lined up on the coffee table. It looked like he had cleaned out the entire refrigerator.

"It's Furtado. We'll have to take your car. Hurry!"

Rudd grabbed two apples and stuffed them into his pockets. He jumped up and followed Steele out the door. "Damn it, Steele, I never get to sit down and eat like a regular person. Where we going now?"

"Furtado has Jenny. At the harbor."

"He has Jenny? Oh, no. But how?"

"Never mind how, he's using her to get me to come to him. We've got to hurry."

"But you can't go. He'll kill you."

"You saved me last time. Don't want to do it again?" He handed the automatic to Rudd. "Put this in your pocket."

"Oh no, not again."

# Chapter 25

*O*n the way to the harbor, Steele handed the radio receiver to Rudd and laid out his plan. "We'll do it just like we did before. When we get to the harbor, I'm going to get out at truck gate six. Do a U-turn and go back to Harbor Boulevard. Drive south to Harbor Village. There are a couple of boat rental places there. Rent the fastest boat you can get. Tell them you just want to tour the harbor for a few hours. Use the radio's earpiece. Listen to everything I say, just like you did when I went into Crueltown. Take the rental boat into the main ship channel and follow it until you see the sign for Unloading Dock Six. There are ladders up to the pier. Moor the boat next to one of those ladders and wait."

'Wait for what?"

"As before, listen to what's going on. If I say the words, 'I've already got the harbor surrounded,' call Pruett and tell him to do exactly that. Surround the harbor. Pruett will have his men waiting close by, over near Crueltown."

"Got it. I wait for the signal and then call in Pruett."

"Tell him to have his men close off all of the ways in and out of the harbor area."

"Okay, but why am I renting a speedboat?"

"In case Furtado tries to get away by boat."

"Oh, right. Uh, and if he does, what am I supposed to do? Shoot him?"

"No. Do not let him see you under any circumstances. If he gets into a boat, just follow him. At a safe distance. Report to Pruett where he's going. He'll send the Coast Guard after him."

"I get it. Keep my head down and wait. Follow Furtado if he tries to make a run for it"

"Exactly. But don't get too close."

Steele directed Rudd to drive over the bridge and out onto Terminal Island. They followed the arrows to the truck-loading gates. Rudd pulled into the right-hand truck lane and inched along in the midst of the empty flat-bed trucks.

Finally, Steele saw the sign for Gate Six ahead. "Pull over here. I'll walk the rest of the way."

Rudd pulled over and stopped. "Are you sure about this? What if they--"

"No time to talk. Furtado won't want to stay in one place very long. I've got to get in there."

"All right, but I've got a bad feeling about this."

Steele got out and leaned back into the car's open window. "Now, don't call Pruett until I say so. I may be able to persuade Furtado to let Jenny go if I agree to cooperate. If he sends her out, I'll tell you. Then you can call in Pruett to pick her up."

Rudd frowned. "If you say so."

Steele held out his hand. "If this doesn't turn out well, it's not your fault. You've already done more than anybody else would have. I appreciate it."

Rudd shook his hand, but wouldn't let go. "Thanks for saying that, but you know I'm scared to death about this. What if you're wrong about Furtado? Maybe he just wants to kill you."

"He won't kill me without talking about it first. He loves to hear himself talk. But if you hear his gun go off, it'll be time to call Pruett."

"Damn it, Steele, this is no time for joking. You're always doing crazy things like this. One of these times, you won't come out again."

Steele smiled at him. "Maybe you're right. Maybe you should go in and I'll go rent the boat."

Rudd hesitated, looking very serious. "If that's what you need me to do. Maybe I should. I could negotiate with him, find out what he wants."

Steele patted his friend's arm. "I need you to go rent that boat. As quick as you can. That's the best thing you can do to help me."

Steele stayed by the side of the road and watched Rudd turn around and head back for San Pedro. Then he hurried along next to the trucks until he got to the gate. He saw a heavy-set man with a shaved head standing outside the fence smoking a cigarette. He whispered into the hidden microphone: "Big man waiting at the gate. Shaved head."

As Steele approached, the man called out over the noise of the trucks, "You Steele?"

"That's right."

"Come with me. And keep your damn hands out of your pockets."

Steele did as he was told and they walked to the guard gate.

The bald man showed a pass and said, "He's with me."

The guard hardly glanced at them. He was busy waving the next truck forward.

The bald man got close behind Steele, his hand in his jacket pocket. "Just walk. I'll be right behind you."

Steele walked past the long line of idling flat-bed semis until the man told him to turn right into a parking lot that was filled with rows and rows of parked semi trailers. The sign said, "Long-Term Storage."

Steele pointed at one of the trailers and said, "They've got a lot of truck trailers parked in this long-term storage lot."

"Shut up. Why are you walking so slow, something the matter with your damn legs? If you're trying to pull something . . "

"I've got a hurt leg. I'm going as fast as I can."

"Well, try harder. And keep walking until I say stop. I know you have a gun hidden on you somewhere so don't make any sudden moves. I'll blow your damn head off, no matter what the boss says."

Steele turned to look back at him. "Is the girl all right?"

"Shut up. Just keep walking."

Steele continued on until the man told him to stop next to one of the larger trailers. It looked old and rust-streaked, but the tires were brand new. Faded letters on the side said "F-M Enterprises."

The man banged on the back doors and they opened a crack. The barrel of a shotgun poked out and somebody inside said, "It's him."

"Let him in." Steele recognized that voice. It was Furtado.

The creaking double doors swung partly open. The man with the shotgun turned out to be Carl, the big man Steele had punched earlier that night. Carl stuck the shotgun in Steele's face. "I ought blast ya."

"Hello, Carl," said Steele, smiling. "How's the headache?"

"Knock that off, Carl," said Furtado. "Get outside and keep

watch."

Carl lowered the shotgun and jumped down next to Steele. He swung an elbow toward Steele's midsection, but Steele saw it coming and moved aside. "Kind of slow tonight, aren't you Carl?"

"Carl!" yelled Furtado.

Carl stuck his face close to Steele's, showing his ragged teeth. "Damn stupid cripple, he snarled. "My turn will come. Just you wait."

"Carl, shut up and send him in here."

Carl stepped back and gestured with the shotgun for Steele to get in.

Painfully, Steele managed to climb up into the truck and somebody closed the door behind him. There was a dim overhead light on and Furtado was sitting on a plastic lawn chair in the middle of the trailer. He was casually holding a large automatic, pointing it more or less at Steele's feet. Two Hispanic-looking men stood against one wall. Both held revolvers and they kept them pointed at Steele.

"All right, Furtado," said Steele, "where is she?"

In response, Steele heard a muffled cry from the dark recesses further back in the truck.

Furtado laughed and clicked on a flashlight. He swung it to spotlight Jenny, sitting naked in the corner. In response to the light, she drew her knees up in front of herself and turned sideways. She was tied and gagged.

Steele moved toward her, but Furtado said, "Uh uh, stay right where you are. Get back against that wall and sit down. If you come any closer, I'll shoot your damn legs right out from under you. They said they wanted you alive, but since you're already a cripple, I don't think they'd mind if I finished the job on your legs."

Steele moved back toward the wall, but he didn't sit down "I'm here, aren't I? Let her go."

Furtado smiled. "But I can't just let a pretty young thing like that walk out of here completely naked, can I? It's getting a bit chilly out there."

"Where are her clothes?"

"Who knows? Maybe some of the boys have them. Maybe they're out there sniffing her panties."

"Then let me at least put my jacket over her."

"Aw, how sweet. Throw it to me."

Steele took off his jacket and tossed it to Futado who searched the pockets. He also felt along the lining, but apparently didn't feel the tiny transmitter in the padded shoulder because he turned and threw the jacket to Jenny. She used her feet to drag it to her and managed to get it up in front of herself.

"What are you up to, Furtado?" said Steele. "Why are you hiding here in this rusty old F-M Enterprises truck?"

"Why did you say that? Now I know you've got a wire on you. Search him boys. Feel for a transmitter hidden in his clothes."

The two men came forward. One of them stuck a gun in his ribs while the other did a thorough job of searching him. Finally, the man pulled up his left pant leg. "Hey, boss, he's got some kind of fake foot stuck to the bottom of his leg. And look at this, a little pistol attached to it." He removed the automatic and held it up for Furtado to see.

"Give it to me. And tie his hands behind him."

The man handed the gun to Furtado and took out some rough twine that he used it to bind Steele's wrists.

"Sit him down," commanded Furtado.

The two men forced Steele to sit down against the wall of the truck. They stayed close, one on each side of him.

Furtado looked at the automatic. "Well, well. A little hidey gun. You haven't changed at all, have you, Steele? But no wire? I'd have sworn you were talking to somebody. I hope you aren't planning anything foolish. I *will* kill your little girl friend, you know, and you too, if I have to. I'm not going back to that prison."

"Let's have it, Furtado, why did you bring me here?"

"Why, to talk to you. I wanted so much to continue our stimulating conversation of earlier this evening. Before we were so rudely interrupted. Who was that ill-mannered person who took a shot at me?"

"I didn't come here to talk. You said if I came you'd let the girl go."

"And I will. Eventually. The problem with you, Steele, is you're too impatient. Is that why they want you? Did you do something rash?"

"Why don't you just tell me what you're talking about? Who wants me?"

"I suspect you know very well who . . . Uh, just a moment." He turned to the two guards. "You two men can wait outside. It shouldn't be long."

The two men left the trailer without a word.

After they'd closed the creaking double doors, Furtado turned back to Steele. "Well, now, what did you go and do, Steele? What did you do that got somebody so upset with you they'd pay a half million bucks just to get their hands on you?"

"So that's it," said Steele. "A lot of money for little old me. I guess you didn't want to say how much it was in front of your men. Don't trust them, eh? It's so hard to get good help these days."

Furtado nodded thoughtfully. "They've been reliable, for the most part. But five hundred thousand dollars is more money than they will ever see in their whole lives. Might be a little too tempting. You know, times are hard for men like them."

"What? The crime business in the doldrums these days?"

Furtado shook the pistol at Steele. "What would you know about hard times? Like most Americans, you were . . . how do they say it? Born with a silver spoon in your mouth. People like you don't have a clue how good you have it."

Steele chuckled and shook his head. "Here we go. Time for the sad poor-me story."

"That comment proves people like you know nothing about what it's like for the rest of us. My ma worked for you people, worked her ass off. She found a job as a nanny and took good care of their kids until somebody turned her in as an illegal. The cops kicked her down a flight of stairs, even though she was pregnant with me. It could of killed me, should have killed me, but I was too tough. They threw her in the back of a van and dumped her back on the streets of Tijuana along with a bunch of wetbacks, as you people call us. She was stuck there with no money and nobody to protect her. She ended up in a cardboard shack out next to the dump. You can't imagine what she went through out there. I was just a little kid, but I remember. I remember the men who came in the night. I kept a sharp knife under my dirty old mattress in case they came at me. At night, when everybody else was sleeping, I stayed awake and sharpened that knife, waiting for the chance to use it."

Furtado stopped talking and stared at the floor.

Steele watched him closely, keeping very still while he worked on loosening the twine that was tight around his wrists. "That's a really sad story, Furtado. And you told it so well. I especially like the knife part. A nice touch. Proves you had no choice but to go into a life of crime. But why are you whiling away the time telling me stories? We're waiting for somebody, aren't we? Who is it?"

Furtado looked up at him. "They'll be here soon. Then I'm afraid it's the end for you. Too bad I won't get to do the job myself, but their money is good so I'll have to hand you over. They promised me you won't die easily."

"And when they come for me, you'll let Jenny go? I'll cooperate with them if you let her go."

"I'll think about it. But maybe she's taken a fancy to me. After those Arabs chop off your head, she'll be needing a new boyfriend."

"Think she'll want to go back to the Tijuana slums with you?"

"Tijuana slums. Listen, Steele, I could buy and sell you any day of the week. I've got a fancier house in San Diego than you could ever imagine having. Five bedrooms. Three full bathrooms plus a spa room. Swimming pool in back. My dear old ma takes a swim in it every morning."

"When they catch you, they'll send her right back to Mexico. I'm afraid she'll have to give up her morning swim. Or do they have a pool at that Tijuana dump?"

"She'll be swimming in that pool as long as she lives. I've made sure of that. She's a legal citizen of this country, just like I am. You see, my old lady learned something working for you rich people. She learned if you are born in this country, you get to be a citizen. She waited down there in Tijuana until she was way into her ninth month and then she snuck back across the border. Walked all night with me in her belly. She hid out in a migrant worker's camp until her water broke, then she had one of the field hands drive her to a big San Diego hospital. Told them she was legal, but forgot her papers in the panic to get to the hospital. They probably knew what she was up to, but what could they do? I was already halfway out of her. After I was born, they sent her right back to Tijuana. She had me wrapped up in a little blue blanket the ladies at the hospital gave her. We lived like animals down there in Mexico, but she never let go of my US of A birth certificate. Kept it hidden away. When I was twelve I took it out of her secret hiding place. I put it in my pocket and lit out. Made it across the border and worked in the fields of your country like a grown-up man. Whenever the INS raided the fields, I pulled out that paper. They usually beat the shit out of me, but in the end they had to let me go. I was legal and there was nothing they could do about it. As soon as I got my hands on some real money, I paid to bring her up here too. Cost me plenty, but now she's as legal as anybody."

"Sounds like you didn't buy her citizenship with the money you made picking strawberries. Apparently you found that crime paid better than working stooped over in the sun all day."

Furtado nodded, not smiling. "Stoop work. What would you know about that? You can judge me all you want, Steele, but I'd of liked to see you make it like I did. I made it on my own, using my own brain." He touched the side of his head with the barrel of his gun.

Steele shook his head. "It's not hard to make it selling heroin to kids in Watts."

"Harder than you think. When you begin to make the real money, there's always somebody who wants to take it away from you."

"Come one, Furtado. You said we didn't have much time, so let me in on it. Why did you kill Culp? You're dying to tell me. Was he threatening to take away your hard-earned money?"

"That dumb old guy? He was a nothing. Came to us with some hair-brained plan to buy some washed-up old casino in Vegas. Wanted to borrow money. What an idiot. The boys dragged him in to see me. Said they'd found a bunch of cash on him, but he wouldn't say where he got it. I told them to get rid of him. But the boys wouldn't give up and they finally persuaded him to admit he stole the money from the casino where he worked. It took some time, but they even got him to say who was in it with him. Some dumb kid who'd been covering up for him at the casino. I called up the kid. Told him I was Culp's son calling from LA. That's when he told me the casino had hired you to look for Culp. All of a sudden, I knew it was fate. I had the very man you were looking for, the perfect way to get you to come to me."

"That's when you killed Culp. To send your little message to me."

"Naw. I wouldn't have bothered. Any more than I'd bother to swat a pesky fly. If you want to know the truth, I could have used him better alive. I was still deciding how to use him to get to you when apparently the old guy did something stupid and one of the boys shot him. I don't know what he did. Pissed somebody off I guess, so they offed him. I wasn't there when it happened, but seeing the old guy lying there dead on the floor gave me an idea of how to send a clue to the great detective, a way to draw you in like a spider does to a fly."

"Then you had your men dump his body at Crueltown with that message on his forehead. But why leave him in a car? That was careless."

"You're right. It was careless. Damn sloppy. Like you said before, it's hard to get good help these days. I wanted to make sure they found the body right away so you'd hear about it from your fat reporter friend. Some stoned-out kid we'd been using as a burro said he'd do it if we'd give him some free fixes. He said he knew a car he could steal. I told him to take the body out to Crueltown and dump it in the middle of the road. But the kid was a complete idiot. He was tryin' to get the big old guy out of the car's trunk when he saw somebody coming. He panicked and ran inside Crueltown. Can you imagine it? You've got a body in the trunk of your car with a bullet hole in his head and you run off leaving the trunk open. Dumb."

"I assumed something like that had happened. But what about Gary, the kid from the casino? How did you get him to come to LA?"

"You're just full of questions, aren't you, Steele? Well, since you're not going to be around much longer, I'll tell you. Can't let you get your head chopped off with it still full of questions, can we? The boys thought the kid might have a bunch of that stolen money stashed away. They even talked about going to Vegas to find him. I told them it was a waste of time, but then I got worried the stupid kid would get caught and tell the cops about the phone call he'd got from Culp's son so I called him back and convinced him I could help him get away. I told him to bring all the money he could get his hands on and meet me in LA. I said I'd get him on a boat to Costa Rica."

"Then you killed him just to send me another message."

"And it worked, didn't it? I knew those panties in his stomach would bring you in. You fell for it, like a big fat fish going for a minnow. You see, I know you, Steele. I know what makes you tick. You think you--" He stopped in mid-sentence when somebody opened the trailer's doors. He swung the pistol in that direction, but lowered it when he saw it was Carl.

"Hey, boss, check out this guy. He was tryin' to sneak up on us." Carl pushed Rudd up into the truck.

"Well, look who we have here," said Furtado. "It's Rudd, the ace reporter."

"Sorry, Steele," said Rudd, hanging his head. "I thought you were in trouble so I--"

Steele silenced him with a raised hand.

"Did you search him?" asked Furtado.

"Yeah," said Carl. "He had this thing. Some kind of little radio." He held up the radio receiver.

"Was he armed?"

Carl shrugged. "Uh, sort of."

"Hand it over."

Carl took the Beretta out of his pocket. "Aw, boss, all he had was this cute little automatic. Can't I keep it?"

"Give it to me, Carl. Put him back there with the girl. Make sure you tie him good. And gag him."

Carl didn't seem very happy about giving up the pistol, but he handed it to Furtado along with the radio. He pushed Rudd toward the back of the trailer.

"Oh, hi, Jenny," said Rudd. "Are you all right? Jeez, what happened to your clothes?"

Jenny tried to say something through her gag.

Furtado yelled, "Shut him up. Gag him."

Carl tied Rudd and gagged him.

Steele was sorry to see Rudd hog-tied like that, but at least they hadn't killed him. He could only hope Rudd had managed to call Pruett before they caught him.

Furtado waved Carl away. "Get back outside and keep watch."

"You sure you don't want me to stay here and guard 'em?"

"No, I can handle it. Wait outside. They'll be here soon. Let me know as soon as they come."

Carl went out and closed the doors.

"Well, now, isn't this cozy?" said Furtado, smiling. "I've got your cute little girl friend and now I've got a fat guy with a radio receiver and another little hidey pistol." He took Steele's Beretta out of his pocket and compared it with Rudd's. "Funny, this looks a lot like your gun, doesn't it Steele? Did you think he was going to come in here and rescue you with this little pistol?"

"He was just supposed to wait for me in the car," said Steele.

"And what was he supposed to be doing while he waited? Listen to this radio? He looked closely at the radio receiver. "I knew you were wired. Is this who you were talking to? Or is somebody else listening in?"

"Only the police. They've heard every word you've said, even your sad story about how tough you and your sweet old momma had it."

Furtado pointed the Beretta at Steele. "Are you trying to provoke me?" He threw the radio receiver into the corner. "If somebody is listening in, they know I've got the girl and I've got you and Rudd too. They haven't come in so far so I guess they must be waiting for something. What is it? Some kind of signal."

"They're busy bringing in the SWAT team They're surrounding the entire harbor." Steele turned to look at Rudd. "Isn't that right?"

Rudd nodded his head vigorously and tried to say something through the gag.

Steele turned back to Furtado. "You see? You'll never get out of here."

Furtado smiled. "Oh, I have a way out. I know this place well. When I first discovered Crueltown, I used walk over here and watch them unload all night. I learned the harbor is a big place, with lots of secret nooks and crannies where you can get . . . well, never mind about that. I think you'd better tell me where the wire is or I'm afraid I'll have to shoot your fat friend."

"There is no wire. You're getting paranoid, Furtado. When you're back in prison, you should try to get some psychological help."

Furtado stared at Steele for a long moment. Then he turned and pointed the little Beretta at Rudd. "Let's see how accurate this little gun is. Do you think I can hit him in the knee from here? Maybe the bullet will shatter and leave some fragments in his leg, like you did to me."

"The transmitter is in my jacket," said Steele.

"Ah, the jacket. So that's why you gave it to the girl. Very clever."

Furtado got up and went to stand over Jenny. "Is little Jenny cold?" He pulled the jacket off of her. She turned sideways again to try to hide her nakedness.

Furtado came back, feeling along the seams of the jacket.

"It's in the shoulder," said Steele.

Furtado squeezed along the seam. "Ah, there it is. Very clever, Steele. Sewn right along the edge so it's almost impossible to find." He threw the jacket down and ground the collar under his heel. Then he turned to Rudd. "I'd still like to try out this little pistol. Where should I shoot him, Steele? His feet. Good target practice I think."

"Good idea," said Steele. "Make some noise. That'll help the police find us."

Just then, the truck's doors opened again and Carl stuck his head in. "Two guys out here, boss. I think it's them."

Furtado lowered the gun. "Send them in."

Two men in expensive-looking business suits climbed up into the trailer and somebody closed the doors behind them. One of them was wearing a hat, something like the hats men used to wear back before World War Two. Steele wondered if he had seen some of the old noir detective movies and thought American gangster still wore hats like that. The hatter had his hand inside his suit coat, in true gangster fashion.

The men stopped near the door and stared at Steele with hard, unwavering eyes. Steele met their stare. They were both middle-eastern, one of them probably in his forties, the man in the hat much younger.

The older one pointed at Steele. "That him?"

"Yeah," said Furtado. "Who are you?"

"Call me Omar."

"You got the money?"

Omar nodded toward the back of the trailer. "Who are these people?"

Furtado shrugged. "I used the girl to get Steele here. The other guy was sneaking around outside. You didn't answer my question." He wasn't exactly pointing the Beretta at Omar, but he wasn't putting it away either.

"You'll get the money," said Omar, "as soon as we get the shipment."

Steele tried to place the man's accent. Maybe Saudi.

"The container is still on the ship," said Furtado. "I've got the bill of lading and a truck waiting. It looks like it will come off in a few hours, but I don't know how I'm supposed to get it through customs. They're real tight right now because of that terrorist scare up in Seattle. They've got dogs sniffing around every container that comes in."

"It is not a problem," said Omar. "We have a truck."

Furtado looked surprised. "Your own truck? What about the bill of lading?"

"No need. Let's go."

"Go?" said Furtado. "Where we going?"

"I want to see the container come off. Truck is already in line."

Furtado stood up. "What about Steele?"

"Bring him. Take care of others."

"Take care of them?"

"Kill them."

"No," said Steele. "If you want my cooperation, leave them here."

Omar pulled out an automatic and began to screw a silencer onto the barrel. "You will not speak."

Steele turned to Furtado. "Listen to me, Furtado. He's about to make the kind of trouble you don't need. Think about how you'd get the bodies out of here. Just lock them in and I'll cooperate."

Omar pointed the gun at Steele's head. "I said you are not to speak."

"You won't shoot me," said Steele, meeting the man's stare. "Somebody important wants me alive, remember?"

"He's right," said Furtado. "The message said Steele had to be delivered alive. That means they want to question him. As long as I hold these two, he'll have to answer your questions. It gives you more leverage over him."

Omar hesitated, still pointing the gun at Steele.

"My men will keep them tied up here until you get what you want out of Steele," said Furtado. "Let's go." He moved to the doors and opened them. Then he gestured with his pistol for Steele to get out.

Steele knew it was going to be hard to get down out of the truck because of his damaged knees, but he didn't have much time to think about it: one of the men pushed him out and he was barely able to get turned in the air before he hit the ground. He did a backward roll and landed without doing too much damage. He quickly got to his feet.

As the two middle-eastern men climbed down from the truck, Furtado called one of his men over. "Lock this truck."

The man did as he was told.

"Now give me the key," commanded Furtado.

The man handed it over and Furtado put it in his pocket. "Carl, you come with us. The rest of you stay here."

"No," said Omar. "We want no suspicion. You and Steele only."

"Carl comes with me," said Furtado. "You have your man," he said, nodding toward the hatter who never took his hand out from inside his jacket. "Carl is my man."

"He must leave shotgun," said Omar.

"No problem," said Furtado. "You got your pistol, Carl?"

Carl took a large revolver out of a shoulder holster and held it up, grinning."

"That's good, Carl. Now put it away. Stay behind Steele and don't take your eyes off him."

Omar led the way across the parking lot. Furtado was next to him, followed by Steele. The other middle-eastern man, the hatter, followed with Carl. As they went across the wide parking lot, Carl used every opportunity to push Steele forward, saying exactly the same words each time: "move it, cripple." Each time, Steele pretended to stumble and that slowed the procession. He was trying to gain enough time to secretly loosen the twine that held his wrists.

Furtado eventually noticed their slow progress and stopped to look back. "Quit that, Carl. Just stay the hell away from him."

As they walked through the rows of parked trucks, Steele sized up the situation. Omar seemed to be leading them toward a huge Chinese container ship that was in the process of unloading. The container they were after must be on that ship. Drugs, probably heroin, must be hidden somewhere inside it. But how were they going to get it off the ship and through customs?

Looking ahead, Steele could see that the big crane was working fast, pulling the big metal containers off the ship one after the other and then swinging them back to the parking lot to lower them onto the waiting flat-bed trucks. Bathed in lights against the dark sky, the crane looked like a giant preying mantis grabbing up prey.

Steele glanced back. The silent man in the hat was lagging behind, but he was watching closely. With the hatter and Carl back there, Steele knew running was not an option, especially not with his hands tied behind his back. And as long as Rudd and Jenny were still being held back there in that truck trailer, he knew had to play along for the time being.

As they got closer to the crane, its surging engine and the snap of the straining cables got louder and louder. Another middle-eastern man was waiting at the foot of the stairs that led up to the crane operator's cabin. Omar went to the man and they whispered together for a moment. Then Omar waved them forward and led them up the stairs.

Furtado was close behind him. "Why are we going up there?" he shouted over the noise of the crane's engine. The container isn't scheduled to come off yet."

Omar ignored him and continued on up the stairs that vibrated and clanged with each of their steps.

Steele was using his sideways method to follow them as fast as he could, but apparently that wasn't fast enough for Carl. The big man got ahold of Steele's arm and half dragged him up. Carl was puffing from the exertion, but he seemed to be enjoying dragging Steele along.

Omar was waiting on the next landing. He impatiently called down to them: "Hurry it up. What's taking so long?"

"The gimp can't make it on his own," said Carl. "I'm helping him."

Steele felt like twisting out of Carl's grasp and throwing the big man down the stairs, but he resisted the impulse. Better to let Carl think he was in control and continue to work on loosening the ropes around his wrists.

Omar shook his head and went on.

When they were finally all gathered on the top landing, Omar took out his gun and pushed open the door. In contrast with the bright phosphorescent lights outside, the only illumination inside the glassed-in cabin was a small light over the crane operator's control panel.

The crane operator, an older man with a lot of gray in his thick mustache, turned to them. "What the hell? You can't come in here."

Omar pointed his gun at him. "Do not move."

The operator put up his hands. "Hey, man, I don't know what you're looking for, but I can't do nuthin' for you up here. My job is just to pull the containers off and drop them onto the trucks."

"Be silent," said Omar. He moved to the crane operator and showed him a piece of paper. "Unload this container."

The operator looked at the number on the paper and then at a chart on the wall. "No can do, bud. That one won't come off for another couple of hours."

Omar shoved the barrel of the gun into the man's side. "You unload. Now."

The crane operator pushed the gun way. "Jesus, man. Lay off with the gun. I can't get that one. It's clear over in the ship's next section."

Steele stepped forward. "I think you should do as he says. It would be best to cooperate with these men."

The operator looked at him and shook his head. "I'd have to reposition the damn thing."

"Then I'd suggest you do that," said Steele.

"Well, hell, I guess I could. But tell that guy to quit sticking his gun in my gut."

"I wish I could tell him anything," said Steele, partly turning to the side to show him his hands. "But my hands are tied, literally."

The operator leaned close to Steele. "What's going on?"

"Shut up," said Omar. "Both of you."

"This man is only trying to do his job," said Steele. "He's cooperating, as I am."

Omar pointed the gun at Steele's face. "Get back. Over there."

Steele backed away until he was against the cabin's wall. He was now close enough to the hatter to reach him, if he could just get his hands loose. The pen gun was still in his shirt pocket. He could feel that the bindings had cut into his wrists, and the coolness on his hands indicated they had started to bleed. But it felt like the blood was causing the twine to stretch a little. He tried moving the bindings back and forth along the areas that felt the most painful, hoping to soak the twine thoroughly with his blood.

A speaker on the wall crackled. "What's the holdup?"

Omar swung around. "Who is that?"

"The yard foreman," said the crane operator. "He's wondering why I stopped."

"Do not stop," said Omar, waving his gun toward the crane's controls. "Continue."

The operator went back to work, but as soon as he had off-loaded the next container, Omar again showed him the paper. "Get this container. Now."

The operator shrugged and began to reposition the crane.

"Hey, came the voice from the speaker, "Why're you movin'? We've still got a whole bunch to do in this section."

"I've gotta answer him," said the operator.

"Get container," said Omar. "I said now!"

"Tell him something," said Steele. "Tell him it's a special order or something."

The operator reached up and pushed a button next to the speaker. "Special order. Got to get it off right away."

"Well, Christ," came the voice through the speaker. "Why didn't you tell us that before we moved down here? Now I got to send these trucks to the back of the line. Which one should I get up here next?"

The crane operator looked at Omar.

Omar moved close to the glass and pointed. "That one. Black truck."

The operator leaned forward to see. "But that's a local truck. All the containers from this ship are supposed to go through customs."

"Load it," said Omar, again pushing the gun into the operator's side. "Now."

"Okay, okay, don't get your bowels in an uproar."

"Now I get it," said Furtado. "That's a hell of a good idea. Get the stuff loaded onto a local truck, like it's from a stateside shipment, and he'll be able to drive right out of here."

The operator maneuvered the crane into position and began bringing the container up from the ship.

"What's in it?" asked Steele. "Heroin?"

"Dolls," said Furtado. "An entire load of cute little Afghan peasant dolls, and my men are waiting at Crueltown to unload 'em. How about that? Who'd ever think to look inside cute little raggedy dolls?"

"Quiet," said Omar. He swung his pistol toward Furtado.

Furtado took a step toward him. "Hey, asshole, don't point that thing at me."

Omar kept the gun on Furtado for a few seconds before turning back to watch the operator lower the container onto the black truck. As the truck pulled away, Omar moved close to the glass to watch it go. When the truck had left the shipyard, he tore the loudspeaker microphone out of the wall and threw it to the floor.

"What the hell?" said the crane operator.

Omar put his gun against the side of the operator's head and fired. Oddly, even as his eyes rolled up into his head, he smiled for just a moment before slumping forward. Steele had seen that strange smile before. It was an involuntary motor response caused by the bullet penetrating the man's brain.

Steele pulled as hard on his bindings as he could and felt the twine stretch a little more. Finally, his hands came free. He resisted the temptation to reach for the pen gun in his pocket. The tiny gun held only one shot. He would have wait for the right moment to use it.

As the dead crane operator slid to the floor, the hatter suddenly pulled out a silenced automatic and shot Carl in the back of the head. Carl fell forward with a grunt and landed hard, his face smashing into the floor. He didn't move.

Furtado instantly realized what was happening and reached for his pistol, but before he could get it out, the hatter turned and pointed his gun at him. Furtado shrugged and handed the gun over. The hatter smiled a strange, almost gleeful, smile and pointed his gun at Furtado's face.

Furtado smiled right back at him. "Go ahead and shoot, asshole. Let's see you get out of this harbor with my men waiting down below."

The man hesitated and Steele realized this was his chance, probably the only chance he would get. He quickly took out the pen gun and fired it at the back of the hatter's head.

As the man fell, Steele grabbed for his gun, but he went down too fast. The gun hit the floor and bounced away. Steele dived for it, but before he could grab it, he heard Omar fire. Immediately, he felt a pain in the back of his shoulder. He turned his head just enough to see Omar taking aim for another shot. He tried to roll away, but Omar's fired quickly, hitting him square in the back. The pain was intense but he knew he had to get up quick or he was a dead man. But when he tried to push himself up, he discovered left arm wasn't working. He slipped back down onto his stomach and heard Omar laugh, the harsh mean laugh of a sadist. Omar came to stand over him. Steele knew the next shot would be to the back of his head. He turned his head away.

But when the sound of the shot came, Steele didn't feel it hit. Could Omar have missed? He fought down the pain in his back and turned onto his side. Omar was lying face down on the floor. A tiny wisp of smoke was coming out of a little hole in the side of his head. Furtado was standing over the man with Steele's Beretta in his hand.

The pain in Steele's back was suddenly overwhelming. He couldn't move.

Furtado came to stand over him. He squatted down to look into Steele's eyes. "How bad it is it? Are you killed?"

"Guess so," whispered Steele. "Can't breathe."

Furtado stood up and shook his head. "Tough luck, Steele, but you knew you weren't going to walk away from this one anyhow. By the way, thanks for saving my life. How come you did that?"

"Mistake," whispered Steele.

"Naw, you saw he was gonna shoot me. You actually did it to save me. Sometimes I can't figure you, Steele." Furtado picked up the silenced gun from the floor. "This is his gun. So what did you shoot him with?"

Steele didn't reply. The pen gun was close by on the floor, but it was good for only that one shot. If only he had another gun. He knew Furtado would soon finish him. With the noise of the crane's engine, the workers down below wouldn't have even heard the shooting. Furtado would be able to just walk away unnoticed. He said he had an escape plan, a boat waiting. All that heroin would soon find it's way onto the streets of LA.

Furtado stared down at him. Steele knew it would be one shot to the head and that would be that. He closed his eyes and waited. He was surprised at how calm he felt. In Iraq, he hadn't seen it coming, hadn't had time to prepare. But this time, he would be ready for it. He was determined to remain calm, to not let Furtado see any fear.

But Furtado didn't fire. What was he waiting for? Steele opened his eyes and saw that Furtado was searching the floor. He soon found the pen gun and picked it up. "Well, look at this, another little hidey gun. So this is what you killed him with. You're somethin' else, Steele."

"Let them go," whispered Steele.

"Who? Oh, you mean your fat pal and your little girl friend. You think I owe you that just because you saved my life? The only thing I owe you is to put a bullet in your head, just like you put that bullet in my leg back then in Crueltown. I'd be doing you a favor. You're a gonner anyhow."

"Let them go. They're no use to you . . . now."

"Well, maybe you're right. No use taking a chance going back to that truck. Might be more Arabs around there. And now I can't even sell you to them. They probably won't take too kindly to me doin' in their main man." Furtado stood up. "How about this? Here's what I can do for you, I'll just leave you here to die in peace. Nobody will find you up here, and I've got the Arab's cell phone so you can't call for help." He glanced at the door. "Do you really have the SWAT team surrounding this place?"

"No," whispered Steele.

"No? That probably means you do. But you should have realized I'd always be one step ahead of you. I've got a real fast boat waiting nearby. I'll be out of this harbor and back home in San Diego in less than an hour.

"Say hello to . . . your mother . . . for me."

Furtado laughed. "I will, I will." He looked at Omar's body. "You don't suppose he had the half million on him, do you?" He rolled over the body and began to go through the dead man's clothes.

Steele realized Furtado was going to get away and there was nothing he could do about it. If only he had another hidden gun. But then he remembered Carl hadn't had time to draw his big revolver. It would still be in his shoulder holster. With Furtado occupied, maybe he could get to Carl's gun.

Steele tried to move toward Carl's body, but every movement caused intense pain and that caused the muscles in his back to clench up. He tried using his legs to push and made a little progress. Keeping his eyes on Furtado, he was able to slither forward just far to reach inside Carl's coat with his good arm. He felt the big revolver in Carl's shoulder holster and got ahold of it. But when he tried to pull it out from under Carl's big body, a wave of pain shot through his back.

But then Furtado finished searching the dead man and stood up. Steele was barely able to turn away from Carl's body before Furtado turned toward him.

"Hey, what are you trying to do, Steele? Make it to the door?"

"Can't move," whispered Steele. "Pain."

"I bet," said Furtado. "I bet it hurts like hell. You sure you don't want me to put a bullet in your head and get it over with?"

"No . . . thanks."

"Okay, up to you." Furtado squatted down to shake the money in Steele's face. "Look at this. A couple of hundred bucks. All this trouble, and for what? No five hundred grand, no getting to see them drag you away to get your head chopped off. What a waste of time.

But you'll be dead soon and I've got all that Heroin. I guess that makes it all worth it. That smack is gonna make me rich, Steele. Real rich."

"Get Momma another . . . pool," whispered Steele.

"I will. In fact, I should get her an even fancier house. That's exactly what I'll do." He laughed again and shoved the money in his pocket as he went to the door. He looked back at Steele. "Well, so long, Steele. See you in hell."

Furtado pulled the door shut and Steele could hear his footsteps going down the clanging metal stairs. Steele quickly reached inside Carl coat and managed to get the gun pulled out. He used his good arm to painfully pull himself up to the window sill. On the other side of the glass, Furtado was just reaching the first landing below. One more second and he would be out of sight. Steele quickly aimed and fired. The shot was very loud inside the small room as it blew the glass out.

Furtado went down hard, but he quickly sat up, holding onto his leg. He looked up at Steele. "Not my leg," he screamed. "Not my damn leg again."

He pulled out Steele's pistol and struggled to his feet. He started back up the stairs, using the metal railing to pull himself along.

"Stop!" yelled Steele. "Don't make me shoot you again,"

But Furtado kept coming, his face filled with rage. "Go ahead and try, you son of a bitch. I'll blow your goddam head off." He lifted the automatic and started firing as he came.

Steele expected to be hit at any minute, but Furtado was firing so fast the recoil of the automatic was making most of his shots go high. He steadied himself and aimed the big gun at Furtado's midsection. He squeezed off a single shot.

Furtado was thrown back against the railing. He looked down at where the bullet had gone in as if he couldn't believe it. He gingerly touched the place where the blood was leaking out and held up his bloody hand to show Steele. "Look at this. My blood. You've killed me."

"Put down your gun," said Steele. "I'll get help for you."

"I'm shot right through the middle. Why did you do that?"

"Throw down your gun. We both need an ambulance."

Furtado turned to look out toward the open ocean. "No . . got to go. She'll be . . . worried about me. Doesn't like it . . . when I come home . . . late." Suddenly his legs gave out and he sat down hard. He shook his head like he was trying to make his eyes focus. He turned to look out toward the ocean. Somehow, he got up himself up onto all fours and began to crawl back down to the landing. "She'll be worried. She'll be . . . afraid." Somehow, he managed to pull himself to his feet using the railing. Then he started to crawl up onto it.

"No, shouted Steele. "Don't do it."

"Too late," moaned Furtado. "Got to get . . . home. Mother . . . waiting." He grimaced, and with one last pull got himself draped over the railing. He teetered there for a moment, looking back at Steele. He seemed about to say something, but then he lost his grip and fell.

Steele leaned out through the broken window and watched Furtado tumble over and over all the way down until he hit the edge of the ship channel. He glanced off it and fell the rest of the way down to the water like a floppy old rag doll.

Suddenly, Steele felt all the energy drain out of himself. He slid down the wall to the floor. He turned over onto his back and stared up at the ceiling. Everything was very bright. It must be the loss of blood. He had a momentary memory of seeing that same kind of brightness in Iraq, after the explosion. He was tempted to just lie still and let it happen. He was undoubtedly losing blood so fast it wouldn't take long. In Iraq, he had blacked out after only a few seconds.

Steele opened his eyes and realized he was still in the crane operator's cabin. Had he blacked out? For how long? In Iraq, he had expected one of two outcomes: he would be executed by the terrorists who had set off the bomb, or the backup convoy would come in time to save him. That time the convoy had come, but here there was no backup convoy. If he was going to survive, he would have to save himself. Could he possibly drag himself down all those stairs outside? It wasn't possible. He could barely move. Omar had disabled the loudspeaker so he couldn't call for help, and Furtado had taken Omar's cell phone. But what about the crane operator. Maybe he had one.

Steele painfully turned over onto his stomach. He slowly began to crawl toward the body of the operator. The pain was blinding but he kept going. It was only a few feet, but it seemed to take forever. He searched the crane operator's body and felt something in the man's inside shirt pocket. It was a small cell phone. Steele forced his eyes to focus on the numbers and started to punch in 9-1-1, but then he remembered Rudd and Jenny were will locked inside that truck. He punched in Pruett's number.

Pruett answered on the first ring. "Is that you, Steele? Where are you?"

"Harbor," whispered Steele. "Rudd and hostage . . . in . . . a truck. Gate six. Long-term . . . storage. H-M Enterprises . . . on side of truck. Guards . . there."

"Got it. I'm heading there now. I've got SWAT with me. You sound bad, Steele. Are you hurt?"

"Shot. Twice." Steele was having trouble focusing. Things seemed to be fading in and out. Breathing was hard. Talking was hard. "Furtado dead. Heroin. In . . . container truck. Black truck. Gone now."

"Are you saying there's a black truck with a shipping container on it? Smuggling heroin?"

"Yes. Don't let it . . . get to . . . Crueltown."

"Okay, I'll have them surround the whole area and put up roadblocks. Where are you?"

"Up in . . . unloading . . . crane. Got to . . . hang up and . . . call ambulance."

"No, I'll call in a Medivac helicopter. They've got a landing pad there. It'll be there in a couple of minutes. Hang on, Steele, hang on."

# Chapter 26

*S*teele was having trouble seeing clearly. He couldn't seem to make his eyes focus.

A voice. "Can you hear me, Steele? You just came out of surgery. They say you're going to be all right."

Steele tried to open his eyes, but everything was too bright. That voice. "Rudd?"

"Yeah, it's me. Do you know where you are? You're in the recovery room. They wheeled you out of surgery just a little while ago."

"You . . . alright?"

"Yeah, Pruett showed up with a whole bunch of his men and got us out of that truck. Look who I've got here with me."

Steele blinked and his eyes cleared enough to see her. "Jenny?"

"Yes, it's me. How are you feeling?"

He felt her take his hand. "Woozy."

"Yes, I bet you are. It's the pain killers they're giving you. The doctor said you're lucky to be alive. One of those bullets would have gone right through your lung if it hadn't hit a rib. They say it's going to hurt every time you breathe."

"Won't . . . breathe . . . then."

He felt her squeeze his hand. "Oh, silly, you have to breathe. But don't worry. They say you'll be better soon. I'll take care of you. You can stay at my place until you're feeling better. Would you like that?"

"Would he? said Rudd. "How could anybody turn down an offer like that?"

# Chapter 27

*T*he next time Steele woke up, it was dim in the room and nobody was there. He was able to turn his head slightly to see that he was hooked up to some machines. Little yellow lights flickered and a bright dot moved across a green screen tracing the steady rhythm of his heartbeat.

He tried to get a full breath, but it hurt too much. An IV was connected to his arm. He wondered what was in it. Probably morphine, same as in that hospital in Berlin. He hoped he wouldn't have to undergo more follow-up surgeries like he did that time.

He woke up again, smelling hospital smells. Why do hospitals always smell like that? All except that military hospital in Baghdad. It had smelled like . . . burned flesh. It suddenly occurred to him that the smell must have been his own burned legs. Why hadn't he realized that before?

He closed his eyes and tried to think about something else, anything else. He felt sleepy, overpowered by the drugs that were moving down that plastic tube and into his arm. The dream-like image of that young boy in Baghdad came again. That boy knew what was going to happen; maybe he had even watched them bury the IED under the road. That boy just stood there, watching, waiting for it to happen. Steele wished he could make that dream go away. Why did those eyes keep watching him? What did they want? He knew it wasn't the boy's fault, he only . . .

But then Steele realized that this time the dream was different: the boy's curious eyes had changed, became older, more afraid. Suddenly, he realized the eyes in the dream were not the boy's eyes; they were

Furtado's eyes, the look that Steele had seen in them just before he'd shot him. They were the eyes of a man who knew he was about to die. In that last moment of realization, Furtado's eyes showed that he was no longer angry and vengeful; somehow, in that last moment of his life, his eyes had become calm, but concerned, as if he had suddenly realized his mother was going to have to get along without him forever. Steele knew he had no choice but to pull that trigger and Furtado knew it too; he was forcing Steele to do it. Is that what the look in his eyes meant? Go ahead and shoot, I know you have to.

Steele tried to stop thinking about it. All this remembering wasn't going to change the way things were. He focused on the feel of the morphine moving through his brain, willing it to take over his thoughts, asking it to carry him away from such images.

The next time Steele woke up, it was bright in the room and he had a vague sense that many people were there. He blinked until his eyes cleared enough to see Rudd over next to the window, talking to somebody. Who was it?

He felt somebody holding his hand. He turned his head toward her. "Loren?"

"Loren? No, it's Jenny. Don't you remember?"

Then he did remember. Whenever he woke up from his strange dreams, Jenny had been there. But sometimes late a night, when the room was dark and the hospital was finally silent, it was as if he was back in that drafty hospital in Berlin with Loren sitting in the bedside chair, holding his hand.

Jenny leaned close and smiled. "You've been sleeping a lot. The doctor says that's good. I hope you're starting to feel a little better now. The doctor says you're going to pull through just fine. Do you feel like talking a little? Someone has been waiting to talk to you."

She turned. "He's awake."

Someone came out of the brightness of the sunlit window to lean over him. It was Pruett.

"So you're finally awake. They say you're gonna make it. Don't know how, all shot up like that. Guess you're just plain lucky, or just too damn stubborn to die. You'd lost a lot of blood by the time they got to you. The doctor told me that bullet in your shoulder wasn't a big deal, but the one in the back was close to . . . well, anyhow, like I said, you're pretty damn lucky."

"Better lucky than smart," whispered Steele.

"Yeah, well, they tell me I'm not supposed to tire you too much so I'll get right to it. We got the smuggler's truck. That container was full of a lot of crap, but deep down inside it was a great big box full of Afghan dolls. And guess what was inside."

"Heroin," whispered Steele.

"Damn right. Pure, uncut heroin. The boys downtown are still adding it up, but it'd be worth tens of millions on the street." Pruett leaned closer. "Listen, Steele, I've got to know who all those dead guys were. There was the crane operator, some of the dock workers identified him. And the big guy, the one shot in the back of the head? Name was Carl Frey. We had a fat file on him. Been in and out of prison since he was a kid. But what about the other two dead guys? Who the hell were they? They looked like Arabs, but we can't find out a damn thing about them. Their prints weren't on record anywhere."

Steele knew they were probably al-Qaeda operatives, but he couldn't tell Pruett that. "Never saw them before," he whispered.

"We couldn't even tell who shot you. No guns to be found anywhere, except for the big .357 magnum you had. And I thought you said Furtado was dead. We couldn't find him either."

"In the water. Fell."

"Oh, we didn't look there. Okay, we'll get busy draggin' the harbor for him. Now, can I clean this case off my docket? You're sure it was Furtado who did both of those 'Keep Out' murders?"

"Yes. Furtado . . . and his men."

"Okay. I'm pretty sure we got 'em all. SWAT rounded 'em up here and there inside the harbor. They were hidin' all over that parking lot, under trucks, behind the big stacks of containers. One was even hiding inside some big pipes on another truck. We took 'em all downtown and they started rattin' on each other soon as we put the screws to 'em. Oh, there was one guy that took off in a speedboat. He got away. Made it out to the open ocean before we could get a boat in the water. But we're not even sure he was part of it. The Coast Guard thinks they've got a line on the boat. They found it abandoned down near San Diego."

Jenny came back to put her hand on Pruett's shoulder "Now, now," she said, "he's done enough talking for today. He needs to rest."

Steele smiled to himself as she shooed Pruett toward the door. Pruett jammed his hat back on with irritation, but he did as he was told. "All right, all right, young lady. I'm goin'" He turned back long enough to say, "You take care of yourself, Steele. We'll talk more later."

Despite the tube attached to his arm, Steele was able to lift it enough to indicate a salute. But Pruett didn't see it; he was already heading out the door.

For the next few days, Jenny and Rudd took turns sitting by Steele's bed. Jenny chattered on about this and that, and when it was Rudd's turn he happily read aloud his serialized newspaper stories about how the famous Detective X had solved the 'Keep Out' case. He said the stories were very popular and his editor had promised him a raise--soon.

Late one night, Rudd was out finding something to eat when Rachel called from Las Vegas. She said she'd heard about what had happened and that she'd be coming to see him on her day off. She also added a surprising bit of news: "My boss sent that report about the Vinellis to the bankruptcy judge. He used a yellow marker to highlight the part about the guy named Vinelli who was killed in Chicago. And guess what?"

"What?"

"Apparently, he knew some other judge in Chicago who checked and found out some things about the Vinellis that were left off of their gaming application. He asked the Nevada Gaming Board to reviewed the Omnivexx application. They held a special meeting and voted against renewing their license to run this casino. They disqualified both Omnivexx and the Vinellis using the old 'associated with unseemly elements' rule that goes back to the fifties. But what's really amazing is what happened next. Mr. Monroe talked to the judge about putting together a management group to buy them out. Looks like the Vinellis won't have any choice. They'll have to sell out for whatever they can get. Monroe says Mrs. Culp's son, James, will be involved too."

"Are you happy about it?"

"Sure. Mr. Monroe says there'll be a place for me in the new management team. How about that? A girl fresh out of college comes west for a job in accounting and ends up in casino management. Well, middle-management, at least."

"Congratulations."

"Yeah, well, who knows? We'll see how it all turns out. Maybe we won't be able to make a go of it, but at least we'll get a chance to try to save this old place. Anyhow, I'll get over to LA to see you as soon as I can. Got to go now. Hope you're feeling better."

After she hung up, Steele thought about what she'd said. If only Culp would have done the same thing, ask the judge to investigate Omnivexx. But his resentment of the Vinellis was so great he wanted to defeat them by himself.

Odd, that James was joining the plan to buy out the Vinellis, the family that had done so much for him and his brother. Or was he joining the buyout effort for some other reason? Could he be working *for* the Vinellis behind the scenes? And what about his brother? Was Craig still in hiding? Or had he heard about what had happened to Furtado? Maybe he had gone back to Las Vegas also.

Steele closed his eyes and told himself to stop thinking about it. He was done with the case. He'd done what he'd been paid to do, find Culp's killers. After Culp disappeared, the Vinellis told Monroe to hire him, not because they cared about Culp, but because they were afraid he would tell what he knew about them. They probably hoped an LA-based detective would stay away from Las Vegas and simply find out who Culp had contacted in Los Angeles. In the end, it was their own paranoia that would be their undoing.

# Chapter 28

*S*everal days later, Steele was sitting up in his hospital bed late at night, checking his home phone messages, when he came across a message from Loren. He'd sent her the phone number of his new cell phone in an email telling her what had happened and that he was in the hospital again. She hadn't called that number; instead, she left a message at his home number. After some preliminary statements of condolences about his injuries, she couldn't seem to decide what to say next. Her voice was halting, unsure. That wasn't like her. Finally, she got to the point: she wasn't coming. She said she had some important exams coming up. But then, after some hesitation, she admitted that wasn't the real reason. The real reason, she said, had more to do with her not wanting to see him "shot up like that" anymore. She reminded him of the time she came to see him in the Berlin hospital, when he was still confined to his hospital bed, unsure that he'd ever walk again. "Remember what I said that time? That I didn't want to spend my life sitting next to a hospital bed? Well . . . there you are again. Not much has changed, has it?" She ended the phone call, simply saying, "Well, goodbye then. I hope you get better soon. If you want to come to Paris sometime, I mean when you're better, I wouldn't mind seeing you. Uh, call first."

Steele sat there for a long time thinking about her message. She was right: she shouldn't spend her life sitting next to his hospital bed. And Jenny shouldn't either. The chances he took were bound to lead him to more hospital beds in the future, or to a grave. Nobody should be expected to spend their days sitting next to either.

The next morning, he woke up early. Staring up at the sterile white ceiling, he made a decision: time to get out of there. He swung his legs out of bed. He grabbed his cell phone and called Rudd. "Come pick me up. I'm getting out of here."

"Now take it easy, Steele," said Rudd. "They said you shouldn't move around too much. Give it a few more days."

"I'm checking myself out of this place right now. Do I have to call a cab?"

There was a long pause before Rudd finally responded. "Aw, Steele, you always do this. Why are you always so impatient?"

"I'll be waiting for you outside. At the front entrance."

"Okay, I'll be there in twenty minutes."

His shoulder and back hurt so much, Steele had trouble getting his prosthetic foot strapped on, but he finally did it. He finished dressing and quietly slipped out of the room. He made it to the elevator without anyone noticing him. He leaned against the elevator wall as it descended to the ground floor. His shoulder was aching and every breath hurt, but it was good to be out of that damn bed.

When the elevator door opened, Rudd was there waiting. Steele allowed Rudd to help him to make it out to the car.

On the way home, he asked Rudd to drive him past Crueltown.

Rudd looked surprised. "Why would you want to go there?"

"I want to see it in the daytime. I have a feeling things have changed."

"Changed? But Pruett said they're still under standing orders not to go in there. Why would things have changed?"

Steele knew he couldn't tell Rudd about his conversation with the Director so he remained quiet and stared out the window. The midday sun looked feeble through the heavy smog. It was time for that trip, time to get away from LA for a while. Maybe this time he should book passage on a ship instead of flying. He looked to the south, toward the harbor. He thought about Furtado falling, falling, until he disappeared into the harbor's dark oily water. Was Furtado's body still there, lying at the bottom of the deep harbor under that murky water?

He shook off that thought and wondered if one of those huge container ships would take on a passenger. A ship like that would take quite a while to get to Hong Kong. A long sea voyage would be good. It would give him time to recover, both physically and mentally.

Rudd drove to Crueltown in silence and then Steele directed him to go to the same place they'd parked the night Steele went in to find Furtado. They got out of the car and Rudd helped Steele walk slowly to the top of the hill. The hole in the fence was still there behind the bushes. They went though the hole and walked to the edge of the hill beyond. Down below, Crueltown looked quiet and empty in the morning mist. The scattered old trailers were still there, but the smoky campfires and barking dogs were gone. Nothing moved down there.

"It looks deserted," said Rudd. "I don't get it. Pruett said he couldn't get a court order to go in, but it looks like everybody's run away."

"They'll be back," said Steele, turning away. "They'll be back."

www.ingramcontent.com/pod-product-compliance
Lightning Source LLC
Chambersburg PA
CBHW070622130626
46556CB00001B/437